# Bear Witness

# Also available by Linda O. Johnston, writing as Lark O. Jensen

# Bear
# Witness

## AN ALASKA UNTAMED MYSTERY

## Lark O. Jensen

CROOKED LANE

NEW YORK

Published in the United States by Crooked Lane Books, an imprint of The Quick Brown Fox & Company LLC.

Crooked Lane Books and its logo are trademarks of The Quick Brown Fox & Company LLC.

Library of Congress Catalog-in-Publication data available upon request.

ISBN (hardcover): 978-1-64385-896-8
ISBN (ebook): 978-1-64385-897-5

Cover design by Ben Perini

Printed in the United States.

www.crookedlanebooks.com

Crooked Lane Books
34 West 27th St., 10th Floor
New York, NY 10001

First Edition: May 2022

10 9 8 7 6 5 4 3 2 1

This book is dedicated to
Linda O. Johnston's husband Fred,
as she does with all her books.
Hey, Lark O. Jensen likes the guy, too.

# Chapter One

I felt my grin explode all over my face. Nothing unusual about that. The tour boat I was on had left the dock from Juneau, Alaska, hours ago on this Monday in May. We were now in the fjord called Tracy Arm, with snow- and ice-covered hills at our sides. And just ahead, in the distance, I could see strings of ice floes bobbing in the water, many with dark spots on them.

Harbor seals. I could hardly wait till we were closer and I could point them out to the passengers—including any pregnant mother seals who happened to be there or, better yet, mamas plus babies. They appeared a lot this time of year.

And I loved seeing them and introducing the tour boat's customers to them.

That's who I am: Stacie Calder, wildlife lover and expert and new tour guide, here in Alaska where there are so many different kinds of wonderful animals to find and see and point out. I even bring my own dog with me—Sasha, a two-year-old husky, who's far from wild. She's been well trained by me, and she also loves to interact with the tourists I introduce, at a distance, to the area's animals.

But Sasha is all mine. My blue-eyed baby, my champion, my protector. In fact, though it's not an uncommon name for people or pets, not everyone knows that *Sasha* means *defender*.

Fortunately, my current employers understand what it means to love animals. When I asked, after introducing my dog and showing how sweet and obedient she was, the Clem-Tours bosses, parents Ingrid and Curt, immediately gave me permission to bring her along while I was on tour duty. That was late summer last year, when I learned what it meant to give these tours. And I just started doing so earlier in May, when tours started again after winter.

I petted my mostly-gray-and-white pup on her furry head between her pointed ears now as I spoke into the microphone, and she wagged her shaggy tail. We were on the top deck of the three-deck tour boat, a mostly open level with chairs in the center, a roof overhead on poles, plus rails around the perimeter so passengers could sit or stand and see the water and the shore while viewing animals I pointed out.

What I said was always broadcast on the deck where I stood at the time, but I could also set the system so I could be heard everywhere—which I almost never did. I talked up here, on the top deck, and kept the other decks silent so tourists could just watch without being bombarded by me if they chose.

Now there were about twenty people up here with me, mostly standing around the edges of the deck, watching what was around us beneath the blue, cloudy sky. Only a few seats in the rows in the deck's center were occupied, by a variety of guests, from seniors to the very young.

Sasha and I stood at the front of the port side, and quite a few people were hanging out with us. I'd been talking almost since we left shore, so everyone knew my purpose on this boat: blabbing info that might interest them about our environment at that moment, especially about animals.

I'd done an introduction at first, as we'd left, so the passengers would understand my references to forward and aft—front of the boat and rear—and port and starboard—left and right—among other important stuff, like being careful.

"We're getting closer, people, but watch those small sheets of ice in the water in front of us. Can you see who's there?"

A girl of about fifteen who'd been standing near me got even closer. She was wearing a parka with its hood hugging her face, though it wasn't extremely cold today. But it wasn't warm, either. The high temperatures in this area in May seldom go above the fifties.

She patted Sasha after getting my okay, then pointed and asked, "Are those seals?"

"You got it," I said, catching the eye of a smiling woman behind her who was most likely her mom. I then asked the girl, "What's your name?"

"Allie," she said.

"Pretty," I told her, then spoke into the microphone again. "I have Allie here with me, a very smart young lady who said that what we're seeing, those spots on the ice that you'll see better as we get closer, are seals. They're harbor seals, and some might be new mamas and their pups."

I'd slung a red fabric bag over one shoulder before and now reached down into it, pulling out a white plastic cup with the name of this boat—*ClemElk*—etched into it in a gold color. "This is for you, Allie," I said, handing it to her. "It's your prize for helping me."

"Thank you!" she exclaimed, then dashed over to her mother, who also mouthed *Thank you.*

I simply nodded and smiled.

I was wearing a navy-blue zip-up hoodie that had a small ClemTours logo on the front over a long-sleeved T-shirt and wool slacks. No, I wasn't cold, but this kind of thing was my uniform on these tours. Especially the hoodie, though I didn't have the hood up right now. That let my dachshund-brown hair, pulled up into a clip at the top of my head but loose below that, blow free. Why dachshund brown? The dog I had as a child, Shorty, and I had matching hair color, although mine was always longer.

I seldom wore gloves despite having them in my pockets, since I had to be able to maneuver my microphone, binoculars, and more.

And the tourists? Their garb, and degree of warm clothing, varied. There were people of all ages on board.

All appeared to be enjoying themselves. And my talk. Although we were finally reaching the area where I hoped to tell them the most about Alaska's nearest wildlife.

We were getting closer now to the seals on the ice. The tour boat had been rocking gently nearly the entire time we'd been on it—more when we'd left the Juneau area, since we were going faster. Now we'd slowed, but the water, though not too bad, wasn't completely calm.

I pulled my binoculars up from where they hung around my neck and looked at the nearest ice atop the water.

A few floes had two or more seals on them—and of those, a couple of the additional seals were quite young, relative newborns.

Fun to see, fun to point out.

Around me, groups began congregating along the edges of the deck, sometimes getting close to Sasha, who knew just to step behind me and snuggle my legs. I was glad about the railings, especially when a couple of young men started taunting each other—in fun, it seemed, but they nevertheless got into a bit of a disagreement. "Easy there, guys," I told them. "The seals don't eat people meat, but I still don't want you to end up in the water."

They both looked at me from beneath their tight beanies, appearing startled at first. And then they laughed.

Before I started talking again, another guy came up to me. He'd joined me before on this tour as I'd spoken into my microphone. His jacket was of puffy pale-green vinyl, and he wore a black knit hat pulled way down on his head, almost to his brown eyes. He seemed quite interested in the area and my descriptions and was full of questions, which, fortunately, I was able to answer.

But of course I'd been a wildlife lover all my life, had studied and worked with wild animals in a variety of ways.

Smiling, I lifted my hand to gently silence him for the moment, and when I lowered my hand, I patted Sasha on the head.

I spoke for a short while about harbor seals and their background in Alaska, particularly Tracy Arm. I'd done a bunch of research. Plus, when I was learning the basics for this job, I'd gone on a few other ClemTours boat trips, listening to and talking to some of the other tour guides. I'd become buddies with a couple of them already, and both were also out giving tours today—but not in Tracy Arm.

For right now, this was my bailiwick. I loved going out on this boat usually five days a week—one tour each day, weather permitting—and telling our passengers all about the wildlife we saw.

I explained that these seals had a bit of stiff fur on them. They could be distinguished from sea lions and other pinnipeds by the fact that they had no ear flaps, just holes. I described their size and some of what they ate.

And then I stopped talking, since we were close enough for our passengers to actually see a bunch of them on different nearby ice floes.

I turned to talk again to that guy who'd sought me out, but Lettie Amblex came up to me. She was my assistant on this boat, and she'd been hanging out on the lowest of the three decks, talking to people about the tour and the wildlife we were likely to see. "This is great," she said as she leaned on the nearest railing and stared at the closest sea lions, another mother with a youngster. "I told everyone on the bottom deck that it would be good to come up here and look, since we can see better. But some are saying it's cold, and others are enjoying a meal or drink or whatever at the galley. They'll be sorry. Anyone who doesn't come up here on these tours always regrets it."

She would know better than I. Even though she was in her early twenties, around ten years younger than me, she'd grown up in Juneau and had worked for the Clementoses since she was a teenager. But she didn't have the broader knowledge about wildlife that I did thanks to my education and background.

Me? I might be new here as a tour guide, but I'm a naturalist. I grew up in Los Angeles, fell in love with the LA Zoo.

I eventually majored in wildlife conservation and management at the University of Arizona. I spent a while teaching kids about the animals at the San Diego Zoo Safari Park till I decided I wanted to see more actually in the wild. That's when I headed to Alaska, a couple of years ago, after landing a job at Juneau Wildlife World. I still work there at times of the year when it's too wintry to give boat tours.

Lettie was taller than me, and I'm pretty much average height. Her black hair was in a pixie cut, though it was pulled back and didn't frame her pretty, youthful face. Her black eyebrows seemed always to be raised in surprise, as they were now.

"Well, you did your best," I said. However, our jobs on board this boat included ensuring as much as possible that all the passengers loved their voyage.

If they failed to see all the wildlife, some might feel slighted.

I'd have to go to the deck below soon, where the bridge was located, to see what wildlife was visible there and also to encourage those stragglers there and on the deck below that to wend their ways up the steps to the top deck if they wanted to get the most out of this trip.

"Yep," Lettie agreed.

"I like seeing all those seals," said the man I'd put off talking to. "But what else are we likely to see? And will we be out here a lot longer? It's really nice here. I hope this excursion's a nice long one."

Interesting, I thought. Everyone who bought a ticket onshore was greeted by ClemTours personnel who gave them a verbal rundown of what to expect as well as the amount of time the tour was likely to take.

"Well, you were probably told this was about a seven-hour-round-trip journey when you got on board," I said. "It took more than a couple of hours to get to this area, and it'll take the same to return. That means we'll be here in Tracy Arm and some surrounding areas for around a couple of hours too."

"Got it," he said.

"And we're going to see more fun animals out here," Lettie added. At my glare, she said, "Or we usually do on these tours. Birds and bears and—well, we'll see."

"Right," I said.

"Fantastic," the man said. "I would love to hear more about all the animals we're likely to see and how you find them. And then how you can make sure the boat goes where you're most likely to see the most wildlife—that does happen, doesn't it?"

"Of course," I said, and briefly explained that in addition to my microphone, I had a system that could communicate directly with the captain on the bridge. "Although the captain and crew there are also always on the lookout for more wildlife and let me know about it too as they head in that direction. But now—"

"But now—well, you can put the animals in danger here by getting too close or making too much noise, right?"

His voice had risen in volume, and I saw others around us looking at him, then me. It was almost as if he wanted the other tourists to think about what this boat could do if handled inappropriately.

"We could, yes—but you can be certain that we don't. Our captain is well experienced in going slowly to keep our wake and noise down, and he is careful to steer far away from any animals in the water, like the seals."

"But what if—"

"Believe me," I said. "We are conscientious and do it right. I'm a wildlife advocate and care a lot about animals, and I wouldn't allow anything else."

Before he could say more, I raised my hand to silence him and walked a few feet away, Sasha behind me. Even when our caution and care weren't being questioned, I never spoke too long with any one passenger, not when I could show a lot of fun stuff to all of them—the more wildlife, the better. I turned away to scan the sea nearby as well as the land around us, hoping to make good on at least some of that right now.

And fortunately the guy stayed silent.

There! The timing was perfect. I was sure the mother bear who lumbered at the foot of a craggy, snow-dotted mountain nearby, cub keeping up behind, hadn't heard anything we were saying on board. Or even if she had and had understood, she hadn't cared, since she certainly looked happy and healthy, at least from this distance.

But there they were, mama and baby bear. And of course I told all the passengers where to look now, and gave a brief dissertation on bears and their species in the area, which included both brown bears and black bears. These two, in the distance, were brown in color and appeared to be, in fact, brown bears—although brown bears could be black and black bears could be brown.

And as I finished, I saw that I now had not only Lettie near me; the head of us all on the *ClemElk*, our captain, Palmer Clementos—one of the owners' sons—was now walking up the stairs from the deck below. Good. I liked Palmer. Even pretended to flirt with him now and then.

That pushy guy was still around too, but not particularly close, and he still remained quiet.

I always watched the shoreline for wildlife and things I could talk about as a tour guide—but I additionally kept my eyes on what was happening on the boat everywhere I could see.

I didn't know if any of our passengers up here had noticed the captain, especially since, as far as I could tell, all of them were watching where my hand now pointed, to the shoreline and the wandering bears. The boat was sailing in the same direction as they walked—avoiding the seals on ice, of course—so the bears remained in our view.

And now the captain was also in mine.

The captain could leave the bridge sometimes, like now, when we were cruising slowly to see the wildlife. He had an assistant, Steph Porter, who hung out with him most of the time when he was in charge, and at times like this she remained on the bridge, running the boat.

I'd met Palmer's parents and siblings, who, like him, each captained a tour boat. There were four siblings: Gustavus—Gus—and Palmer, and Kate and Craig, all named after Alaskan towns, although Kate was named after the town of Kake. Their parents mostly captained a ClemTours boat together, but if they were busy enough, Ingrid and Curt each ran a separate one. There was a bit of family resemblance among all of them. Like Palmer, they were each of moderate height. Their hair tended to be shades of light brown, and Palmer's was among the darkest. He wore it short, as most of the Clementos men did. Palmer kept his face shaved, although his male siblings seemed inclined to wear anything from fuzzy facial hair to beards—and the latter was what their dad did.

As captain of this tour boat, Palmer wore their standard uniform of beige slacks and jacket. The large ClemTours logo on the back seemed to show small ocean waves with a large eagle soaring over them.

I loved that logo. It was the same as the small one on my pocket but a lot more visible that size.

Anyway, right now, I was glad to see Palmer. As he did on some outings, he'd soon take the microphone from me and give his captain's perspective on the tour, what we'd seen, what we were likely to see, and why we had to go slowly around here—so as not to make too much engine noise and scare the wildlife, as I had confirmed before when questioned. His saying so would prove it, and I loved his family's perspective on wildlife protection too.

"Hi, Stacie," he greeted me, his voice a bit raspy as always. I assumed that was at least partly from his inhaling the wind and air at the bridge, which he kept mostly open. "How's it going?" He turned slightly and gave Sasha a pat on the head.

"Just fine," I said. "Are you going to talk about what we'll be seeing and how long we'll be out here? That gentleman over there—"

I started to gesture toward the guy who'd begun hanging out with me and asking his difficult questions, but he was edging away, head down. He didn't get far, though, since there were so many people standing on the deck looking around. He seemed to be heading toward the steps, but they blocked him.

"Hey," Palmer said, and there was a sharpness to his voice that surprised me. He began edging his own way toward the guy. And then he reached him, moving around so he was the one to block him.

Which made me curious.

I spoke into the microphone again and told everyone to keep watching those bears, since they might disappear back from the shore and into a snow-surrounded hill.

Then, Sasha beside me, I quickly joined Palmer and the passenger. They were now in the rows of seats in the middle of the deck, apparently to get a bit of privacy. None of the other passengers were there. Palmer was speaking very quietly but clearly angrily. Fortunately, the nearest passengers had done as I'd suggested and moved to the edge of the deck to watch the bears.

"What the hell are you doing here again today, Truit?" Palmer demanded. "And why are you dressed so different from usual, with that jacket that makes you look fat and your hat practically covering your face? Are you attempting some kind of disguise so you can hide out on this boat?"

"Nah, of course not," the man—apparently Truit—said. "I just had some time to myself and used to love being on this boat, so I bought a ticket, and here I am. And I was chilly enough to wear a thick jacket and hat."

"Yeah, right," Palmer said.

He used to love being on this boat? I wondered what that meant.

Although he did look a little familiar, but I could be imagining that.

Okay, I was nosy, but I wanted to know more. I joined them and said to the captain, "This gentleman did seem to be enjoying this tour." I didn't mention that he'd asked how long it might go on but said, "He asked what other wildlife we'd see, and if we're being careful not to harm them, and—"

"He knows all about what wildlife we're likely to see and what we do to keep them safe," Palmer snapped back at me. Uncharacteristic fury lit his brown eyes. The change from his usual amused, sometimes flirtatious expression startled me. He didn't turn away from Truit. "He used to work on the ClemElk as a deckhand."

"Really?" I couldn't help nearly exclaiming. In the short time I'd been with the guy, he'd acted as if he knew nothing about this boat or how it was handled.

"Yeah, really. And he's taken other tours with us. But right now his outfit suggests he didn't want us to notice him." Palmer glared at me, as if he was shooting his anger toward me for daring to question him. That gave me pause—especially since I'd thought he liked me. Or maybe I'd just blown that. Then he turned back to Truit. "So I'll want to talk to you later. You can tell me the truth then about the rumor I heard—that you intend to start your own boat tour company to compete with us."

"Even if I did," Truit said, "so what? There are lots of competing boat tour companies here in Alaska."

"So you admit it?" Palmer sounded even more outraged. "One that's cheaper, of course, is what I heard, so you can maybe put us and a lot of those other companies out of business, even though you'll do a lousy job of it."

I wanted to throttle the guy myself, since I really thought a lot of the ClemTours company and all it did for its passengers, even if it wasn't the cheapest of tours available. I liked the whole Clementos family.

No wonder Palmer was upset.

But just then Al Sherter showed up on the stairway from the below decks, hanging on to the rail and hurrying. He was one of the boat's couple of deckhands, and he looked like he had something on his mind.

Palmer must have seen him out of the corner of his eye as he continued to glare at Truit, since he now turned toward him. "Everything okay?" he asked.

"Sure," Al said, reaching the captain's side, "but Steph's a bit concerned about the length of your absence without giving a tour talk. Everything okay here?" As usual, he wore a ClemTours sweatshirt with that same cute logo on the front pocket as on mine.

Palmer turned to glare once more at Truit, then looked away. He clearly had to force his expression into normalcy, but he smiled slightly at the deckhand. "It's fine," he said. "I'll go talk to her now."

"Good," Truit said. "I'll just continue to enjoy this tour." He had the gall to wink toward me, and I wanted to kick him in the shins . . . or elsewhere.

"Good—for now," I told him. "Of course, we can always just sail our way to shore and let you off right here, since you know what this tour's all about anyway."

"What!" Truit looked outraged and perhaps a bit uneasy.

And Palmer, who'd started toward the steps, turned to look back at me and smile.

Naturally, I wasn't serious. Who knew when anyone would come out here to pick up a dumped passenger? Would be too dangerous, even if he deserved it.

"Just kidding," I said. "But why don't you just sit here and listen, if you must. I have to get back to giving my tour."

And with that, I turned my back on him as Palmer had done and, with Sasha, returned to the front of the deck, where Lettie still stood, talking to some passengers about the harbor seals that were now nearest to us. I gritted my teeth as Truit joined them, wondering if he was about to try to recruit Lettie for his nonexistent tour company.

But fortunately, she soon walked away, and some of the tourists followed her as she stopped at another area at the edge of the deck.

I pulled out my microphone and began to talk once more. "And now, ladies and gentlemen, let's look at our nearest companions. Do you know how harbor seals live in the winter?"

No one seemed to, so I continued my spiel—and avoided looking at that ass Truit, who was wandering again.

Eventually, when I grew quiet for a while, he came over to me. He'd taken his hat off, and I saw that his short hair was light brown. "Look," he said. "I can't help loving this place and its wildlife. Can you?" Before I could answer—affirmatively as to loving them, of course—he continued, "You obviously enjoy sharing what you know about it with visitors. Me too. And I'm just looking into the possibilities of how I can do it. Let's exchange information later. You already know I'm Truit—Sheldon Truit. Who knows? If I do start a competing tour boat company, maybe you can come work for me."

Oh, so he was attempting to recruit me. "Don't bet on it," I countered, then turned my back on him, patted Sasha, and began speaking into the microphone about why our tour boat continued to go so slowly: to avoid disturbing the seals and other nearby animals by too much noise and movement.

And when I turned slightly and looked back toward where I'd last spoken with Sheldon Truit, he was gone.

# Chapter Two

I looked around the deck and its groups of people for Lettie again. I wanted to take a bit of time out from up here and go below, both to give the passengers on the other decks a brief talk on what I could see from their levels and to say hi to my onboard buddies and any tourists I'd met before. And maybe just to take a brief break.

Lettie was now on the starboard side in the middle of a bunch of people who were all looking in the same direction. Sasha and I headed over there, and I couldn't help smiling. We had just gone by a few seal individuals and couples, but now we were passing a small herd of seals. Or pod of seals. Or a colony. Different words were used to describe them in a group. My preference? *Herd* worked fine.

This herd contained five on a couple of nearby floes. They included a mama and pup.

"Aren't they adorable?" asked a lady who held a little boy's hand—very wise up on this somewhat open deck. Despite the railing, I was always concerned that people could slip off, so I made sure to give a brief warning in my introduction. And first thing we did before leaving port, or soon after, was to have Captain Palmer—or whatever captain happened to be in charge of the tour boat we were on—state some rules and regulations relating to safety. Both good ideas in my estimation. I tended to be a worrier.

Last thing we—the Clementos family and all their employees, including me—wanted was for anyone to fall off and get hurt . . . or worse.

"They most certainly are." If I hadn't been planning to head right downstairs to the other decks, I'd have given another talk on the habitat and habits of seals. Maybe later. Right now, I just told Lettie I was heading down, which she knew meant I wanted her to hang out here and keep an eye on our passengers.

"See you in a while," she said.

"Right." I'd put my bag that contained prizes and more in the closed wooden box beneath the microphones, and I was soon on the stairway headed down with Sasha. I held on to the railing, of course, on this moving boat. I passed by the second deck, aiming for the one at the bottom—which also had the galley. I wanted some coffee and to get Sasha some water.

Not that I was tired, but the idea of a bit of caffeine and added energy sounded good.

This deck was almost completely enclosed with glass around the perimeter so our passengers could still see our environment. Also, I was able to unzip my jacket beneath my binoculars. The seating area was nearly filled, as it often was, mostly with people who looked familiar, since I'd seen them upstairs while I was talking. Now they were eating—and also conversing. The acoustics in this encircled area weren't too great, so it sounded a bit loud.

There was also a walkway around the galley at the front of the boat where the kitchen and some storerooms were, though it was narrow and behind doors on each side that were sometimes locked. But it was a good way to see the surroundings. Mostly only crew members went out there, unless they invited a tourist or two to accompany them.

Partway around the galley was a counter with stools, and behind it was a serving area, then the galley's actual preparation place. The person in charge of the galley here was Betsy Jones, a very nice, very efficient lady. She always seemed to be serving someone a drink or snack or even a small meal— sandwiches, fruit, salads—some prepackaged and often healthy. Or not.

I went up to her and planted my butt temporarily on one of the stools.

"Hey, what can I get you, Stacie?" she asked in her high voice. She was about my age, early thirties, and her golden curls framed her face as if she were a lot younger. Her glasses were quite visible and were apparently gradients, since she often lifted or lowered her head to look out of different parts of the lenses. "The usual?"

"If you mean black coffee, the kind I get here each time I give tours on this boat—and some water in Sasha's special bowl—then yes, the usual."

She laughed, and so did I. She turned her back to go grab a paper cup and stick a sleeve on it, then pushed the tap on the large coffee brewer that sat on the back counter.

In moments, I was able to put a lid on and take a sip. "Aaah," I moaned in temporary ecstasy at its heat and flavor. "Perfect. Please put it on my tab." The latter was unnecessary.

We were all entitled to food and drink while on duty, as long as we didn't go overboard. With the ordering, I meant—not literally.

"Everything okay on our top deck?" Betsy asked as she handed me the metal bowl I kept on board for Sasha's water. I bent down and put it on the deck, and sure enough, my smart pup took a quick drink while she could. "Lots of wildlife to show to our guests?"

"Lots of wildlife, yes," I told her, waiting for a short while till Sasha was done drinking. I then put the nearly empty bowl back on a paper towel on the counter that Betsy had left there for sanitation purposes.

"Hey, Stacie," said a male voice behind me, and deckhand Rafe Pedros sat down on the stool beside me.

"Hey, Rafe," I said. "Break time?"

He looked at his wrist to check his watch. "Yeah, for maybe three minutes. Coffee, Betsy, please," he said. Rafe's dark hair swept his ears, and he had a short beard. Nice-looking guy, and he seemed to do a good job on the boat, always busy checking on things when he wasn't working on engine stuff.

"The coffee's good today," I told him. Not that it ever wasn't. And I ran into him a lot here also getting java.

"Glad to hear that." This time it was a female voice from behind me that I recognized: Steph Porter, Captain Palmer's assistant. Evidently he was back on the bridge running the boat, and I figured Steph might be getting not only herself a treat but Palmer too.

Sure enough, she ordered one cup of coffee, one bottle of water, a bag of pretzels, and two of the healthy prepackaged meals containing veggies.

And Betsy, knowing whom the stuff was partially for, hurried to fill the order fast, including her normal routine of unwrapping the packaged meals and putting the contents into a large paper cup to make it easier to eat. She then put the plastic packaging into a recycle container.

Steph was thin and agile and a bit older than the rest of us, but that didn't slow her down. Her brown hair was short, with touches of gray here and there, and her lined hands looked older than her almost-smooth face. I wasn't sure how long she'd worked for ClemTours, but I'd gathered she was a long-term employee, and I could understand why they kept her. She always seemed to be busy doing something to help Palmer or someone else.

She left quickly, and I turned back to Rafe. "You staying around here for a while?" I asked, more to make conversation than to hint that I wanted to hang out with him, though I wouldn't have minded maybe another minute.

"Nope, I've got to go." And soon he was gone.

I turned back to Betsy. "Any chance I can get you to warm this before I go?"

"The usual way?" Which meant putting a bit more of the hot stuff into the cup that had begun to cool. More coffee that way.

"Of course."

She accommodated me, and I said good-bye for now. "Guess I'd better get started back up to my deck—the long way around." As I turned to head back to the stairs, I noticed that my non-buddy Truit was sitting at one of the small tables nearby. He wasn't wearing his hat, so I could see his short hair was almost light enough to be blond. He had his head down, as if he was studying his phone on his lap. Near him was a glass of water, which he clutched in his right hand as tightly as if it were beer. I'd never asked if tour ships were permitted to serve alcohol, but I knew the policy for ClemTours was not to allow it. Safer that way, I figured.

I considered saying hi to him again, but why? Just because we'd met? Not a great idea.

I'd been told the guy had once worked on this boat as a deckhand. Had any of the others—Steph or Rafe—recognized him? Had Betsy? She'd most likely seen him most clearly. And all of them had worked for ClemTours a lot longer than I had.

Palmer had known who he was, of course, although Truit had been up and about then rather than hiding his face.

If the others here had recognized him, would they have said hello? Well, it didn't really matter. I wasn't going to say hi.

He did turn and start talking to a woman at a table nearby, though. I wished I could hear what he said. Was he bad-mouthing this boat again? I certainly hoped not.

As I started walking the other direction, I saw Hansen Horwitz, someone else I'd met on other tours. He immediately approached me. He was big and paunchy, with a round face and gray hair receding at his forehead.

"Hi, Stacie," he said, giving me one big smile on that overstuffed face. He held a sandwich in one hand—salami, maybe?

"Hi, Hansen. I didn't know you were with us today. Didn't see you before."

He looked a bit abashed and glanced down at the wooden deck. "Sorry. I haven't gone up to deck three today, and I assume that's where you've been."

"That's right." I took a sip of my coffee, which was nice and hot—for now. "Have you seen much wildlife? I've mostly been pointing out seals and bears, but I'm going back up there. I'm hoping some otters and birds will appear before we start back."

"Sounds good." He still didn't look at me, but he took a bite from his sandwich.

I had to ask. "Is everything okay?"

"I hope so. Maybe you can tell me. You know how I love these ClemTours, don't you?"

Since I'd seen him on many tours since I'd started, I wasn't surprised. "Sure," I said, puzzled about why he'd mentioned that.

"Well—is it true that there's some kind of trouble with this boat?"

"What? What kind of trouble?" I was floored by the very idea. I loved not only ClemTours but this particular craft. I thought Palmer did a great job as captain, and I liked the other crew members too.

"Er . . . forget it. Just some stupid rumors I heard." Hansen now looked apologetic. "Hey, that coffee looks good. I think I'll get some too—and some more snacks." He took another bite of his sandwich, then finished it. "Care to join me?"

Normally I'd just have said no right away, since I needed to get back up to the third deck. And I did reject the idea of joining him in snacking, although I wanted to stay near this *ClemElk* fan and find out what the heck he was talking about.

Instead I said, "Unfortunately, I do need to get back upstairs. Promise you'll come up there too?"

"Well, sure. I want to hear your talk and see your wildlife."

My wildlife? Maybe, in some ways, it was.

"And you can tell me then what else you'd like me to talk about," I told him. "So I can get you to come on other *ClemElk* tours and show you that all's well with this boat."

"Great!" Hansen said. "I'll join you up there soon."

Which was my cue to leave. Although I couldn't help peeking down at the galley area from the third step. I saw Betsy serve Hansen a drink and more. I saw Truit still sitting there, no longer talking to anyone, although he raised his head and peered around, apparently glancing toward Hansen and Betsy. And I saw a lot of tourists sitting there eating and drinking.

I'd make a callout when I started talking again on the third deck, and maybe some of them would come up. Hansen, probably. Some of the other tourists too.

But hopefully not Truit.

Sasha and I climbed only the first set of stairs initially, then I looked around at the tables and chairs in the middle—and, of course, the windowed perimeter of the second deck with its rails where people could also peek out. Not many here. They were mostly hanging out upstairs where I was heading, and then there'd been the few on the first deck.

We walked around and said hi to the people who stood staring out at the inlet around us, pointing out the nearest floes and seals now and then.

I'd no intention of staying long. *Up to my top deck soon*, I kept telling myself.

Even so, I led Sasha to the bridge, at the bow of this level. It was enclosed with glass so visitors could see our captain and his assistants at work without barging in to bother them.

I nevertheless rapped gently on the glass at the door. Palmer glanced over, smiled, and opened the door.

"Hi, Captain," I said.

"Hi, tour lady," he responded, then stepped back so Sasha and I could enter. He was alone now. Steph wasn't there, unsurprisingly. I'd just seen her near the galley.

"So I'm delighted to see we're getting close to the end of Tracy Arm," I told him.

"Me too. It's always enjoyable to get as close as possible to those twin Sawyer glaciers there. Wish I could be off the bridge more hearing the oohs and aahs of our passengers, but even though Steph does fine near them, I always feel I need to stay in charge most of the time—but I will join you eventually."

"Got it," I said. And I was glad to hear that. Not that the glaciers were about to attack us. We did occasionally see one of them calving a bit, but a large piece of ice separating from the rest and dropping into the water wasn't that dangerous, since we were never too up close and personal. Still . . .

"Speaking of which—" Palmer said.

By which he meant *whom*, I realized, as Steph used her key and stepped into the now-crowded bridge room. "Hi again," she said to me. "And I assume, Palmer, that—"

"Yep, I'll take a short break now so I'll be back here to say hello to the Sawyers."

Food break, potty break, just a break from this small room? I didn't ask. But we walked together till we reached the stairway. I started heading up, and Palmer started down—which was where he'd find the first two of those break goals.

He'd also find—

"Just so you know," I said in a low voice, aware that there were a few passengers sitting at the tables within hearing distance. "That person you weren't thrilled to see is down there."

"Unfortunately, he has to be somewhere till we land. But thanks for letting me know."

Then we both continued in our respective directions. I, of course, had company, since Sasha followed me, still leashed and obedient and wonderful.

When we arrived back on the top deck and I zipped up my hoodie again, I was delighted to see that people were still clustered in various locations near the outer rail. Sure, it was chilly up here, but the view of the sometimes bare and sometimes snow-covered mountains nearby was spectacular.

But I didn't immediately see any wildlife. Darn. Although I could always talk about the view and the glaciers we would soon see, I preferred being able to show the passengers everything at once as I spoke.

Oh well.

I took my place at the bow of the deck, this time choosing the starboard side. Good. There were a few seals on floes visible here, and I of course pointed them out to people, who all seemed delighted to see them.

We kept going for a while. I would soon prepare our tourists to get close to the Sawyer glaciers—only I suddenly heard something that sounded distant. Something that got Sasha to sit up and move her ears.

A possible wolf's howl.

I moved my binoculars to my eyes and looked around. Sure enough, off to our right were some mountains that hadn't much snow on them. Craggy slopes with some greenish vegetation on their surfaces.

And moving, near the top, were several canines. Wolves. And one of them must have been the howler.

"Hey, everyone," I said into my microphone. "Look over there, toward our starboard side, up on the mountain!" I pointed toward the wolves and reveled in the thrilled expressions of my tourist crowd as they looked and also pointed and even cheered.

I used my on-boat communication system to call the bridge to let Palmer know to go even more slowly through this area, although of course he was already keeping the boat's speed down so as not to startle any of the closer wildlife.

"Hey, that's wonderful," responded a voice from the bridge—not Palmer's but Steph's. Hadn't the captain returned there yet? Didn't matter. He'd hear about it from his assistant. When I told her to slow the boat, she immediately agreed.

And sure enough, I felt our minimal speed reduce even more. We even stopped, though not for long.

I talked a little about Alaskan wolves, explaining they were generally a subspecies of gray wolves, but soon got back to discussing glaciers, since we were nearing the end of the arm where the Sawyers existed.

And then there we were. Not too close, of course, but the rivers of ice ahead seemed to flow toward us, though they actually weren't moving. Not even any calving was happening at the moment.

I lectured a little about glaciers and received lots of feedback from the awed passengers. Fun!

I wasn't surprised to see how many of our passengers were now on the top deck viewing our surroundings. Asking me questions—including that cute teen Allie again. Taking lots of pictures, of course. And some petted Sasha.

I even saw Hansen again, in the middle of a crowd, talking and pointing and apparently really enjoying himself—maybe not too surprising, since he'd taken quite a few ClemTours journeys. Even some of our crew came up here to see where we were, though none stayed very long.

I didn't see Truit there, but I gathered he'd seen it all before. Maybe he was still in the galley area hiding out or talking to someone—or making notes about what he could do to achieve his nasty goals.

But all good things come to an end, including the time allotted for this tour, so we eventually turned and started back down Tracy Arm. I took a small break from talking—and wasn't too surprised to see Hansen, who'd been among the crowd before, come toward me. He had a plastic bag hanging from his arm. More goodies from the galley? He'd seemed to be eating quite a bit before when I'd seen him there, so I wouldn't be surprised.

And now he wanted to talk to me? Good. I'd wanted an answer from him. What had he heard about the *ClemElk*?

"This has been great fun, as usual," he told me. He would know, since he took this tour often.

"Thanks," I said. I edged a little closer to him so hopefully no one else would hear. "So tell me what trouble you've heard about this boat."

He leaned down farther, causing Sasha to stand and look at him as though she were protecting me, and I expected a great, horrible revelation. "Not a lot, really. Only I gather there's word out there that some people want to add to the

ClemTours competition, maybe starting mostly in this area where the *ClemElk* cruises. I hope not. I love taking these tours. I want to take a lot more."

"I see," I said. And I did. I'd heard that too, of course, when I'd met that Truit, thanks to Captain Palmer. "Well, we'll just have to see what happens. But this is one really good tour boat, as are all of them in ClemTours. I'm sure it'll all turn out just fine."

And since my fingers were glove-free as usual . . . I looked toward the hillsides we were now passing, and saw Hansen's gaze go that way too.

Which meant I was able to quickly cross my fingers behind my back.

# Chapter Three

As we continued back through Tracy Arm, I didn't shut up—me? never!—but I didn't see a whole lot in the terrain or wildlife that was different from what I'd talked about before. Still, I pointed it all out again, in case anyone hadn't been listening—or was interested enough to hear similar descriptions again, with a few fun changes and twists drawn from my knowledge.

Which actually did appear to include a lot of the passengers, since the upper deck remained fairly crowded.

That seemed to be the way it was on most of the *ClemElk* tours I'd talked on, and others too—including most ClemTours I'd gone on to observe before I started taking charge.

Did I get bored saying the same things at the beginning of every tour? No way. Nor did I bore myself with my own repetitions as the tour went on. I tried to vary how I phrased things and point out differences, for both our passengers' benefit and my own.

Things changed anyway thanks to my passengers' ongoing and interesting questions and comments. And the wildlife, of whatever type, included different individuals and groups in different locations. I always had fun and did all I could to ensure the tourists did too.

I noticed when Lettie arrived up here. She must not have had many people on the galley deck to talk to, and I was happy when she started nosing her way into a group here, a group there, interacting with the tourists as they still watched the areas around us. She caught my eye several times and clearly was pointing toward the animals I mentioned in my ongoing talk—acting, as she should, as my backup.

Eventually we reached the end of the approximately thirty-mile-long Tracy Arm fjord and started on our way back to Juneau, a distance of about forty-five miles. Of course I hoped we'd see some sea life soon—humpback whales or orcas, maybe, or porpoises. But for now, I decided I could take another break. Get some more coffee. See where most of the passengers who'd been up on my deck had gone now that we'd left glaciers and Tracy Arm behind.

I'd enjoy what was left of this cruise, as I always did—and do all I could to make sure our tourists did too. Sure, I'd talk a lot more a little later. But a short time to myself was fine.

Only . . . okay, as I said, I'm a worrier. I'd heard Captain Palmer argue with passenger Truit, who'd once worked here and now might be devising a way to compete enough to put ClemTours out of business. That could be an exaggeration, of course, since ClemTours was a well-established tour company. But someone with that goal in mind could hurt the business, even if it wasn't ruined. And Truit seemed inclined to criticize this boat and how it was run, possibly to more of the passengers.

Also, Hansen's hints suggested that word was out that maybe ClemTours actually was, or could be, in trouble.

We had a little while out here, and taking that bit of time to reassure myself that all wasn't potentially dire could be a good thing. As a result, Sasha and I stopped on the bridge deck on the way downstairs. We walked forward, since I wanted to pop in at the bridge and talk a little with Palmer about it all, but when I peeked through the glass, only Steph was there. Again, no problem. Palmer had undoubtedly set our course back toward home, and Steph would just have to ensure we were doing okay. She was skilled enough to have set the course herself and steer that way anyhow.

But I clearly wasn't going to get this opportunity to ask Palmer any questions. Maybe later. Or maybe I'd ask someone else in his family when we were back onshore. Or several someones.

Still . . . well, not only am I a worrier, but I'm also filled with compulsiveness and determination.

If I couldn't talk to Palmer about it right now, I wanted to speak with someone else who'd have answers. That wouldn't be Hansen, since he had expressed concern and given some info about where that concern had come from. No, the person I decided to approach was the person on board who might be the root of this potentially unwelcome future.

And so, tugging Sasha's leash gently, I started down to the bottom deck. Hey, two great goals were possible there.

More coffee.

And a discussion with Truit.

What was his first name? Oh yeah, Sheldon. He'd mentioned that himself, though Palmer had called him nothing but Truit. That, therefore, was how I thought of him.

Sasha and I had to stay to the right of the stairs on our trip down them. A bunch of tourists were heading up, and they all patted Sasha on the head as they passed by.

"Enjoying your tour?" I asked them. There were two couples I'd seen hanging out together, and they'd remained mostly on my deck for our outing.

"Loving it!" exclaimed one of the women, a pretty college-age lady. In fact, they all looked about that age, and I assumed they were traveling together during a school break.

But I tended to make a lot of assumptions, some of which could be wrong.

"So glad to hear that," I called over my shoulder as Sasha and I reached the bottom of the stairs and the others continued up.

The seating area on this part of the deck was crowded. Apparently not everyone wanted to watch the water from above as we returned to Juneau—or to hear what I said about where we were and what we saw. That was fine.

I got coffee first. Betsy raised her blond eyebrows when I first requested it and tossed a meaningful glance toward the area where the restrooms were located, but she got me a fresh cup without saying anything else.

And yes, I did head that way, to the ship's head—the term for its bathrooms—and not just because she'd suggested it. No problem carrying my coffee there either.

I assumed Betsy visited this area now and then, too, and left the galley alone at least momentarily, or even visited the kitchen behind the galley area, but I'd never failed to see the busy lady behind the counter.

When Sasha and I came back to the seating area, I looked around for the person who was my current target. But I didn't see Truit.

I did see Palmer, though, and walked to where he was sitting.

"Hi, Captain," I said. "Can we go over there and talk?" I nodded toward the side of the galley's serving area where one of the doors to the prow area was—nice and nearly private over there.

"Sure, but only for a minute. I need to get back to the bridge."

"Of course."

He carried a bottle of water and joined Sasha and me where I'd indicated. Very quietly I told him I was looking for Truit to talk to him about what he planned in the way of competition for the Clementos fleet. "I realize it's not really my business, but I care about all of you and your company. You may already know all you need to do to counter whatever he's up to, but—"

"No," Palmer said softly, "we don't. And I'd usually tell someone in your position to just back off and let us handle it anyway, but . . . well, I appreciate your concern and will be interested in whether you do learn anything helpful. Not that we're unused to competition."

No, they definitely weren't. There were a lot of other companies providing water tours from all of the many Alaskan ports. But in my opinion, ClemTours was among the best.

Palmer hadn't stopped talking despite my mind's diverting to ponder his competition. "Something about the way this guy seems to be approaching it, though—learning what he could as one of our deckhands a while back, though I understand he now also works for other tour companies on and off. But now he specifically mentions that he wants to be our adversary and succeed at it. I don't get it—and we don't want it."

"Got it," I said, then asked, "Do you happen to know where he is right now? Last time I saw him, he was sitting in this area and seemed to be somewhat hiding."

"No, but if I do see him, I'll contact you and let you know where he is."

"Thanks."

Palmer rose and started up the steps toward the bridge. I found it interesting that he had encouraged me in my quest to learn what I could from Truit. Maybe he and members of his family were doing the same thing, finding out all they could so they could determine the best way to confront him and keep him from injuring their business.

Well, I wasn't sure I'd be able to help much, but I was certainly going to look into it.

And right now, I wanted to find him. Once we docked and he left, he'd go do whatever he was going to do, and I wouldn't learn anything.

Okay, I hadn't seen Truit on my deck, nor on the middle deck when I'd gone to the bridge to talk to Palmer, though I hadn't really looked for him then.

But now I was definitely looking.

Not that I could determine if he was in the men's head, but I'd been on this deck long enough that he was likely to have come out if that's where he was.

He had to know his way around this boat, since he'd worked here before as a deckhand.

*Deckhand.* I headed with Sasha to the stern of the ship on this deck, where the deckhands generally hung out near the engine when not working on other stuff. I wasn't aware if Rafe or Al knew who Truit was or that he'd previously had the same job they did, but when I found them together, I asked if they'd had any visitors here from among the ship's passengers after we'd started back toward Juneau. Both indicated they'd stayed in this area of the boat since we'd left Tracy Arm and hadn't seen anyone else.

Okay, so now where should I check? I looked around the seating area again but still didn't see him there.

Time for my sweet, calm Sasha and me to go up to the next deck.

Palmer and Steph were both on the bridge. The seating area in the center of that deck was fairly empty. People were apparently hanging out at the first or third deck, which was the usual.

In any case, I didn't see Truit there.

Next? Back up to my top deck. Where, by the way, I had designated a small, enclosed area with special pads at the bottom as Sasha's head.

It was still busy here, with groups of tourists still looking over the side. Lettie was in charge, visiting the groups again—still—and reminding them to stay careful as they stood near the rails.

I went over to talk to her. She was my closest buddy here as well as my assistant on board, and I knew she'd tell me if she had any helpful info.

"Sorry, Stacie," she said, her brows knit in a concerned scowl after I told her what I was doing—and why I was getting a bit worried. What was the guy up to?

"It's weird that you can't find him," she continued. "Since I learned he's the same Truit who used to be a deckhand here, I've wondered what he's up to, too, in disguise like that." I might tell her what I understood about it later, but this wasn't a good time. "But since he was a deckhand, he might know all the possible nooks and crannies there are to hide in."

My sentiments exactly. But—

"Are you aware of any?" I asked. "I'm not."

She wasn't either.

Strange that I hadn't located him anywhere. Was he somehow determined to avoid me, using the other set of steps near the aft area to go up as I headed down, and vice versa? But if so, why?

"Hey, Stacie," Lettie said then. "Look!"

She pointed off the port side of the boat, where a small pod of Dall's porpoises was swimming, most breaching simultaneously, then going back down into the water.

My job and love of wildlife kicked in, and I picked up the microphone to point out our new companions and fill the tourists in on cetaceans, Dall's porpoises in particular.

The black-and-white porpoises hung out with us for a while, occasionally riding our boat's bow waves. I thought almost all our passengers had joined me on the top deck to look and listen and call out about how cute the porpoises were. But then those adorable cetaceans swam away as we continued back toward Juneau.

Still no sign of Truit, watching the porpoises or otherwise. "I'll be back up here before we land," I told Lettie, leaving her in charge on this deck again. I considered telling her to watch out for Truit for me in case he somehow was successfully sneaking around and avoiding me but decided I didn't want to let her know how obsessive I was starting to get about this.

And so I walked around the third deck with Sasha at my side, stopping when she wanted to, including at her head station, and then we went down the rear set of steps to the second deck. There I again looked around at the few people seated in the center and up at the bridge.

No Truit.

Next, down to deck one, where I'd last seen him—but had looked for him unsuccessfully just a while earlier.

No Truit.

How strange. Just in case—since I was sure he knew about the locked but open area at the prow around the galley—I took the key from its hook just inside the galley and opened one of the doors. I then walked around that pathway. Fun to be that close to the water as we pressed forward.

But no Truit.

Now I felt really baffled. I locked the door again as Sasha and I headed into the galley area, recognizing that Betsy had seen me, but so what? I could have been out there just looking for more sea life. I returned the key and once more looked around at the seated and standing passengers here who were talking to one another.

I even kept my gaze downward for a while, in case he was somehow hiding beneath the tables, but still didn't see him.

So now what? I returned to the bridge, knocked, and went in. "I've been looking around for Truit," I told Palmer, "and I can't find him anywhere."

"He's probably trying to pull some stupid trick on us," the captain responded, his usually good-humored face squashed into an expression of exasperation—and anger. "Well, we're not playing his game. Forget about him. We'll grab him to talk to after we dock and everyone gets off the boat."

Which seemed like an entirely sensible idea to me. But I was still irritated—and confused—by the fact that despite all my efforts, I'd seen no sign of him.

Even so, I returned to my deck, sat down, and listened for a while as Lettie talked about the sea, the skyline, the distant shoreline. She did a great job. I figured she'd eventually take over as a tour guide on one of the ClemTours boats, although she didn't have the kind of background on wildlife that some of us who narrated the tours did.

But I'd be glad to help her out if she ever needed it.

We grew closer to Juneau and the place we'd dock. I petted Sasha, who sat on the deck beside me, and tried not to think about my frustration regarding Truit.

Where the heck was he? How had he hidden so well?

But at the back of my mind, a horrible thought had taken root and begun scratching at my brain.

Had he somehow fallen overboard?

Nah. He was an experienced sailor. He knew this boat and where we'd gone.

And he hadn't purposely jumped overboard—had he?

Yes, that scratching at my brain was becoming even more destructive.

Why would he do such a thing? It might hurt the ClemTours' ability to remain successful, but killing himself certainly wouldn't help him start a competing company.

I wasn't about to mention that possibility to anyone. I wasn't even about to mention the fact that I couldn't find Truit to anyone besides Palmer.

I'd just get off the boat as quickly as I could and stand on the dock, watching for him.

We reached Juneau a short while later and soon pulled up to our specified docks, where some of the ClemTours boats berthed till their next outing. Only one other was there now.

I'd planted myself near the forward stairway and didn't wait for passengers to start saying good-bye to Sasha and me there. Instead, after retrieving my versatile prize bag from its box, I grabbed the rail and Sasha's leash and hurried down both flights, then through the galley area on the lowest deck to the now-open exit area.

There we were among the first to disembark, walking down the gangway to the wooden pier. I moved away from the gangway then, and Sasha and I turned and waited to see who else got off.

I did do my duty—my fun duty—of saying good-byes to our tourists and thanking them for joining us . . . and inviting them to join us again. Many expressed pleasure at what they'd done and seen, and some even said they'd be glad to return for another visit to Alaska and tour with ClemTours.

Which made me smile and internally cheer—especially when Captain Palmer, wearing his ClemTours jacket and a big, hearty smile, joined me in our farewells.

At one point, during a lull, he asked, "Has Truit disembarked?"

"I haven't seen him," I said. "But I've been watching."

I was soon engulfed in a big hug from Hansen. "Great tour," he said. "But—is everything okay? I haven't seen Truit for a while. Did he fall off the boat?"

He knew Truit. Interesting. I hadn't noticed them together on this tour, but that didn't mean they hadn't talked to one another.

I definitely didn't like Hansen's suggestion of where Truit might be.

I started to force a laugh at the very idea, but before I did, another nearby passenger exclaimed, "What!"

Unsurprising. Hansen didn't exactly have a soft voice. It was almost as if he'd wanted others to hear.

People began asking more questions then as they continued to disembark. Some seemed quite upset. "Did someone go overboard?" asked one of the women in that pair of couples I figured were college students.

"Not that we know of," Palmer said, which was sort of true. We didn't really know.

Other crew members, including Lettie and Steph, Rafe and Al, and Betsy, joined us one by one and also helped with our farewells.

Still no Truit.

Eventually, no one else seemed to be getting off the boat.

Palmer said to the deckhands, "I'd like you to go back and make sure we don't have any stowaways hiding onboard. We'll be doing this again tomorrow, after all."

Both Rafe and Al looked at each other, then at their boss. This was the first time I'd heard of this request too, and I was sure it puzzled them.

Not that I was going to explain why.

Palmer let the rest of the crew go, but of course I remained there waiting and watching, curious and hoping . . . and very, very concerned.

Especially when, maybe fifteen minutes later, Rafe and Al reappeared.

"Ship's empty, Captain," Rafe said. He was being fairly formal, since we all used each other's first names most of the time, except sometimes in front of tourists.

"Okay, thanks, guys," Palmer said. He looked at me and shrugged his shoulders. Then he pulled his phone out of his pocket and called 911. "I guess we'd better get some official help, since we don't really know what happened," he said. "And of course I'll wait till they come. Can you too?"

"Of course," I said. I knew I had to, and not just because of my curiosity. I'd kind of gotten this concern going, since I'd been the one to start looking for Truit.

It didn't take long for an official vehicle to pull up on the road near the docks. It said *Alaska State Troopers* on the side. A couple of troopers got out and joined us near the boat. At least there were now appropriate officials on the job, trying to figure this out.

But where on earth—or sea—was Sheldon Truit?

# Chapter Four

I was tired of looking. And worrying.

But I realized I'd not get Truit out of my thoughts till he was found.

Even so, I didn't need to stay here to do my worrying. And leaving the boat behind might help my state of mind.

What I wanted to do now was walk away quickly with Sasha, take her to my SUV parked in the nearby lot reserved for employees of the tour boats, and drive off quickly to the dog-friendly apartment I rented in Juneau. I often stopped to pick up takeout food, or at a grocery store, so I'd be sure to have a good dinner.

Sasha? I always kept a good supply of the healthiest of dog foods at home, as well as an assortment of special treats— some of which I brought on our tours, both as rewards for her wonderful behavior and to keep her from getting hungry.

But I was nearly out of the ones I kept in my pocket. And I figured, with the Initial Response Section here now—which I'd just overheard Rafe and Al talking about as a very special arm of the Alaska State Troopers that sometimes took part in search-and-rescue missions—my ability to leave with Sasha was likely to take a while.

Drat it.

Even so, my tote bag over my shoulder with my binoculars inside, I started leading Sasha away from the port area. A lot of the piers along the currently still, blue water were occupied by other tour boats, including another ClemTours vessel. We were near the paved ground where our tourists gathered as we got ready for a tour, and I headed toward the parking lot. I didn't slink along the ground or anything else sneaky. But I hoped the troopers would let me go.

One of the two was talking to Palmer, who I assumed had identified himself as the person who called them. I was glad I'd already moved away from where my fellow crew members stood near the *ClemElk*'s gangway. A few of our tourists also hung around, standing on the pier area toward the aft of the boat. The second trooper had approached them.

Only—as I held up my hand slightly in a wave good-bye to everyone, the first uniformed trooper left Palmer's direct presence and approached me. He was tall, in a long-sleeved beige shirt with a thick blue vest over it and long navy pants with a stripe up the side. A badge on the vest identified him as Liam Amaruq, Alaska State Trooper, Initial Response Section. "You're Stacie Calder, the ship's tour director on this outing, right?"

"Yes," I said, wishing I could say no without possible repercussions. Palmer must have identified me.

"Mr. Clementos—Palmer—said you were the first one to notice that Mr. Truit was apparently missing."

I finally made myself look up into his face, after giving Sasha a stay order to remain sitting beside me on the concrete ground. It wasn't too cold out, so she should be at least somewhat comfortable. And as she sat near my knees, I touched the top of her furry head between her pointed ears.

This Liam was a good-looking trooper, with strong facial features and a wide brow between smooth, dark hair and deep brown eyes that appeared to want to dive right into my skull and check out my brain.

Yep, I studied him as if he were one of the wild creatures I most liked to see and analyze. But what I wanted to analyze was what he thought about the situation—and my connection to it.

"Yes, I guess so," I told him. "I knew we were about to head back to shore, and I'd spoken briefly to Mr. Truit before. I wanted to ask if he'd enjoyed his ride today, since I understood he likes local tours. So I started looking for him but didn't find him." And that was all I intended to say about my contact with him. I didn't want to mention what I'd heard about how interested he was in existing Alaskan boat tours around here. Or what his purported plans were.

Just in case something had happened to the guy, I didn't want to be considered involved with it, other than as a remote observer.

"I see," the trooper said. "Well, I'm going to have more questions for you, so please hang around. I'll be discussing the situation with those of you who work for ClemTours, and my fellow officer will continue to question the tourists who are still around."

Just then, I heard a helicopter in the distance, and as I looked up, it got closer till it was right overhead. It had a logo on the side similar to the one this guy had on his vest. "Is that—"

"Yes," he said. "We don't know how concerned to be about this missing tourist, so the copter will cruise around the tour route just in case the guy fell off the boat and is swimming in the water."

If he'd fallen off the boat, I suspected Truit wouldn't be swimming. Even though the air wasn't too cold, the water we'd motored through had some pretty cold areas—as evidenced by the ice floes I'd been able to point out wildlife on.

On the other hand, I wasn't exactly sure where we'd been when I'd last seen Truit, and if it had been closer to this pier, the water was most likely warmer.

Which didn't necessarily mean he'd just be able to have a fun outing swimming back to shore.

"So, are you ready to answer some questions soon, Stacie?"

Stacie? We were on a first-name basis? Fine with me, although I assumed that he thought the friendlier we were, the more likely I was to tell him what he wanted to hear.

"Sure, Liam," I said, and he shot me a wry grin as he motioned for me to follow him back to where my *ClemElk* cohorts stood. An intriguing grin. But no way would I let myself feel attracted to this guy.

Sasha trotted beside me as I complied with Liam's beckoning. So much for hurrying home for the evening. I wasn't sure what my next step here was, how my next tour might go tomorrow. But I couldn't help wondering what Truit was up to. Was this a real, dangerous disappearance—or was he playing games to harm the boat he'd once belonged to?

Soon I stood there with the group while Liam took one of us aside at a time, Palmer first. The captain had to be most important. I just wished I could hear what they said.

Then he drew Steph, Palmer's assistant, off to the side and they talked, and I realized these discussions were pretty brief, at least for now. That was the good part. But I'd no doubt the trooper would schedule something a lot more detailed if any of us came up with something he wanted more info about.

Next, it was Betsy from the galley. Then my assistant Lettie. Then deckhands Al and Rafe.

Meanwhile, those of us who were free for the moment exchanged comments, mostly about how upset we were—not necessarily because Truit was missing, but because he might be somewhere laughing at us.

Then it was my turn. Sasha and I walked with Liam toward the aft area of the boat, and we stood on the land away from everyone else.

The questions Liam shot at me weren't fun at all, and I had to watch myself to make sure I didn't accuse Truit of wanting to become a ClemTours competitor. It was up to Palmer to reveal that, if he hadn't already. I didn't know the actuality or details of it like our captain might.

But Liam kept interrogating me, longer than he had the others, maybe because I would have seen Truit around the passengers more. He asked when I first noticed Truit, what tourists were around him, when I first met him, whether I was introduced to him and by whom, and more, and I had the impression he hoped I'd reveal I'd immediately disliked the guy.

He also asked if I recalled seeing Truit talking to any specific passengers, particularly those who'd taken this tour before. The only one like that I was aware of was Hansen, but I didn't recall seeing them together. Still, why did Liam ask?

Had one of those he'd already questioned suggested some relationship between Truit and Hansen he'd be checking into?

I answered the questions he asked me honestly but briefly without saying what I felt or disclosing anything I'd learned about Truit. And I couldn't help but remember my comment to our now-missing passenger when Palmer was around and I'd first learned who Truit was—that we could head for a shore far from here and let him off there, since he knew what the tour was all about.

Had Palmer mentioned that to Liam?

Well, I wasn't about to mention it myself—but I could start interrogating Liam back in other ways.

"Do you realize that Mr. Truit might be doing this to ruin upcoming tours on our boat?" I demanded.

"Why would he do that?" Liam asked, one hand on his narrow hip as his look again seemed to bore inside me.

"I don't know, but I had the impression he had something against this boat. I heard he once worked on the *ClemElk*." Okay. I'd revealed something—but hoped that Palmer had mentioned it first.

"That's what I understand," Liam said, and I tried not to show it as I issued a sigh of relief. "Do you know why he no longer does?"

"Nope," I said. "He hasn't been a deckhand since I started working here last year." In other words, talk more with Palmer about it.

"Got it." Liam had a few more questions—and then he did something I hadn't expected. "I've called in some more of my fellow patrol members to come and inspect the ship and look for Mr. Truit. But since you were the first to report him missing and I gather you looked for him first, I want you to accompany me on a walk through the *ClemElk* while we look for him again. Okay?"

*No, of course not*, I wanted to shout.

But if I did that and something had in fact happened to Truit, I'd undoubtedly appear involved—and guilty.

"Okay." My response was appropriate, but my tone sounded like I wanted to throw up.

And maybe I did. Particularly because I was worried about why this law enforcement guy had chosen me to grill on a longer-term basis for the moment than anyone else. I was neutral. A near newbie. I didn't know much.

I shot a glance at Palmer as we walked by where he still stood with the rest of our crew. Yes, he was watching us. Did he trust me not to say anything that could harm him or his family members—or anyone else affiliated with ClemTours, for that matter?

And why did Liam want just me, and not the captain, to accompany him? I wasn't about to ask.

It certainly was my intention to protect every one of the Clementoses as much as I could. I had no reason to feel that any of them had harmed Truit—or if someone had, I'd no information to point any fingers at them.

And okay. I remained highly curious about Truit. If I walked around our tour boat with this law enforcement officer, who apparently worked a lot in search and rescue, and a clue remained on board, I might learn something about what had happened.

Which might be a stretch, but what the heck? I'd try to help while absorbing all the info about search and rescue I could. Or at least search. I figured that if Truit was still on board or somewhere else around here, we'd know it—so the likelihood was that Liam didn't intend for us to rescue him.

Though I'd be glad to try to help if he did.

We now walked briskly, Sasha leashed at my right and Liam on my left, to the boat's gangway. It was usually blocked off when this much time had passed since we'd docked, but not now. I figured our deckhands had either been told in advance not to touch it or they'd removed the usual barrier in anticipation of further boarding, this time by law enforcement.

And, it appeared, Sasha and me.

"So," I said to Liam, "how do you want to do this—start at the main deck and go up, or start on the top, mostly open deck?"

"Not sure it matters, since there'll be people down here, including my partner, who'll be able to watch to see if Truit does show up and get off." He looked up and studied the boat from this angle, at the side. "What all is on the top deck?"

"It's mostly a viewing area for tours, open around most of the outside and seats in the center."

"Good. Let's go there first. It should be fairly easy to eliminate it as an area where he's hiding—or lying injured."

So this truly could be a possible search and rescue in the trooper's point of view. Fine. I didn't need to tell Liam how I'd looked all over the ship and would most likely have seen Truit if he'd been hurt and shoved somewhere.

And if he'd just been hiding—well, I wasn't the only one who'd ultimately looked for him. Was it possible he was still there, purposely staying out of sight?

Anything was possible, but I doubted it.

But I still had no idea where he'd gone or how he'd gotten there. So I led Liam up the ramp and onto the boat's lowest deck, then up a stairway to the topmost, open-air deck with its canopy roof.

Anyone who might be in the center seating area would undoubtedly be visible. I saw no one.

"I assume this is a good place for tourists to be when the boat's moving or when you're giving a talk, right?"

Good. This cop apparently knew what was done on tour boats. "I certainly think so. It's my favorite place to be when I'm lecturing or pointing out wildlife or glaciers or other things to see while we're out in the water."

We'd started walking along the starboard side near the waist-high railing. I looked off to the side and pretended we were out to sea and I could see seals or bears or wolves and not just the groupings of people on the nearby shore. And—well, yes, I kind of kept watch to see if any of those people could be Truit.

But I didn't see him.

"This is very nice," Liam said. "I can see why it would be a good deck to be on while you're out on a tour." Gee, could he read my thoughts?

"Absolutely," I said, and at his further questions, I explained how the small mounted box at the prow on this level contained microphones with cords that I could plug in at various places, or I could just use them with batteries, so I could be nearly anywhere on the boat and still provide talks about what we were seeing that came over the designated loudspeakers.

As we walked, a bank of clouds passed overhead. The deck had been illuminated a lot more brightly by the sun moments before, and the change must have spurred Liam's next question. He was looking up, as I did. The clouds were bright white and didn't seem to indicate a storm rolling in, but nevertheless he asked, "What do you do up here when it starts raining or snowing?"

"Depends on the amount and how hard it's blowing. I'll go downstairs to one of the other decks sometimes, since even with the roof, this deck is open enough for precipitation to blow in if we're moving." I tried not to sound as if the answer was obvious and the question a dumb one to ask. It wasn't, really. There was at least one other alternative, which I told him. "We also have a few clear plastic tarps that can be attached here and there around the perimeter if the conditions aren't too bad."

"Where do you keep them?"

As if I kept them anywhere. "Our deckhands fetch them from the rear of this deck."

"Can you show me where?"

"Sure." I began leading him down the center of the deck from the bow, where we currently were, through the rows of seats, with Sasha tied at the bow for now. I'd been told pretty much everything about this boat and its nearly identical ClemTours siblings in case I was asked by our tourists, although I hadn't been on one yet when the covers had been used. I did point out a couple of the pipes along the sides that held up the roof and could also have tarps attached when needed.

The prow of the boat was pointed, but the stern area was longish and blunt. An enclosed area near the aft stairs, along the starboard side at the back, was where Sasha's pads were, and fortunately the deckhands often replaced them for me. Also, a long metal box lay within the most forward part of that enclosure—where the tarps were kept. I showed that to Liam.

"Was this opened to look for Truit?" he demanded immediately. His tone was sharp, as if he was accusing me of failing to do something critical.

"I didn't do it," I said. I didn't even know if the thing was kept locked. But on looking at it now, it did appear to be a size that could hold a human body—stuck there by someone else. Or hiding.

Could Truit have removed the tarps somehow and . . .

"Damn," I whispered, hoping Liam didn't hear it. Had the jerk, who obviously could know all the hiding places on the boat, hidden here?

But there were other places he could have hidden too. And no one had seen him.

Still, I reached the box first and grabbed the top, yanking it up.

There wasn't a whole lot of empty space with the folded tarps there, but yes, Truit might have been able to hide on top of them.

If so, he wasn't there now. But a black knit cap was.

And I recalled that a black knit cap was one of the first things I'd noticed about the man asking me tour questions when I'd initially met him.

Who'd turned out to be Truit.

"Damn!" I said again, louder this time. I reached toward the cap, then stopped. I had a law enforcement guy with me, and the cap could be evidence of . . . something. Truit's possible presence right here sometime, at least.

Or it could be someone else's.

Still, I told Liam about having seen Truit with a cap like this.

"Interesting," he said, pulling his phone from his pocket and taking some pictures. "Glad you didn't touch it. We'll need to keep this place secure, just in case." He didn't say just in case of what. "Maybe this entire deck, until we're certain Mr. Truit is okay and someplace else."

I doubted that would happen right away. And—it struck me then. "Do you mean this boat won't be able to take any more tours till we know where Truit is?"

"Probably." The gaze Liam leveled at me was challenging, as if he expected me to object.

Which I did, in a way. "I certainly hope he's okay—somewhere," I hissed. "But if he's done this on purpose, figuring he'd be ruining our ability to sail for now, take no further tours out till he's found—" I didn't finish, but I did see Liam nod slightly, and I quickly looked away and closed my mouth, knowing I'd better not say anything more against the guy. At least for now. Till he was found and it became clear he'd gone missing in order to hurt this boat, this company.

And I hoped it was something as nasty as that but that he'd staged it all—and remained unharmed somewhere.

Liam stepped away and made a call on his phone—undoubtedly to someone official who could come up here and take charge of the box and the cap and whatever else might be appropriate as evidence. Maybe one of his colleagues he'd said were on their way to conduct their own checking of the boat. Of course, that presupposed there was some crime it contained evidence of.

If someone had harmed Truit, sure. But would he be guilty of something if he was just playing vicious games against ClemTours by pretending to disappear?

"Let's continue with our examination of this boat," Liam said, his voice low and cool, as if he hoped to calm me. I assumed whoever he'd called would do what was needed to make sure no one else came on board for now.

"Fine," I said through my teeth. "The deck below us next."

I let him close the lid of the box, not wanting to touch it again and figuring it was inappropriate for me, a civilian, to do so when it contained something that might be important to . . . whatever.

Then I quickly walked along the port side of the deck till I reached Sasha, unhooked her leash from where I'd hooked it, and waited for Liam at the top of the stairs we'd used to reach this deck before.

Down the stairs to the next level—where the bridge was. I showed Liam that first. The room curving around the prow on this deck was locked, but there were enough windows that we could see no one was inside.

There weren't any further rooms on this level, but we walked around the perimeter, checking out the tables and chairs inside and the railings here too, which were surrounded by glass.

"This looks like the right place to be if you've got rain or other precipitation on one of your tours," Liam noted. Which of course was the reality I'd been fed when I first was taken around a couple of the ClemTours boats to introduce me to them. No tours were given in the late fall or the winter, times when it would probably snow.

"Certainly likely to be more comfortable than the one above us," I acknowledged. "I've only been out in a few rainstorms, though, and mostly could have stayed above, but I did come down here sometimes to give my tours, since more tourists gravitated to this level or below."

"Yes, below," Liam said. And that's where we headed next.

Of course this deck had a lot more places where someone could hide—in the galley at the prow and in the rooms behind it, including the kitchen, and in the enclosures toward the aft area where the deckhands kept equipment and hung out, plus the meeting areas. I explained that to Liam on our way down. "But this is the level I assumed Truit was most likely to be hiding, so I looked in all those places and didn't see him."

Nevertheless, Liam had me lead him from one area to the next and describe what each was used for.

He seemed fascinated. And maybe not because he was searching for Truit, since it was clear right away that many of the enclosures were empty, though Liam still checked them all out carefully.

I didn't ask why. I wasn't sure I wanted to know.

We finished checking out all areas—after I opened the ones that were locked, since I knew where the keys were kept.

"I like cruising," Liam told me. "Which is a good thing, since there are a lot of boats in Alaska where I can take trips and tours. Maybe I'll even buy a boat someday."

"Great," I said, almost without thinking. "Do you want to become a competitor of ClemTours too?"

We had reached the top of the ramp leading off the boat, and we both stopped. And looked at each other.

Yeah, this Liam was one good-looking guy. One I could want to get to know more under other circumstances. Too bad, in a way, that we were foes of sorts, at least right now. He might not suspect me of having anything to do with Truit's disappearance, but he probably suspected Palmer or someone else connected with my ClemTours employer.

And unfortunately, he could be right. I had no idea what had happened—or if someone I knew had in some way harmed Truit.

"Maybe," Liam said, his grin growing wider. "Or maybe not. I like what I do. So let's go ahead and leave the boat." He scanned the shore. "I think I see some more of my fellow troopers down there, and we need to talk about what's next."

Of course he did. I didn't have to be happy about it. Sasha and I led him off the boat, and he refastened the onboard gate behind us. Then we all walked down the gangway.

Palmer met us at the bottom along with a woman in a similar uniform to Liam's, but she seemed to have more brass on her vest. Her name tag introduced her as Sergeant Peggy Frost.

Frost? An appropriate name for Alaska, I thought.

"Find anything?" Palmer asked, glancing from me to Liam and back again.

I started to tell him about the black pull-on cap we'd seen in the tarp box on the top deck, but Liam beat me to it. "There's something that we found that might belong to Truit." He looked at Sergeant Frost, who might be his boss. "I already reported it."

"So that's why—" Palmer began, but this time the sergeant beat him to it.

"We'll be checking it out tomorrow," she said. "It's getting late today." Which it was—nearly seven o'clock. Of course here in Alaska in May, there was still a bunch of waning daylight left.

I knew what Palmer had started to say. "Then the *ClemElk* won't be able to give a tour tomorrow?" I also knew I sounded angry, but I liked giving my tours. And the company counted on me—and the other guides, and having the boats busy on all scheduled days.

"No," Palmer said. "But fortunately, it was a day off for the *ClemWolf*. We'll have our regular outing but on that boat instead."

"Oh, I'm so glad," I responded. I wanted to ask if there'd been any progress in finding Truit elsewhere but figured I'd hear about it somehow—if not tonight, then tomorrow.

"Me too," Liam said. "Oh, and by the way, I'll be taking your tour tomorrow on the *ClemWolf*."

"Really?" I again looked at Palmer as I felt an unwelcome shimmer of interest tickle my mind.

Palmer didn't look thrilled, but he nodded. "Really," he responded.

# Chapter Five

It was finally time to head home. I led Sasha around the dock area as I said good-night to Palmer and my coworkers—and my interrogator Liam. He had given me a business card so I'd have the info to call him if I thought of anything useful. But I'd already told him the little I knew.

I'd see him and the rest tomorrow. Like it or not. I wasn't certain how I felt about Liam hanging out on board, listening to my tour, watching again for the missing Truit, who surely wouldn't be there—especially since it would be a different ClemTours boat. I supposed Liam just wanted to see how the tour, and the boat, were run and look at different possibilities of how someone could disappear.

Well, okay. I'd deal with him then, if necessary. And not allow myself to feel any unwelcome interest.

This evening, at least, it was just Sasha and me.

The walk to the parking lot didn't take long, although of course I let my energetic husky, who'd been appropriately calm all day, sniff along the way and do what else she needed to, with my cleanup assistance. I even ran with her for a short while to help her ease off some of that energy she'd stored inside on the ship.

When we reached our car, the parking lot was fairly empty. Most of the tour boats had undoubtedly returned a while back and the crews been allowed to leave. I let Sasha pull me toward one of the few cars left there, my medium blue SUV. I'd chosen it because white ones would be impossible to see at times during snow season, black ones were too common, and heck, I really liked this shade of blue.

And I needed a car as large as this to ensure my protective pup would have plenty of room in the back seat as I drove.

I let her hop in, then fastened her to the seat with a doggy seat belt. She never appeared to mind the enforced immobility. Maybe she somehow knew it was for her own protection.

Yes, I protected my protective pup as much as she protected me.

Our drive wasn't particularly long. My apartment was in a residential area of Juneau near downtown, also not far from the shoreline area from which most boat tours departed. I'd have liked a place farther away, in a nearby but less developed area where there'd be more wildlife visible—but I was in town sometimes when the weather got bad, and I didn't want to be marooned anywhere that it might be difficult, or even impossible, to get around.

Besides, I could always visit Juneau Wildlife World, the nearby theme park where I'd worked before joining Clem-Tours and still did in the winter months when no tours were given.

On the way home, I did my frequent thing of stopping to pick up dinner at a fast-food place—one where the sub sandwich was cut into segments and contained lots of good veggies along with the roast chicken. Sasha stayed in the car when I went in to get it. The temperature was cool enough, of course, that it wasn't unhealthy for her.

Soon we were home. It was still daylight, though it was eight o'clock at night. The sun wouldn't begin to set till nine-ish here in May in Juneau. Our place was in a small but nice development, and I'd been able to rent a comfy and convenient unit on the ground floor—the better for taking Sasha in and out. And my lease absolutely permitted my pup to live with me.

I parked right outside our door, then walked Sasha briefly again. I got her dinner ready as soon as we entered the house. Next, I poured myself a glass of wine—I needed it after that strange, upsetting day—and sat down on the fluffy beige living room couch with the TV mounted on the wall across from it, though I didn't turn it on. I put my section of sandwich on a plate on the coffee table in front of me.

Before taking a bite, I pulled Liam's card from my pocket. Liam Amaruq was his full name. Out of curiosity, I also pulled out my cell phone and Googled his last name. Interesting. Amaruq was a gigantic wolf in Inuit mythology.

No wonder naturalist me found him interesting.

Time to eat and turn on the TV. I didn't always like to watch the news or sitcoms or suspense shows and preferred looking at shows featuring wild animals, but I didn't find any tonight, so I tuned in to a game show.

Sasha lay on the floor beside me, and I bent over often to stroke her fuzzy back. And when I'd finished eating, I took her out one more time while dusk was arriving. Then I got ready and went to bed—with Sasha on her doggy bed on the floor nearby.

I didn't fall asleep immediately, even though I'd pulled the heavy drapes shut to block out the light outside. Too much to think about. That mind of mine kept circling around the possibilities of where Truit was now—and what condition he was in. Laughing? Probably. But instead he could be decomposing somewhere after death, and—

Nope, I didn't want to think about that. Nor did I want to think about how interesting I found Liam . . . forget that. I picked up a book on Alaskan wildlife from my nightstand and read myself to sleep.

The next morning worked as usual. I was awakened early by a husky head on my bed as Sasha acted as my canine alarm clock. I threw on some clothes to take her for a brief walk— not the outfit I'd wear to work that day.

Then, back inside, she got her breakfast. I got mine too— healthy cereal and 1 percent milk, which I ate while sitting at my tiny kitchen table on its really pretty blue-and-gold-tile floor. I'd wait till I got to the boat to get my first cup of coffee.

After that, I showered and changed into my nice tour giver outfit, designed to keep me warm in the morning while the temperature was in the forties—a blue ClemTours hoodie over a long-sleeved blue T-shirt, also with the ClemTours logo. Then I took Sasha for another walk and got us both into the car. I brought my tote bag over my shoulder, the one that contained necessities—like the prizes I'd be giving out and my binoculars.

Back to the parking lot. Then back to where the boats were docked.

Would I know which one to go to? The *ClemWolf*, probably, but all I knew for certain was that it wouldn't be the *ClemElk*.

The six ClemTours boats were each named after a different animal native to Alaska: the *ClemElk*, of course, and the *ClemWolf*, plus the *ClemBear*, the *ClemSeal*, the *ClemBison*, and the *ClemMoose*. Each of them generally provided tours five days a week, weather permitting, leaving from the Alaskan towns of Juneau, Anchorage, and Skagway. That meant they each were empty for a couple of days, like the *ClemWolf* would have been. They were all similar in structure, and it was therefore easy for the crew to change from one to another. Sasha and I soon arrived where the *ClemElk* was still docked. I was delighted to see Steph standing nearby.

"What are we doing?" I asked our captain's assistant.

"*ClemWolf*," she responded, using both her arms, clad in her beige hoodie's sleeves, in a decisive gesture to point to the ClemTours boat docked right next door.

"Wonderful!" I said. We were slightly, but not very, early, since the tour left around nine. Although I wondered who else had already arrived, I didn't ask. I'd soon find out. I assumed that would include Palmer, who'd undoubtedly confirmed which boat we were using first. And probably Betsy, who tended to arrive even earlier to start coffee brewing and food preparation in the galley.

*So,* ClemWolf, *here we come.*

As I'd known, this boat was almost identical in size, configuration, decks, and amenities to the *ClemElk*. I'd been on this one before too. I led Sasha up the ramp onto the bottom deck.

First thing, I wandered around on that wooden deck, Sasha at my side and my tote still over my shoulder, to see who was already on board. The galley at the prow was nearby, and sure enough, Betsy was there.

"Everything you need available?" I asked her. If it wasn't, I didn't know how I'd help, but I'd try.

She'd been drying a platter and stopped to look at me, squinting a bit through her glasses. She wore a blue long-sleeved ClemTours T-shirt. "I'm fine," she said. "I'll spend the time before our passengers come on board making sure things are clean, but I do that a lot even on the boat I'm spending time on. And so far I haven't found anything in too bad condition."

"Great. Well, I think I'll head up to the top deck to see if everything there appears like what I'm used to. It probably will, of course."

"Of course," Betsy said, and let go of the platter enough to send me off with a wave.

Sasha and I headed toward the stairway at the location we usually used. On the middle deck I stopped long enough to look around. I saw deckhands Al and Rafe rearranging chairs in the middle and stopped to talk with them briefly, then peeked forward to see that Palmer was, as anticipated, behind the glass at the bridge.

Soon we were on the upper deck. After placing my tote bag in its wooden box below the microphones—yes, there was a similar box here—I immediately started walking around it with Sasha beside me, although I tucked her leash into her collar. I'd hold it once more when our tour goers began to arrive, but right now she could do pretty much what she wanted up here—including visiting her pad soon, which I'd asked the deckhands to move here from the *ClemElk*. I figured they'd get permission to board briefly for something like that.

Yes, this did look very much like the *ClemElk*, including the smaller box attached at the prow containing a microphone and related equipment. I used one of the sanitary wipes kept in the box for the tour guides to clean it off.

We continued around. Also yes, there was another box at the back that should contain tarps if they became needed up here.

Had anyone . . . ?

Okay. Maybe I was being obsessive, but I got close, held my arm out straight, gently lifted the lid of that box—and looked in.

Tarps! No bodies. No caps. I breathed a sigh of relief.

Time to go back downstairs and check with Palmer about the route he intended to take so I'd have a better idea about the wildlife we were likely to see. I thought about securing Sasha up here, but I figured she'd enjoy seeing the captain too.

Just as we were about to head down, I saw Lettie coming up. She too wore a ClemTours blue T-shirt, and she smiled as she saw us. "Everything okay up there on this *Wolf*?"

"Everything's okay, as far as I can tell," I assured her. Sasha and I waited while Lettie reached the deck, she and I high-fived, and then my dog and I headed down.

Palmer was exiting the bridge enclosure as we arrived. He wore his usual beige jacket with the logo on the back over matching beige pants. I found myself echoing what Lettie had just asked me. "Is everything okay on this boat, Palmer?"

"Looks just fine," he said. "Gus is going to join us on this trip. He's the one who usually captains the *ClemWolf*."

"That should be fun," I responded. And I meant it. Palmer's brother was a good guy.

*   *   *

I'd first met all the Clementoses and visited all the boats while I underwent training to become one of their proud tour guides. I'd memorized them easily, as I did wildlife, since they were important to who I was and what I was doing.

And I did feel as if we were revered by the family members. They all seemed to love wildlife too, as well as Alaska's amazing vistas, like expanses of water in inlets, glaciers, and ice floes. But the family position was that they didn't have the knowledge of someone who'd studied nature, especially native animals, and really knew the different species—as I did. Someone like me was, in their estimation, a worthy tour guide. They were right, of course. And I was proud of it, so I didn't shrug off their praise.

As I considered all that and tried not to smile too much, I turned to look out the windows on the port side of this deck toward the area along the shoreline where customers who'd be taking our tour would be congregating now. Sure enough, I saw a bunch of them.

I glanced down at my watch; it was what I would use most to tell time on this tour. I often needed to know what time it was and didn't want to rely on dragging a cell phone from my pocket, since there would seldom be enough of a signal out in the water to use it in the places we'd be.

Palmer seemed to read my mind—not hard to do under the circumstances. "It's about eight twenty. We'll let them start boarding now so we can leave on time." He ran his hand through his medium-brown hair as if a tad nervous, which wasn't like him. Nor was he being even a tiny bit flirtatious or funny, which he teasingly was sometimes, though he and I didn't really share an attraction. But I didn't think it was the timing of the tour that affected him today.

On time meant nine o'clock on this Tuesday in May. From what I understood, another large cruise ship had docked in Juneau overnight, so some of the folks traveling on it could have signed up for this ClemTours outing today. Possibly others on the ship had registered with other ClemTours boats or competitors. Tour companies tended to do similar but not identical things, so ours was far from being the only one providing enjoyable excursions. But I thought ours was the best, of course.

Anyway, I decided to go get my first cup of coffee of the day in the galley, stay down there for a short while to relax, and then head back up to my favorite tour deck to prepare for my talk.

I told Palmer what I was up to, a normal routine on a day like today. "Can I bring you anything from the galley?"

"No, thanks. Steph'll be boarding in another twenty minutes or so, and she'll stop and pick up some coffee for me."

"Got it," I said. "I'm looking forward to today as usual, but—" Okay, I'd done it. Hinted at our problem. I decided not to finish.

Still, Palmer knew what I meant. "But we're all going to be thinking about what happened yesterday and where Truit could be now. I've had several more calls from the Alaska Initial Response troopers asking questions in a cool way, but I sensed the heat and accusations they weren't saying."

"I'm so sorry," I said, meaning it. "I just wish—"

"That we knew where the miserable son of a cheater was? Yeah. Well, hopefully he'll show up soon—maybe in the clutches of one of the bears or wolves you love to point out." The smile on his moderately good-looking but currently furrowed face told me he was kidding.

Unless, of course, he actually had done something to make sure Truit was off the boat in the vicinity of one of those—

No way. I'd surely have seen it.

"Anyway, see you in a bit," I said, then began leading Sasha to the forward stairs again.

Betsy was still in the galley, of course, behind the counter, doing whatever she did to get things organized. Rafe and Al were now standing near the counter.

And they weren't the only ones. The tourists might only be starting to board now, but Liam now stood with the deckhands. He had claimed yesterday he wanted to join us on board as a tourist, but he had managed to get here before any of the others. Probably so he could start doing what he did all the time: nose around and attempt to solve crimes, I assumed—not that I knew how the Initial Response team of the Alaska State Troopers handled its cases.

Trooper Liam Amaruq held a cup of coffee and toasted me with it as Sasha and I approached. "Good morning, Stacie."

"Good morning, Liam." I signaled Sasha, beside me, to sit and raise her right paw. It wasn't a salute, but it kind of resembled one.

Unlike everyone else around here so far, Liam wasn't wearing something with the ClemTours logo. But at least he was wearing casual civilian clothes—a black sweatshirt over black jeans—and not his uniform.

A lot of questions flipped through my head, like how he'd come on board so early—although I assumed Steph had helped with that, treating him like one of us staff members just because he'd probably requested that she do so. He was, after all, someone in authority. But before I asked anything, Liam drew even closer and petted Sasha on the head. My dog appeared to love it and nuzzled his hand.

Liam looked up at me, a smile that seemed kind of teasing on his face—which I enjoyed despite my doubts. I couldn't resist smiling back, just a little, as I ignored the twinge of interest that passed through me.

Then he leaned on top of the curved galley counter and said, "So here I am, kind of an in-between visitor to your boat. I'm not one of you crew members, but I will be working here today, and I'm willing to help you or anyone else."

"I assume that's because the more you learn, the more you may be able to help figure out where Truit is, right?"

"Hey, good idea," he said.

I swallowed my snort when I saw Betsy approaching us from behind the counter, carrying a cup of coffee. "I assume you'd like one of these," she said, holding it out to me.

"Excellent assumption," I said, taking it from her. "Thanks."

"Anything else for either of you?" she asked.

"Not now," I responded, but I looked at Liam in case he had a different answer.

"Not now," he agreed, and then we both said our temporary *See ya*s to Betsy and turned toward the stairway. "Time to go up to your top deck?"

"That's what Sasha and I are about to do." I gently pulled at my pup's leash with the hand that didn't hold coffee—which was nice and hot, so I didn't want to spill any on her. We started walking back toward the steps we'd come down before, in the location we were used to on the *ClemElk*. I didn't look back but felt Liam following us, and soon I heard his footsteps on the stairs behind us.

It didn't take us long to get to the top. As I'd assumed, no one else was there. I checked my watch.

Didn't need to, as it turned out. "It's eight thirty," Liam said as he reached my non-Sasha side, clearly seeing me check. "I think your tourists have started boarding."

"That's right."

"Well," he said, "I think I'll just take a quick walk around the perimeter here, then head back down to the bottom deck and watch them join us." Made sense to me. It was his first time on this boat, the first time he could visit this deck, so why not?

"Know what? I just had the same idea." I watched Liam look at me as if I'd said something surprising. "Greeting the tourists, I mean. I do that most of the time anyway." As if I needed to explain to him. But it always seemed like a good idea to see some of our passengers and say hi before I started communicating more with them.

"I'll bet you do. Do you ever pick out tourists you particularly want to focus on during your tours?"

"Sometimes—like little kids who'll be most excited about the seals and dolphins and all. And then there are occasionally guys who clearly are here looking for someone to date in Alaska."

His brows rose dramatically. "Really?" Was he considering doing that?

Like maybe asking me on a date . . . Certainly sounded interesting, but it definitely wouldn't work. Not under these conditions, when I was someone he had to interrogate about matters concerning one of his cases.

"Not really," I countered, hurling a grin toward him. I then started walking slowly around the deck yet again with Sasha, just for the fun of it, and left my tote in its box at the prow. Nothing different could be seen from up here yet. And I wasn't going to find even a clue about Truit on this boat.

I gathered nothing had been found on the now-empty *ClemElk* either. Or at least not something Liam was about to reveal.

I glanced at my watch once more when we got closer to the stairway. Yep, it was a good time to go down to the lowest deck and observe our incoming passengers.

Not that they would provide any clues about our missing passenger and possible foe.

And as I reached the steps, I was met by Lettie. I wasn't sure where she'd been, but it couldn't have been far. "Good morning again, Stacie," she said, then looked behind me briefly toward where Liam stood. "Er—and hello, Officer."

"Lettie, right?" Liam questioned. He'd obviously memorized the names of everyone working on board.

"That's right."

"I'm Liam."

Before they began a conversation—which I supposed they might—I led Sasha closer to the steps.

Liam followed us, apparently still planning to head to the lower decks.

Sasha and I preceded our visiting trooper. And when we reached the bottom deck, passengers had indeed started to come on board.

Since I was here, my job was to greet them alongside Palmer. After all, the two of us were at least theoretically the most important people on this boat—captain and tour guide. Of course, to us the most important people were those who helped us.

When I joined Palmer, he wasn't alone. With him was his brother Gus, who resembled him and usually captained our current boat, the *ClemWolf.* They were about the same height. Gus's short hair was a lighter brown than Palmer's, and he had a slight beard and sported the same beige uniform as his brother.

Highly appropriate for the dual captains of this tour boat to greet our passengers.

\* \* \*

"Glad you're here," Palmer said to me.

"Thanks," I said, then smiled at Gus. "I'd say welcome on board, but this is your boat."

"Then let me say it," he said with a smile that looked as good on his face as a similar one did on Palmer's. "Welcome on board the *ClemWolf,* Stacie. Oh, and also welcome to—" He stopped and looked down at my dog, who was standing beside me wagging her tail and pulling a bit on her leash as if she wanted to go say hi. Or, more likely, get petted. Gus had seen her before but must have forgotten her name.

"This is Sasha," I said. Gus took a step toward my husky and stroked her back.

Then, because the dribble of people getting on board was becoming more of a steady flow, we all stepped back and started smiling and calling out welcomes.

Although I stopped when I saw that one of our new passengers was also an old one—or at least he'd been on board yesterday, and I'd seen him on a lot of our other tours as well: Hansen Horwitz. And it had been his careless comment that had caused the other guests to learn about their missing fellow passenger. Plus, I now wondered how well he knew Truit.

I noticed that Palmer and Gus also grew tense at my side. Of course they'd know who this frequent tourist was. And he'd also apparently been repeating rumors about the condition of ClemTours.

Would my nearby employers toss him off the boat this time?

Or maybe—would he have any info on that missing passenger?

Gus approached Hansen first.

"Hi, Gus," gushed our visitor. "I wondered where you'd be when I heard your brother would be in charge here today."

"Right here, of course." Gus's tone was curt. "Welcome on board. Glad to see you." Hah, he meant just the opposite, if I was any judge of that tone and his glare. "We'll want to hear all about where Truit and you are in your attempt to start your own tour company."

Really? Truit and Hansen? That was how they knew each other? No wonder this man toured a lot—for research, possibly. But to do something worse? Like undermine the ClemTours company along with Truit?

Did he know where Truit was?

Well, this could definitely be one interesting expedition.

And when I glanced off to my side, where Liam had been standing, I saw him also looking intensely toward this passenger, with an expression that suggested he too would be very interested to hear anything Hansen might say.

# Chapter Six

Washed ahead in the stream of oncoming passengers—undoubtedly intentionally—Hansen continued entering the boat, making his way toward the stairway. Lettie, who'd just shown up on this level, now ushered everyone in that direction. She suggested they all head for the top deck to watch our departure in the most enjoyable way—or the second deck if they were concerned about the chill or wind.

I had an urge to follow Hansen and bombard him with the torrent of questions now circling my mind—but right now my duty was to say hi to a bunch of strangers who counted on me to make their trip enjoyable.

I'd have an opportunity to talk to Hansen later. I'd create that opportunity, even if he didn't like it.

He must anticipate such a thing, though, coming onto the boat like this, knowing the captain and crew were the same people he'd seen yesterday, aware that someone had disappeared from that tour boat—someone he apparently knew.

Oh yes. I would talk to the guy. With or without Liam's presence.

Preferably without, since I might not act politically correct in conducting my amateur interrogation.

But for right now . . . "Welcome to the ClemWolf," I called to a family just getting aboard. I looked at the two young African American boys. "I hope you like seeing all kinds of Alaskan animals—seals and bears and birds and . . . well, I can't promise any particular sorts, even though we saw a lot yesterday, but we'll have fun with those who are near us."

"Yay!" said one of the small guys.

"Can I pet your dog?" asked the other.

"Of course." I glanced toward Palmer to make sure it was okay, since that would delay the family in boarding the tour boat. He just smiled and nodded. The smile wasn't the happiest, but I assumed that was more because of the trooper on board and the reason for it than concern about Sasha getting attention from tourists' kids.

Their parents soon ushered the boys toward the nearest stairway, and I continued to hang out as a greeter. Both Palmer and Gus, old hands at this, seemed to enjoy themselves—or at least they knew how to welcome their customers.

And Liam? He wasn't greeting anyone, of course. He stood near the galley counter, watching closely. Or at least it appeared to me that he was studying each newcomer as well as he could from that short distance away.

Did he think Truit would reappear here in disguise?

Or was that just my own imagination and wonderment? For I did look closely at the men who came by us—and the women to some extent, in case the guy was an expert at disguise.

We stood there for about twenty minutes, and in that time I saw no one who reminded me of our missing passenger.

Which really wasn't a surprise. Why would he come back on board this sister ship after conducting his suspicious disappearance yesterday?

Assuming he had done it intentionally . . .

"Okay," Palmer eventually said, loud enough for me to hear. He'd just held his phone up to his ear, so I wasn't surprised when he continued, "Steph is on her way. She said there aren't many more tourists arriving now, so she won't need to direct them here. One of our deckhands will hang out there for another five minutes till it's time to take off. I'm heading for the bridge. Coming with me, Gus?"

Of course he was. And I used that as my incentive to head back to the top deck with Sasha.

I glanced toward Liam but didn't tell him my plans. I figured he'd wind up on that deck sometime soon, so I'd see him anyway.

I thought about grabbing another coffee, since I'd finished my earlier one, but decided to wait till we were on our way to Tracy Arm to get a fresh cup.

Walking from one deck to the next had been pretty quiet before with no tourists on board yet. Now there was a roar of background conversation accompanying Sasha and me up the steps.

And when we reached the top deck that was my usual hangout, I was happy to see the crowd. Many people were standing, but I figured at least some would want to sit on the center seats later. A few of those seats had bags or jackets on them already to save them.

Our visitors were of all ages, some apparently in family groups or friend groups or couples. I didn't see any who were obviously there alone.

In other words, I didn't see Hansen.

I assumed, therefore, that he was on the bridge deck. Would Palmer confront him?

Not initially, most likely. Our captain would be busy—captaining the boat, getting it out there heading toward Tracy Arm, my favorite, wildlife-rich fjord. As we had yesterday and on most of our tours around here, we'd be motoring along between Juneau and Douglas Island along Stephens Passage at first, then beyond till we achieved our goal, passing a variety of bays, ports, and inlets. Would we see wildlife on the way? Quite possibly. Birds, at least. I'd point them out, but the best of the tour didn't really start till we reached that wonderful fjord.

For now, I started walking around the perimeter outside the seating area, where most of the passengers up here stood.

There was another glaring absence I noted besides Hansen's. Where had Liam decided to hang out for now?

Well, I wasn't going to hunt for him now any more than I would Hansen. I'd have a little time for looking for both of them soon, after the boat left port.

But as it turned out, I didn't have to seek out Liam, since he arrived on this deck via the aft stairway just a short while after Sasha and I did. He looked around, and when our eyes met, he nodded, as if he had been seeking me out. I didn't head toward him, though. We could talk soon, at least for a little while, when the boat was on its way.

He wended his way through the chairs and crowd toward me. "Hi again," he said. "Anything interesting to report?"

"Just that we're here on the *ClemWolf* and—" I glanced down at my watch. It was eight fifty-five. "And we're about to get going."

"That's great!" exclaimed a young lady near me who'd been staring across the water toward Douglas Island. Now she turned to look at me. She appeared to be in her twenties and had a guy with her who beamed at her. Her husband? "We're on a cruise, and Juneau is our stop right now. I've been looking forward to this tour since I booked it as our shore excursion. Seeing local animals is one of the main reasons I wanted to take an Alaskan cruise."

"Well, you chose a good day to come," I said. "The water is fairly smooth and the weather is good. No guarantees on which wildlife we'll see, but I've got a feeling it'll be a fun tour."

"I'm so glad. Thank you. Your name is Stacie, right? I saw you when we boarded the boat and you and the captains were saying hi." She bent over and petted Sasha's head. Apparently she liked other animals in addition to craving wildlife.

"That's right," I said.

"Well, I'm Charlotte, and this is my husband Brad." Her grin grew till it took over her entire face. "We're on our honeymoon."

"Congratulations!" I exclaimed. Just then, I felt the boat hiccup. Well, not really, but it moved a little. "Guess we're taking off now. I need to do a couple of things, but I'll be back here for most of our voyage to Tracy Arm."

"Wonderful," said enthusiastic Charlotte. "We put some stuff down to save our seats, but we'll mostly be hanging out here near the railing so we can get the best view of the animals you introduce us to."

"See you in a bit." I waved my hand in a brief good-bye as Sasha and I headed toward the forward stairs. We passed Lettie on the way, and I let her know I'd be back soon.

Yes, I'd decided to grab another cup of coffee. But first thing, I wanted to find out where Hansen was. Not that it mattered—but I did intend to quiz him sometime today about what he knew about Truit.

I heard Palmer give his usual spiel about rules and safety over the boat's public address system. We were on our way.

"Hey," said a voice from behind me after we'd gone down about six steps. A now-familiar voice.

I stopped, and as I turned, I said, "Hello, Trooper Liam. Have you started following me?" ·

"Nope. Not unless what you're up to is to find that guy Hansen." He'd caught up with me and kept his voice very low so no one else could hear it, I figured. Which should work. No other person was close to us, and Sasha didn't care what we said—unless we used words she knew, like *food* and *treat*.

I tilted my head and attempted a smile, but it felt anything but cheerful to me. "Are you a psychic as well as a cop?"

"So we're on the same mission. Well, why not? The guy seems like a talker, so he's likely to converse with both of us together. But if he doesn't—"

"Yeah, I know. You're the one in charge. But you'll have to promise to tell me what he says if I have to leave."

"I'll bet you're aware I can't make that kind of a promise." Now he was the one who smiled, apparently a bit amused.

"Right. You're the cop on a case." I started walking again with Sasha beside me. Sure, I might be required to reveal everything I knew if I learned anything useful, but not Liam, the trooper.

"I do promise," he said from behind me, "that if I hear anything I believe you'd be interested in and it's not something I need to keep confidential under these circumstances, I'll reveal all. All I can, that is."

"Thanks," I shot back over my shoulder, knowing I sounded irritated. Which I was—and I wasn't. At least this way, I might learn something.

Or not.

"Of course, that's on the condition you do the same with no conditions," he said.

Although I pretty much agreed, I didn't respond, since Sasha and I had reached the middle deck, and I led her into the center where a few of our tourists were hanging out. And I almost did a happy dance. Who was among them?

Hansen.

Liam must have noticed at the same time. "Well, who do I see here?" he asked softly from behind me.

"Same guy I see, I assume," I said over my shoulder. Sasha and I wriggled our way around some of the occupied chairs toward good old Hansen Horwitz. "Hi, Hansen," I said as we reached him, my tone bright and friendly and excited to see him—falsely, of course, except maybe for the last part. Yes, I was excited to see him, because I'd been looking for him.

"Hello again, Stacie." By contrast, his tone was cool and bland and not especially friendly. But what had he expected—not to see the tour guide on essentially the same tour he'd taken yesterday with the same crew aboard this different boat? And he'd taken other tours with us before.

And what was he doing on this deck, where Palmer undoubtedly could notice him if he looked through the windows at the back part of the bridge enclosure? Did he want to talk to our captain about Truit's disappearance or their purported intent to become competitors, or to accuse Palmer of doing something to make Truit disappear, or—

Well, yes, my mind was soaring around the possibilities.

"Hi, Hansen." This time it was Liam talking. He didn't wait for Hansen to talk or invite us to sit down with him or anything else. He simply grabbed a seat next to the big guy, leaving me to sit even farther away.

Well, that was okay. I'd still be able to participate. And this way Sasha could sit on the floor right near my feet, which she did.

Fortunately, the rows of seats in front of us and behind us remained empty, although a few tourists were around, and some kept checking out Liam. Or maybe Sasha and me, but that wasn't where their stares seemed mainly to be directed.

Liam flashed his badge briefly so Hansen could see it, then stowed it back in his pocket. "So what brings you onto the *ClemWolf* today?"

"Hey, tell him, Stacie." Hansen stuck out his lower lip— large, like the rest of him. "You've seen me on a lot of the ClemTours, right? I love to take the boat rides, look at the wildlife Stacie and the other tour guides point out, just have fun on these boats. And that's why I'm here today."

"Sightseeing, then," I stated. "And is there any other reason?" Like, did he want to know more about what had happened to the man he'd apparently considered becoming a business partner with, at least according to Gus?

"Well, yeah. I didn't intend to sit by myself here but thought I might be able to talk to the captain. He's busy now, though, so maybe later. And I'll talk to others on this boat too—and listen to them. Because . . ."

"Because?" Liam prompted, when Hansen didn't finish right away.

"Because I'm hoping someone will drop a hint about what they did with Truit yesterday, of course."

"Of course," I responded. But that didn't mean he didn't know where Truit was—or wasn't involved in his disappearance. And his being here might be a ploy to take suspicion off him.

In fact, I found myself chomping my tongue—not hard enough to draw blood, fortunately—to keep myself from demanding that Hansen tell us where Truit was and what the man was up to by pretending to disappear.

Or not pretending.

"That sounds like a good idea," Liam said, leaning more toward Hansen. "Why don't you drop us a hint like that?"

"Me?" The word exploded from Hansen, who partially lifted his large body from his chair. "I'm looking for him. I want him to be okay. I certainly don't know what happened to him and if anyone else did something to him."

"Of course." Liam's voice was low and soothing now, but when I moved to look at his face, I saw that it contained one big, skeptical question. "Have you seen or heard anything that gives you a clue as to what happened to him?"

The official interrogator at work, I figured, even though his cool tone continued and his expression quickly morphed to mirror its blandness.

"You should know I didn't," Hansen grumped. "Some of your people asked me a bunch of questions when I got off the *ClemElk* yesterday. They pounced on other people who'd been on the tour too. From what I gathered, they didn't learn much from any of us."

I figured they wouldn't with most of the tourists—but they just might have been able to get something from Hansen. At least that he'd known the missing man. But maybe he didn't even admit that.

"But what about later?" I asked as I leaned forward to look Hansen in the eyes past Liam's shoulder. My turn to question him. "Did you talk to Truit at all last night?" Not that I figured he'd admit it even if he had.

"No," Hansen said, "even though I tried contacting him when I was on shore last night, even drove past his condo—and saw a police presence there, so I wasn't surprised when I couldn't reach him."

So Truit lived in Juneau. I wondered where. Was he a neighbor of sorts? Not that it mattered.

"What about any relatives or other friends here? Did you talk to any of them?"

"I don't know if he has any relatives in the area, so I definitely didn't contact them. And I don't consider us good friends, so I don't really know who else he might be closer to."

But they were potentially going into business together to rival at least one successful tour company, and potentially many others. Didn't that mean they had to be friends? Or were they only remote business associates—without fully trusting one another?

If they'd somehow had a falling out, that could certainly provide a motive for Hansen to do something to Truit.

But how could I ask that in a way that wouldn't be accusatory? Not that I didn't think he could be guilty—but accusing him might make him stop talking to us altogether.

Just then my small ship radio made a noise. I pulled it from my pocket and answered. It was Lettie.

"Excuse me," I said to the men. I stood, leaving Sasha with Liam for the moment. "Everything okay?" I asked my assistant. We were still a distance from Tracy Arm, where I'd start my talk.

But Lettie gave me a good reason to head back up to the top deck. "Just saw a few marbled murrelets along the shore here and there, and I think I see more ahead. I've talked about them, but—"

"Yep, that's my job. Be right there." I was eager to see the birds and talk about them.

I returned to take Sasha's leash. "Got to go up to check out some wildlife from the top deck. Come on up and see them too," I invited them. Then Sasha and I headed for the aft steps.

Most everyone in the crowd up there was hanging out along the starboard railing. Sasha at my side, I hurried to the prow area, where Lettie stood with the microphone. My very able assistant didn't say anything, but she pointed off to the side of the boat toward the not-too-distant shore.

Sure enough, I saw a pair of murrelets in the nearby water and another pair more in the distance. As usual, they weren't in large flocks. They were shaped vaguely like small ducks, with white underbellies and mottled brown backs and wings and even a bit of brown on their heads. Their bills were pointed, and they were apparently feeding on whatever they found in the water—most likely small fish.

"Hi, everyone," I said into the microphone. "Glad Lettie was here to introduce you to our first wildlife on the tour. Anyway, I hope you've seen those marbled murrelets off our starboard side. Now let me tell you a little more about them. They're an endangered species, partly because their habitats have been affected by timber harvest."

I continued a little longer, talking as well as listening to the excited gasps and cries of some of our tourists as we passed the birds and a couple more came into view.

The two kids who'd talked to me as they'd boarded came over and began asking a lot of cogent questions, like where the birds went when the weather was bad, which to the best of my knowledge was the shore as opposed to the water. Some other people besides the boys' parents joined them, so it was a fun session, though I had to keep it short.

It was just a prelude to the tour I'd narrate once we entered Tracy Arm. We eventually reached the fjord, and the first thing we saw were some ice floes with harbor seals on them, just like yesterday. The same seals? Some could have been, and a few were mothers with babies.

There were lots of oohs and aahs again as well as questions from people who seemed quite interested in what we were seeing, including the two kids and others who'd come up to me before. I'd added the other decks to the range of my microphone, and other passengers began to join us up here.

Including my buddy Hansen Horwitz.

Better yet, Liam also came up to this deck. He started wending his way around the tourists, looking at them. Apparently he still didn't see anyone he thought could be Truit. Even though he'd never met the man, I figured he'd seen plenty of photos of him, including his identification pictures for his driver's license.

Liam also passed Hansen and said something to him, though I couldn't hear what. And since Hansen remained there and didn't clench his fists or otherwise appear threatening, I figured it couldn't have been too bad a question or comment.

Sasha perked up beside me, and I realized she was hearing howls way in the distance—which I also heard as I listened for them. Soon I was able to point out some wolves.

Palmer must have been listening to my narration too, since he aimed the boat toward the shore and drifted into one small inlet, then another, where it was easier to see the wolves.

And soon thereafter he even came up to my deck, took the microphone to welcome the passengers, and pointed out some bears along the ice-decorated mountains along the shore as well. Plus some furry otters floating on their backs near the shoreline. And more birds—kittiwakes.

What a delightful outing! And our tourists seemed to really be enjoying it. Palmer smiled at me as he headed back down to the bridge.

Break time for me. We'd nearly reached the end of the route near the glaciers at the far end of Tracy Arm. I was going to head down to the bottom deck to refresh my coffee when I saw a mama seal and baby flippering along the edge of one of the small inlets.

Well, we had to see more of them. I pointed them out on my microphone, then used my onboard communication system to contact Palmer and ask that he follow. Sure enough, we soon turned and headed slowly down the narrow inlet, mountains rising gently at first along the sides. Would our captain be able to turn the boat around to get out?

Sure! We'd headed down the same inlet yesterday. And it could have been to see the exact same mama seal and baby.

I stood near the rail, talking into the microphone and pointing them out. We moved very slowly to stay behind them, given that this vessel was so much larger than them.

I was amused that my husky pup stood on her hind legs and leaned on the rail, tall enough now to watch the seals too. She did that occasionally when wildlife was around; she must smell them even from a distance. But mostly she seemed to be happy to be with me, on a boat, with other people around.

The seals soon maneuvered away from the shoreline, which was fine, since I also saw a couple of brown bears heading up the hillside as we reached the far end of the inlet, and I pointed them out as I viewed them with my binoculars, which I'd retrieved from my tote. I knew we'd soon be backing up just a bit to start turning, as we had yesterday and at other times we'd been in this inlet. And Sasha seemed ready to get down again.

Only Sasha's nose suddenly went up in the air as she rose even more. And then she started barking.

She never did that. "Hush," I told her. "No barks." And my usually obedient dog ignored me, still sniffing. What did she smell? She was acting very unusual. What—

I stood up taller, looked over the rail, and gasped, even as I heard people around us start talking loudly.

"Is that someone lying down there?"

"What's going on?"

"Who is that?"

For on the uneven shore, partly in the water, lay a man.

A man who wasn't moving.

His head lay to the side. No hat. A familiar-looking gray vinyl jacket.

I could be mistaken, but I doubted it.

And despite the difficult angle, I confirmed my suspicions as I looked down through my binoculars.

Truit.

# Chapter Seven

"Oh no!" I cried out without thinking. Sasha was still barking, and people kept exclaiming and asking each other questions. Several had followed Sasha's lead and looked overboard, then begun shouting at others about what they viewed.

I pulled my radio out of my pocket and called down to Palmer.

"What's going on, Stacie?" the captain asked. He must have heard the noise from this deck.

"I—I'm not sure from up here, but I think we've found Truit. Someone's lying very still, half in the water below us, and it definitely looks like him."

"What?" Palmer got off the radio, and I heard him shouting to Gus and Steph. They all must have looked from the open forward part of the bridge. They couldn't lean too far over the side from that level thanks to the rail around the edges, so I wasn't sure what they could see. But the boat stopped moving nearly immediately.

"What's going on? Has Sasha seen something?" Liam elbowed his way beside us, and I pointed downward.

"Definitely. Or smelled it. It's—well, it looks like Truit. On the ground."

"Damn. I need to go talk to the captain."

"I've just contacted him on the bridge. Sasha and I can accompany you there."

I motioned for Lettie, who was farther down the side of the top deck, to join me. Fortunately, she'd been talking to people, looking down, and glancing at me, probably for guidance. She headed my direction as quickly as she could with the crowd of people along that side of the deck.

"What happened?" she asked softly into my ear as soon as she could.

"Did you look down at the shoreline?"

"Yes." Her black brows folded into an arch over her eyes. "But how—"

"We need to find out." I turned to glance at the trooper at my other side, who stood near Sasha. "Well, someone needs to find out, and we have to help. I'm going down to the bridge with Liam. Could you try to keep things calm up here?"

She shrugged her narrow shoulders beneath her blue ClemTours shirt and said, "Sure—as long as *try* is the operative word."

I managed a wry grin. "Right. Anyway, I'll be back here as soon as possible."

"Right."

I coaxed Sasha down from the rail and gave her a quick hug, then turned and motioned for Liam to follow me. "Come," I told Sasha, and she followed as I wended my way through the crowd toward the steps.

Rather, Liam wended his way, moving people in a helpful manner for us, and we followed as best we could. It wasn't particularly easy, since word must have spread to the lower decks and people were starting to climb up to the top deck for a better view. Wonderful. And one of those making his way up was Hansen. Did he know what he'd see from there? I didn't stop to ask him, but he had a serious expression on his bulky face, maybe the most serious I'd ever seen.

It took a little while, but as soon as Sasha and I reached the middle deck, we hurried to catch up with Liam, who was nearing the bridge. I noted that he was talking on a gadget I recognized. It resembled a phone or radio and allowed the holder to talk or send and receive text messages via satellite. I'd considered getting one but didn't really need to reach people much while I was out on tours and out of cell phone range around the Inside Passage and other water routes.

I suspected the trooper was calling his office to report what he'd seen so far and to request help.

I hoped so, at least. Even if Liam had the authority to do something official about checking out what appeared to be a body beneath us, no one else on this boat did, and he couldn't get to the shore from up here without having somewhere to settle the gangway for disembarkation.

I was right. Palmer and his brother Gus stood outside the bridge, leaning against the rail and looking over it, down toward the water. Steph remained inside, undoubtedly ensuring we didn't move in any direction right now. Did she know what she was missing? Most likely, and she was probably glad to be doing what she was instead of joining the rest of us on board in a staring party.

Liam joined Palmer and Gus, and they turned to face him. I caught up quickly so I could hear their conversation.

"You have to get me down there," the determined trooper said. Even though it was his job, I couldn't help admiring him for jumping right in, so to speak, to start the official investigation. "I've called in a report, and I'll have backup here soon to take control, but I need to get started as soon as possible."

"We'll lower you in a lifeboat from the bottom deck," Palmer said.

"Anything quicker? Liam asked. "Any ropes I can climb down? Or—"

"Sure, but nothing as safe," Gus said. When he stood beside Palmer, apparently on the same wavelength, the family resemblance seemed even more obvious.

"You want to kill yourself too?" Palmer growled. So he assumed what had happened to Truit was suicide? Or was he just hopeful that was what had happened? "We have a couple of rope ladders that are used when necessary. I'll get my deckhands to grab one and tie it where they sometimes do on the deck below us. They can show you how to use it too, and even go down it ahead of you to make sure it's as safe as possible. And—"

"Glad you have that rope ladder. I won't want anyone else down there with me as I start this investigation, but thanks for the suggestion. Now, please call your deckhands, and let's get started."

"That's not going to work," Gus objected as Liam pivoted and started making his way toward the stairs. Like Palmer, he was following the trooper, whom I admired for what he was taking on, job or not, but I was starting to get really worried about him. Especially since we didn't know what had happened to Truit to get him down there, unmoving . . .

And there would be danger just in using that stair ladder.

"Our company policy is not to let any of our passengers do things so unsafe," Gus continued. "And—"

Liam turned once more. "Thanks, but I'm not just one of your passengers. I assume you're related to Palmer?"

"Yes, his brother, and—"

"Well, I appreciate your concern, even if it is just to protect your family. I'm a state trooper, not just one of your sightseeing passengers. We apparently have found your missing passenger from yesterday, and my department still has to determine what happened and why. I assume the body washed up on shore today, since the helicopters didn't find him yesterday."

Of course, this was a small waterway, and helicopters might have missed it. And Liam didn't get into the fact that he undoubtedly would attempt to learn if it was merely an accident or, yes, a suicide—but what would engage him most would be learning whether Truit had been killed by someone else. And finding any clues to help him determine who it was.

That's what law enforcement officers did in circumstances like this. Even tour guides like me knew that.

"I understand," Gus said. "But—"

"No buts. Please get me one of your deckhands. I'll meet him on the next deck below."

Obviously Liam disliked this conversation. And to him, apparently, it shouldn't have been a conversation. The others should have been following his orders, even though they weren't officers reporting to him. I understood and admired him for it.

He was on his way to the forward stairs, and although Sasha and I followed him, we got behind Palmer and Gus. I didn't want us to get in the way, and the captain and his brother were clearly in charge. Well, in charge after Liam, who'd taken over.

And what I heard made it clear they didn't like it, even though they did as Liam said.

"This is only going to make things worse," Gus muttered. "All our passengers have seen too much already. And now this cop may be harming himself because of it."

"He said he called for backup," Palmer said.

"Then he should wait for it. Our passengers will see that anyway. And—well, whatever actually happened, the more they see, the more they're likely to blame ClemTours. We might get put out of business by this, even though we had nothing to do with what happened to Truit."

We'd reached the steps and descended the enclosed stairway. I'd wondered before if Truit, who apparently wanted to start his own tour company, had initially made it his goal to harm ClemTours by disappearing.

I still couldn't believe he'd appear to commit suicide to do that. And if he'd wanted to start a competing business, that wasn't the way to do it. Maybe he'd just wanted to get off the *ClemElk* and find a way back to the dock but had somehow injured himself.

The others reached the lower deck before Sasha and me, and I saw Palmer go into the rooms in the aft. He soon reappeared with Al and Rafe, who carried a rope ladder. Both Gus and Liam got into the conversation with them.

I headed for the galley. I had no idea how to hook rope ladders up safely, let alone where they were stored.

I needed something else to hang on to. Like another cup of coffee.

Betsy accommodated me immediately as I watched Rafe go back inside the storage area.

"What's going on?" she asked, staring at me curiously through her glasses. Her curly hair appeared a bit frizzed. "I've heard a lot of noise, and hardly anyone's staying on this deck now. I gather it might have something to do with Truit and his disappearance, from what I overheard some people talking about here just now—like Hansen, the guy who takes our tours a lot—but I don't really know what's happening."

I wished I didn't have to talk about it, but the situation wouldn't go away even if I said nothing, and so I told her. Patting Sasha on her furry head between her ears, I said, "This wonderful dog of mine, who never barks on board, started barking. I'm pretty sure she was the first on the boat to become aware of it because of her amazing sense of smell, but when I looked down at the shore where she'd stood up at the railing, I saw . . . I saw someone lying there half in the water, not moving."

Betsy gasped. "Was it Truit?"

"Looked like him to me."

Betsy aimed her gaze toward the far end of the deck, and I saw then that Liam, the two deckhands, Palmer, and Gus were all heading this direction. Rafe still carried the rope ladder. It was all wound together but appeared quite large.

I wondered how they'd fasten it to the boat and soon found out.

They made their way to the middle of the deck, halfway to where I was standing, where the gangway was pushed below the wooden surface and could be pulled out when people were entering and exiting the boat. There were tall rails at the side, clearly long and attached well, since they needed to be strong to deal with the ramp. And although most of this deck's sides were enclosed by glass, this area was usually covered with a tarp.

When the men reached it, Rafe and Al pulled off the tarp, unwound some rope apparently intended to connect the ladder to a stabilizing point at one end, and knotted it to one of the rails. They checked it a few times, and when they seemed satisfied with how it was attached, they picked up the ladder together and tossed it over the side.

I couldn't help heading for that side of the boat and looking down through the glass. Yes, the ladder had unwound and now did in fact look like two long, strong ropes attached by multiple rungs.

The bottom part reached the water not far from the shore. "Thanks," Liam said to the deckhands, reaching for one of the rope sides tied to the rail.

I was glad to see he also grasped the fixed rail at first as he swung himself around to the outer part of the boat and positioned himself on the ladder. He moved on it a bit, as if assuring himself it was attached well, which also made me feel better.

Only then did he let go of the rail, holding on to the ropes at the sides, and start climbing slowly downward.

I realized I was holding my breath as I waited near where the ladder was attached, stood on my toes, and looked down through the glass. I figured that, in the unlikely event one of the deckhands had been involved with Truit's jumping—or falling—off the boat, they wouldn't want the same thing to happen to Liam. Not with all these witnesses, including me.

Even so—well, it wasn't that I knew Liam well, of course, but I didn't want anything bad to happen to him, whether or not I was watching, and not just because I felt attracted to him.

He climbed down slowly, which seemed good, since he was less likely to fall off. He was in the water when I heard the rumbling of a helicopter in the distance—though it was clearly approaching.

Liam turned to look for the copter, too, before swimming the short distance to shore, then moving closer to where the body lay. I bet he was happy to see his backup arriving. I certainly was. For them to have gotten here so quickly, I assumed this copter had already been on patrol.

Liam didn't wait for the copter to land on the rugged, rocky coast before walking quickly to the body.

Since it apparently hadn't moved at all since Sasha's reaction informed me of its existence, it had to be a corpse—assuming this wasn't all some kind of trick of Truit's, with a pretend body lying there that he'd left to dupe everyone. I doubted that, though.

People had spotted the body thanks to Sasha, who'd smelled it. A life-size doll wouldn't smell like the real thing, unless whoever left it had figured a dog might be the one to discover it and somehow added a scent.

I couldn't see Liam dripping water from here, but he reached the body quickly and bent down, touching the throat, grabbing an arm, and holding the wrist. He didn't act excited, like he'd found any hint of life, but he nevertheless quickly began performing CPR—just in case, I assumed.

He was still at it maybe five minutes later when people from the copter joined him after it landed a little way down the coast. A couple carried bags like EMTs, and one took over the CPR.

Nice of them, I thought, but if there'd been any possibility of bringing Truit or whoever it was back to life, I figured they'd have seen some kind of reaction before this.

Liam now stood beside a couple of the others who'd just arrived, and they were clearly having a conversation. I wished I were down there for that. Were they surmising what had happened, how that body had gotten there? Liam hadn't met Truit, but I'd already figured he would probably recognize him from his ID or other photos online. There would undoubtedly have to be some official kind of identification performed, but Liam would know if it was Truit's body lying there.

Right now my dog still wasn't lying down and relaxing, but she did sit relatively calmly beside me, nose in the air. Whoever it turned out to be down there, my Sasha deserved a whole lot of praise for finding him. Otherwise, who knew how long the body would have lain there, decomposing? It was possible he'd never have been found.

I realized then that Betsy had left the galley area and was standing beside me, also looking down. "How horrible," she gasped. "That's Truit?"

"We think so, but those guys who just landed here are probably part of Liam's state troopers. They'll have to handle the identification."

"But how did he get there? I heard he disappeared from the ship but everyone thought he was hiding. Did he jump, or was he pushed, and why didn't anyone see it?"

"All good questions. We'll just have to see how it all gets sorted out."

If it did.

I didn't like just hanging out here. Time to go back up to the top deck so I could help Lettie deal with the undoubtedly freaked-out tourists there. I wasn't sure when we could leave this area, but I needed to do all I could to help the passengers cope with this difficult situation.

On the way back to our original boarding area, whenever we headed that way, should I behave as if nothing had happened? In other words, should I point out any sights and wildlife as if I were giving a regular tour? Would anyone want me to?

Sure, I thought. We'd be hurrying, I felt certain, but I might as well attempt to distract our passengers from what had happened as much as possible.

But I also wanted to talk to Liam and his cohorts about what would happen next—with Truit, and with our tour boat.

\* \* \*

Before I reached the top deck, I decided I'd go check with Palmer, maybe get his take and his brother Gus's on what was going on.

But before I headed toward them, I looked back down again and was surprised to see that Liam had started climbing back up the rope ladder.

He was coming back on board? Why?

Well, now I'd have to remain on this deck and be available to discuss it with him as soon as he got here.

If he'd tell me anything at all.

# Chapter Eight

I did manage to speak with Palmer and Gus as I waited.

"This has to be even more awful for the two of you than the rest of us," I said. "Until the authorities figure out what happened, I guess people who look at this wrong and hear about Truit's attitude could assume ClemTours, or someone who works for you, had something to do with it."

I spoke softly and sympathetically—but I also watched their respective faces. Gus hadn't been around us yesterday, of course, so the chances of his being involved were slim, even if he knew what Truit was up to.

And I liked my boss, Captain Palmer. I didn't want to even imagine he could be involved in what had happened to Truit. But I gathered now that the two of them hadn't been getting along, and yes, ClemTours was Palmer's company too. And the rest of his family's. What would Palmer do to try to keep it safe?

Kill someone?

I hated to surmise that possibility. Yet I didn't know who else on board might have had as good a reason to get rid of the potential tour boat rival.

But maybe that was it. I didn't know.

"Yeah." Palmer looked first at Gus, then back at me. "This is pretty hard on our whole family—not because we're protecting anyone but because our reputation is at stake here. I just hope the authorities get things right when they determine what happened and keep us out of it."

"As much as possible," Gus said, "since one of our boats was involved. But hey, yes, the authorities need to figure out who did it, assuming someone pushed the guy overboard and he didn't jump or fall over a side railing, though they tend to be high."

"Right," I agreed.

"Good thing this is such a small inlet," Palmer said, "and you didn't see a lot of wildlife here, did you?"

"Well, we were following a seal with her pup," I reminded him. "And we also saw some bears while we were there. But not a lot of animals, no."

"Good, since I doubt we'll be able to come into this one again for a while."

I had a slight urge to kick him, to remind him that though not being able to follow wildlife meant a lot to me too, figuring out what had happened here had to take precedence.

How had Truit gone overboard?

Where had he gone overboard? Had it been in the middle of the inlet? Had he been able to swim to shore but not get out of the water?

Either Palmer saw my perturbation or his own mind took control. "That didn't sound right, did it? I'm not sure I'll even want to come back here ever again. I may not have been overly fond of Truit, but I'm definitely not happy about what happened to him, and returning to the location where he died . . . not a good thing, for many reasons."

"True," I said, feeling somewhat relieved. He did apparently give a damn about this particular passenger's death and where it occurred, and not just because the next tours to Tracy Arm might have to bypass this inlet. I was going to say something else, but then, seeing movement out of the corner of my eye, I turned and saw Liam near the top of the ladder. "Talk to you later," I said to the Clementos brothers. Which I would—talk to them, that is. It might not be my responsibility to determine if Palmer was at all involved in Truit's demise, but I wanted to find out anyway.

And if he was, would I report it to Liam or any other authority?

Probably . . . though it would pain me to have to do so.

I hurried the few steps toward the opening in the side panels where I'd glimpsed Liam. Sasha had no problem following me right away. My dog had remained alert, waiting for my next command.

I soon noticed Liam starting to climb aboard. He had just reached the deck and was swinging his leg over the top to get himself onto it and off the ladder.

He made it look so easy. And I was definitely interested in what was happening down there on the shore.

But would I ever heave myself over the side and make my way down the ladder? No way.

For one thing, Liam's official cohorts who were investigating down there didn't need a wildlife tour guide's help.

And I could hopefully learn all I wanted to from Liam. Assuming he was willing to talk to me, of course.

I figured I wouldn't be the only one aching to learn what was happening from Liam, so I glanced to see how close Palmer and Gus were. I had to let them lead any discussion. They were certainly more involved than me. And they were in charge of this boat and the even more vital *ClemElk*.

But they'd disappeared. Gone back up to the bridge?

To avoid Liam?

No. Why would they? They needed the facts so they could work with them.

But they'd probably also noted Liam's arrival back on board at about the same time I did . . .

Anyway, I'd see them later. We'd still be on this boat for at least a couple of hours.

The two deckhands had materialized from somewhere, either a storeroom or the middle of the crowd. They hurried over to greet Liam, and their presence prevented me from getting too close.

They didn't say much, though they did ask the trooper if the rope ladder had worked out okay. The answer seemed obvious. Liam was back on board, standing there, dripping a bit and hugging himself, probably for warmth, but not rubbing any wounds or faltering as he turned to look back over the side toward the shore below. Al handed him a towel, which he immediately began to use.

As Rafe and Al pulled the ladder back onto the boat, I moved around them to greet Liam. "I assume your colleagues are taking control of . . . of what you found down there." Okay, I could have said *body*, but somehow I didn't want to.

"That's right. And they'll conduct an initial investigation there."

I was a bit surprised, yet glad, that no one had joined us for this conversation. I couldn't be the only one on board who was curious. And concerned.

And anyone who knew Liam had gone down to check out the body would logically assume he might have at least a few initial answers.

Although maybe the tourists were being held back from this area.

I'd already observed that Palmer and Gus weren't here now. I noticed that Betsy had returned to the area behind the galley counter while I was talking to them. A few passengers were even hanging out around there, apparently wanting something to eat or drink.

Maybe even something alcoholic after this, notwithstanding the fact that it was still morning—late morning. It didn't sound too bad to me, after all. But ClemTours didn't serve any alcohol.

Meanwhile, the deckhands were doing their duty and not asking questions, though perhaps they would later.

The only other staff on board were Steph, who was undoubtedly still up at the bridge, and my assistant Lettie. Would they be curious? Sure. But I doubted they'd ask Liam any questions.

"Hey, Stacie," Liam said. He'd been scanning the deck but now stopped and glanced back toward the rail, then at me. "Would you go up and tell Palmer I'd like him to turn the boat back to the port at Juneau now?"

Good idea, for the passengers' sake. And I figured those in charge didn't want extra people around while they conducted the part of their investigation that would take place in this area.

"Sure," I said. "But once we're underway, I'll need to head up to the top deck and at least attempt to provide my tour guide services and let our passengers know what wildlife they're seeing. In normal times this tour wouldn't be quite over yet."

"Sounds good. I'll meet you up there in a while."

Fine. Then I'd be able to start asking my questions.

I hoped.

Liam put the towel over a chair and headed toward the stern of the boat. Toward the restrooms? Or did he want to follow Rafe, who was now carrying the big bundle of rope that was the ladder?

The answer didn't matter. And I figured it was for the benefit of everyone if we actually got going.

I led Sasha yet again toward the stairway up to the bridge deck. I assumed that was where Palmer and Gus had gone. If I was wrong, I could still make the same request—demand, since it came from Liam—to Steph.

But all three were in the enclosed bridge area. Sasha and I headed there. I didn't need to knock on the door. The brothers were at the wheel, but I didn't feel the boat's engine running. Steph opened the door, and I asked if we could come in.

She allowed us to, and Sasha and I approached the two men. I told them what Liam had said. "He apparently wants to return right now."

"Got it," Gus said.

"That's just what we were talking about," Palmer added, shaking his head. "I don't think it makes much sense to keep this tour going today. I suspect we'll even offer the passengers their money back."

Sounded like a good idea to me. At least they might have something good to remember about this outing besides the wildlife we'd seen and would see on the way back. I knew they wouldn't forget the horror of having the body of a missing person found off the side of the boat. "Great," I said. "I'll let Trooper Liam know."

"We'll leave right away," Palmer said.

Liam knew I was going to the top deck, and I didn't really want to wander the rest of the boat first to find him and let him know his orders were being followed. He'd feel the engines and know I'd delivered his message.

"Thanks," I called over my shoulder, as Sasha and I made our way out of the narrow bridge area.

In moments, I felt the boat vibrate. Time to go. Sure enough, we started moving, backward at first, probably better for getting turned around to get out of this inlet.

As Sasha and I neared the stairs, I saw that Hansen had come down here to the middle deck and now sat in one of the forward-facing chairs near the enclosed railing on the far side. This deck appeared to be his favorite, or at least it was where I'd seen the large man most often. Maybe it was because fewer other people hung out here than on the other decks.

He was looking toward the water. For once, he had no drinks or food near him. Or other people.

Was he mourning his potential business partner? Or was he quietly celebrating Truit's death?

Until I'd heard Gus mention they were thinking of going into the tour business together, I hadn't realized Hansen had known Truit. But they sounded more like co-schemers than adversaries.

Maybe. But I knew no details of their relationship, whether they were friends or simply business associates.

Did Hansen have something to do with Truit's going overboard—and dying? Well, all I felt certain of was that, if so, he wouldn't admit it to me.

And so I turned to continue up the steps with Sasha.

Only—

I still saw Hansen out of the corner of my eye and realized he'd stood up and was coming toward us, maneuvering quickly around the few other people who stood in the way. His action made me wary, so I moved away from the stairs, standing with my back against the nearby wall. I hoped my expression remained entirely neutral.

"Stacie," he said as he drew closer. He looked down at me with sad brown eyes set deep in his round face. "Today has been . . . It's been . . ."

His voice sounded sad, too, and he didn't seem able to finish the sentence.

"Difficult," I prompted, assuming he wasn't about to say how wonderful it had been because the body had been found. Maybe sooner than he'd anticipated or wanted.

He nodded. "Yes. Difficult. And life changing."

Today certainly indicated a change in Truit's life, but I assumed that wasn't what Hansen meant.

Could I get him to admit something?

"Obviously you won't be able to go into the tour business— or any other kind of business—with Truit now," I said.

He shook his head, and those eyes actually teared up.

For real, or was the guy a good actor as well as a wannabe tour company co-owner? And he hadn't denied they'd been thinking about it.

"The thing is—well, darn it all." His tone sort of exploded, but he lowered his voice again. "I really want to know what happened to him. Do they know yet how he was killed?" He stared straight at me as if he wanted to chisel into my mind, though his head was tilted.

I told myself to trust his attitude—but my suspicious self disobeyed. Was this just an attempt to learn what the troopers now knew, since he'd seen me with Liam and was aware Liam was a cop? Or was he truly innocent and hurting and crying for answers?

I didn't know, of course. But at least I could tell him the truth this time. "If they know what happened, I'm certainly not aware of it. I gathered from what Liam said, though, that since the investigation is just beginning, there's not much information yet."

Well, part of that was just an assumption. I did want to ask Liam more about what was known and what was being sought. But leaving it all the big mystery that it still was to me made sense now as I spoke with one of the possible suspects—if Truit had been murdered. I couldn't reveal what I didn't know.

Not that I'd any idea of what motive this potential business partner might have had—but neither did I know anything that would clear him.

"Please, Stacie, will you tell me if they learn anything? Assuming you hear about it, of course. I'll give you my card so you'll have my phone number."

Yeah, right. Sure, I'd tell this possible killer what I heard from the state troopers about whether they suspected him and were coming after him. Or let him know they were following up on some kind of lead and chasing after someone else—even if that other person was innocent.

"I don't think that's up to me, Hansen," I replied. "I'd suggest you talk to Liam and make sure he knows you and Truit were considering starting a business together. He'll find out anyway, if he doesn't already know, and if you're not keeping it secret, you're less likely to be considered a suspect." Maybe. But that might also send him right to the top of the suspect list.

"You think I did it, don't you?" Now the lowering of his thick brows and the straight, angry line of his mouth let me read his emotions once more, maybe by design.

A small wave of fear washed through me. I felt safe enough here, on the boat, with fellow crew and staff and even passengers around, at least so long as I didn't get too close to the railing with no one close by.

But could this guy stalk me onshore?

I figured a few lies or exaggerations might be in order to potentially save me.

"Hansen, I was amused by my first impressions of you. You seem like a nice guy. When I learned you were intending to go into business in a way that might harm my employers, I wasn't thrilled, but I didn't assume you were a killer—not even when Truit went missing. And since you intended that he become your business partner, that's all the more reason for me to figure you weren't guilty of his murder. But were you two arguing, or—" I stopped. Maybe that kind of question would make him angrier.

But he responded, "No. We were just taking various ClemTours tours to check them out, sometimes together and sometimes on our own. And we also wanted to see if we could tempt their passengers into wanting something even better someday. A lot of this was Truit's idea. I wanted to participate, and I'd kick in some of the seed money." Interesting. He might be wealthy, which would explain why he could spend so much time taking not-so-cheap tours and not working. "I was relying on Truit. I liked Truit."

He took a step closer to me, and I moved sideways out of his way.

"I get it," I said. "The last thing you wanted was for something to happen to your potential business partner." Maybe. But I didn't add that.

"Exactly." Now he was smiling grimly, but at least he seemed to consider us on the same wavelength.

"Well, not that I have anything to say about it, and not that I'll be involved in the investigation into what happened to Truit, but I'll keep that in mind. And if it ever seems appropriate, I'll mention it to Liam or any other cop I'm in contact with."

Those thick shoulders of his appeared to relax within his puffy gray sweatshirt. "You do understand," he said softly and even emotionally. "Thanks, Stacie."

"Sure," I said. "And now I really need to get onto the top deck and see if there is any wildlife I can talk about." We were now moving faster and should reach the main waterway soon.

I quickly got my pup moving beside me and once again headed into the forward stairway. And breathed a big sigh of relief.

Hansen might just be one big—very big—emotional potential partner, or he might be attempting to save himself from accusations and arrest.

Not my business. But I figured I'd let Liam know about this conversation, just so he could determine whether or not to keep an eye on Hansen.

Sasha and I hurried up the steps. Fortunately, no one else was going up or down, so we reached the top deck quickly.

It was still full of tourists. Calm had settled through the crowd. Most of them were amassed along the port side, and Lettie was at the front of them, holding a microphone.

I felt proud of her. She'd been up here, in charge of giving the tour. Sure, she'd been working for ClemTours for a while, but only recently had she decided to learn how to give tours herself by taking over now and then for me or one of the other tour guides. And she seemed to be doing a good job with all aspects of it now, including taking care of our passengers and their states of mind. I'd watched her before and believed she could do a good job; otherwise I wouldn't have left her on her own for so long.

"We usually don't see a lot of wolves on our tours," she was saying. "We saw a few on the tour we gave yesterday, and I was really excited. These are probably the same ones. Aren't they amazing?" She was pointing to the craggy hillside not far from the boat's prow as we began slipping into the main part of the Tracy Arm fjord.

I heard a lot of passengers ooh and aah and make delighted comments as they took pictures. I was delighted, too—not just because the official tour had started again but also about the great way Lettie was conducting it.

And maybe, just maybe, a return to lecturing would shift the tourists' attention at least a little away from the horrible things that had happened on this voyage.

Plus, the wolves were some distance from where Truit had been found. If they'd been closer, who knew what might have happened to his body?

Okay, I didn't need to think about that. But I was thinking about Truit.

And still wondering what had happened to him.

And who'd caused it . . .

"Hi, Stacie."

Startled, I turned toward Liam. I'd been concentrating on wolves and tourists and hadn't expected to see Liam now, although he'd known I'd wind up on this deck.

"Hi, Liam."

Should I tell him about my conversation with Hansen? Probably.

Right now?

Maybe, since if he wanted to talk to Hansen some more, this would be a good time.

First, though—

"Can you come over here with me?" I nodded to a deserted area away from Lettie and her audience. She could keep control of the tour for now. And I had some questions to ask Liam.

My discussion with Hansen had indicated to me that he probably wouldn't become a competitor to ClemTours, at least not right away and without another partner, since Truit wouldn't be around.

But . . . well, I liked working for this company. Still, I figured that Palmer and maybe others might be considered suspects in Truit's death.

Could the company continue to operate during the investigation?

"So what's up?" Liam asked me as we sat down on a couple of chairs at the end of a row, on the side opposite where most of the tourists stood watching the wolves.

At the moment, my concerns were more important than my discussion with Hansen. And so I asked, "How will you and the other troopers deal with my bosses and ClemTours while you're conducting the investigation into what happened to Truit? I mean, I like the Clementoses. I don't believe any of them are involved, though you might think one could be." Like Palmer, who'd been on the *ClemElk*, but I didn't mention that. "I just hope they're treated with respect, at least until you find some evidence that suggests they shouldn't be."

"That's the point," Liam said.

He leaned toward me, and I tried not to stare at the good-looking masculine cragginess of his face. His looks were irrelevant to what I wanted to know—like, would I continue to have a job?

"I'm sure you recognize that Palmer Clementos is near the top of our suspect list," he continued. "He was obviously on this boat and had an issue with Truit and how he was acting on board and the fact he was looking into starting a competing company. If we find evidence against him or any of the others, we'll need to request that they cease their operations till we complete the investigation."

"All boats? I mean, you're already checking out the *Clem-Elk*. And maybe you need to check this *ClemWolf* out more, since we're on it now. But not the rest." I knew I sounded whiny, but I was worried.

Heck, I loved showing off wildlife. And equally important, I needed my income.

I figured the Clementoses needed theirs too. And they deserved to earn it—or at least most of them did, even if one of them was guilty in Truit's demise. But it was premature to speculate on that right now.

Or at least I hadn't heard about Liam or anyone else finding evidence against them.

"That's not entirely my call," Liam said, and now his expression hardened.

"Entirely?" I questioned. In other words, he would have some say in it. "Then—"

"Then nothing. Look, I'm not thrilled that you seem to be doing your own snooping into this and would like you to stop."

Of course he would. He was a cop. And did I want to just stand down altogether, even though it would be safer?

"But I know the people involved a lot better than you do," I said. "They know me and might talk more. And—"

He raised his hand to silence me. "Right. I figured. Plus you were there when the victim disappeared. You might learn more, in different ways that I can. So if you're not going to keep your nose out of the situation, please keep your nose in it. Sasha's too. But you do need to stop if anything makes you feel uncomfortable in any way. And you need to promise to keep me informed. Okay?"

No reason not to, I figured. And I gathered Liam might even appreciate me as a resource.

"Okay," I agreed.

"Good," Liam said. "So, right now, why don't you and I have a little chat with the two Clementoses on this boat? With Sasha along, of course. She might help calm everyone down, like a therapy dog. Or at least distract them."

Really? He wanted me to come, along with my dog? Then maybe he really did want to use me as a resource. Did cops do that? Maybe this one did. Or maybe he just wanted to have Sasha along, with me keeping quiet.

He continued, "We can go grab coffee at the galley with them and have a nice, friendly chat—unless we learn something I need to follow up on. There's that nice Steph on the bridge who can handle the boat in the meantime, right?"

"I think so," I said. "And I'm supposed to be narrating our tour, but Lettie can keep up with that. So sure. Let's go see if we can talk to Palmer and Gus."

As we started out, I pondered what Liam had just said even more. Would I continue to snoop, as he called it? Possibly, especially if it could help my employers.

And would I keep him informed?

That might depend on what I found out.

# Chapter Nine

I had already talked to them—as an employee and interested party, not the law. And I wasn't the law, but Liam was, and maybe my being included now, along with Sasha, would keep things casual.

I'd participate in the conversation to the extent it made sense. But Liam would be in charge.

At least it should be pleasant in some ways—grabbing coffee together, with other people around. Liam wouldn't be confronting or accusing them privately, as he might consider doing in the enclosed bridge area.

So, nudging Sasha gently, I led her to the steps once more. Liam followed us.

Only before we got there, a few of the passengers approached me—a couple of families, maybe, since they included two couples in their thirties plus five kids all younger than their teens.

"Are we going to get to see some more animals on this tour?" one of the women, in a bright-orange jacket, asked. "I mean—well, it's been a little hard keeping our kids' attention on the good things, especially because we haven't seen much wildlife since we . . . since we came into this area."

"It'll help them have good memories about this tour," said the other woman. Her jacket was beige. "We've of course kept them from looking—well, you know."

"Yes," I said, nodding. "This has been a very difficult venture. As far as I know, we'll conduct the rest of the tour as we always do on the way back to the dock."

The women smiled and glanced at each other, then at their kids—who also wore jackets in different colors. No surprise there. This was Alaska.

"I can't guarantee anything," I continued, "but we should see some more seals, and otters, and birds—probably of several species. And maybe more bears or wolves or even deer on the shore." I hesitated. "My assistant Lettie"—I pointed to where she stood near the bow—"will be talking to you for a while, since I have something I need to do below, but I'll be back here soon and will give you all sorts of fun information about the animals we do see. Okay?"

"Okay," said the woman in orange. "But—will it be all right, then, to let our kids look away from this boat? I mean—"

"I understand your concern," I said, trying not to shudder. "Believe me, this has never happened before. In any case, there should be no problem with the rest of our outing. There may be some authorities asking questions after we dock, of course, but the rest of our tour should be just fine."

I felt like crossing my fingers, hoping I was speaking accurately.

Well, I was, to the extent of my knowledge—and that knowledge didn't include any other missing people whose bodies might show up on our way.

"Is there anything we should know about now?" The woman in the beige jacket faced Liam. He might not be in uniform, but, arms crossed and nodding, he did appear as if he could be more than a passenger.

"Yes. You should know that it's time to enjoy yourselves."

The adults all smiled, though somewhat hesitantly. "Thanks," they said, as they turned to head back toward Lettie.

"I just hope I didn't mislead them," I said to Liam. "We've all had such a miserable day. And—well, I'm sure word will get out to the media. I heard while I was boarding earlier that some of the local online sites were questioning Truit's disappearance last night and this morning, so they're bound to follow up and let the world know what happened to him—to the extent they can get info."

"Our department is media friendly, but we keep things mostly quiet till we have something to say that contains as much as we can tell of the truth. Of course, a lot usually needs to be kept confidential, especially when a crime has been committed, and we'll want to arrest and prosecute the perpetrator once enough evidence has been collected—but we don't tell the world that."

Liam was now behind me again on the steps as he spoke, with Sasha just ahead of me. What he said made sense to me, of course. And—also of course—I'd seen situations where the media took whatever was out there and ran with it, making guesses that might turn out to be true. And might not.

I wondered how much Liam would be able to tell me, since I was in the middle of things.

One thing I did know was that I didn't want to talk to anyone, media or otherwise, about what I'd seen. And especially not about how Truit's body had first been found thanks to my wonderful dog's keen sense of smell.

Sasha had reached the middle deck, and I guided her by pulling her leash a little so that she exited the stairway. She waited till I was by her side, looking up at me with her delightful blue eyes as if to ask, *What's next, Mom?*

"This way," I told her, and we started toward the bridge.

Steph let us in right away. She looked at Liam, who stood beside me at the door. "Hi, Liam," she said to him. "How can we help you?"

So they'd apparently talked before. At least she knew who he was. Not a surprise. I assumed Liam had talked at least a bit to all of our crew when I wasn't with him. Yesterday, today, or both? And how had he done it so far? Just friendly, or had he begun grilling them?

I gathered it couldn't have been too nasty, given Steph's friendly attitude.

"Well," Liam said, "I'd like you to take over control of the boat for a little while. I'm going to invite your bosses to join us for coffee in the galley." He said it loud enough for them to hear, and Gus quickly joined us near the door.

"I assume that if we accept your invitation, you're going to be asking a lot of questions and giving us a hard time." He looked around Liam toward me, as if I was the one who should be given a hard time. Or maybe I shouldn't be here now. But Sasha should, so I was staying.

"Nope," Liam said. "At least no to the last part. I do want to ask you some questions, which is why I want to get together. But I won't give you a hard time. So, are you coming?"

Gus turned to glance toward Palmer, who was now behind him. Steph had moved to the center of the control area, obviously anticipating what the answer would be.

And she was right. We soon headed outside of the enclosed area and toward the nearest stairs.

I'd noticed before that this deck still had the fewest people on it, although there were a few groups here and there, seated at the tables. Of course I'd also noticed how many were upstairs listening to my assistant's wildlife talk. The assistant I was currently jealous of . . . but I hoped to help out in the investigation of what happened to Truit.

Could I really be of assistance? Maybe not. I was essentially an outsider, an onlooker. But I did give a damn about my bosses and hoped that the Clementoses—and even more importantly to me, ClemTours—would be exonerated from any involvement in or liability for Truit's demise.

And I could continue as an employed tour guide for them on their successful, popular boats . . .

Once we reached the lowest deck, I couldn't help noticing that Hansen was sitting alone at one of the tables, his head bowed over whatever he was drinking. I figured I'd better let Liam in on the conversation I'd had with the guy.

Hansen was the one here who'd apparently known Truit best. His sad attitude suggested he hadn't harmed his would-be business partner, but then, even if he had, I wouldn't have expected him to admit it to me. Or to Liam. That could have even worse consequences for him. It still could be true that he'd done it.

Those of us who'd headed here together soon reached the galley counter—the humans standing, Sasha sitting at my side. Betsy greeted us with a smile and asked us what we wanted. "Black coffee for you, Liam?"

Okay, so like with Steph, I figured, Liam had introduced himself and at least begun to ask questions in a pleasant enough way to cause our galley manager to stay pleasant with him too.

She also knew I liked black coffee and got other drinks ready for each of the Clementos brothers.

And then the group of us, led by Palmer, went into a small, closed room at the back of the galley where crew members sometimes ate. We passed Hansen as we headed that way, and as Liam and I entered the room last, I leaned toward him and said softly, "I had an interesting conversation with Hansen a little while ago."

When he bent his head up to answer, warmth heated my face, and my pulse jumped when our cheeks almost touched. I liked the possibility of the close contact, but now wasn't the time or place to test my instincts.

"I'll want to hear about it," he replied, also softly.

"Of course." Maybe while Hansen was still in the galley area, Liam and I could both follow up on my conversation with him.

I sat with Liam and Palmer at my sides and Gus across the square table from me. Sasha lay down behind me.

"So," Palmer said, looking at Liam. "What did you want to talk about? As if I couldn't guess."

"I'm sure you can," Liam responded calmly. I had told him on our way downstairs that I'd spoken with these two briefly before, relaying that they were highly concerned but that I had nothing to report about them in regard to Truit. "And I understand that Stacie and you have had a conversation or two on this topic just recently here on the *ClemWolf*."

Both my bosses focused their eyes on me, and my stomach twisted. They knew I'd seen Palmer's anger. Did they think I'd made accusations?

"I think it's up to you," I told them, "to let Liam know how you really feel about Truit and what happened to him— although I told him that nothing you said to me makes me believe you decided to do away with the passenger who intended to compete with you and maybe put you out of business." I smiled as if I were kidding about the potential description, though I wasn't. The knots in my stomach hadn't eased.

"Glad to hear that," Gus said wryly, but his expression did seem to relax a bit.

Palmer took a large sip of the latte or whatever he had in front of him. Then he looked directly across the table at Liam. "Look," he said. "I'd heard what Truit was up to. Did I like it? Hardly. But my family has seen plenty of other tour companies start up as competition since we began, and some we knew about in advance. Even though this was a little different, since Truit and his would-be partner kept spending time on our boats—"

His voice rose a bit, and Sasha stood up. Good pup that she was, she headed in Palmer's direction—and he began gently stroking her head before he continued.

"—and though I would have preferred that our experience and skills convinced him to change his mind, I certainly wouldn't, and didn't, do anything to ensure he couldn't get into business. Neither did Gus or anyone in our family."

"Absolutely true," Gus agreed.

"So, then, what did you first think when you discovered Truit was a passenger yesterday?" Liam looked at Palmer as he took a sip of his coffee.

"Not much," Palmer replied. "Oh, I didn't like that he wore a kind of disguise, but he must have known we'd recognize him anyway. But he'd been an employee, and we'd seen him taking tours on this boat afterward plenty of times." Probably why he'd looked a little familiar to me, but he hadn't stood out as a tourist to make me remember him. "Plus he worked for other tour companies to make some money and might have learned more about how they operated. I realized who he was and what he was up to, but he wasn't hurting anyone, or our company, by being here. At least not that I was aware of, although I assumed he was collecting ideas on how to compete." Shaking his head, he pursed his lips, then continued. "He might have been lying about us to the passengers, and maybe his collaborator Hansen too, but I never heard it, and none of our passengers ever mentioned such a thing either."

That sounded utterly reasonable to me. I kept my eyes on Liam to try to read his thoughts, but he kept his expression blank.

"Got it," he said. "And I know others in my department talked to you onshore yesterday, but I wasn't part of the conversation. Did you speak much with Truit while he was on the *ClemElk*?"

Palmer looked down at his cup and slowly shook his head. "Too much, I suppose. I—well, I argued with him when I first saw him on board. If you ask people who were on the boat yesterday, they might tell you that."

Actually, I was one who could confirm it. But did that mean Palmer had killed him?

Anything was possible, I supposed. But I preferred not to believe it of Palmer.

"I see," Liam said, dragging out the sentence. "Then you had a potential motive to harm him." He seemed to be watching the captain carefully to see any reaction to that.

And he got one. Palmer looked up and stared Liam in the face. I noticed his eyes were damp, as if filling with tears, and his lower lip quivered. "I suppose you could say that." His tone wasn't sharp but sad. "But as soon as I realized he was missing, I felt horrible—for that very reason. I hoped he was just playing games to make me and possibly my family look bad rather than anything worse. His disappearance didn't make me like him more. He was presenting us with a potential challenge, but I was certain ClemTours could counter it just fine. In fact, the idea of showing him how good we were—and how bad he was—sounded great to me."

He looked at me, then down at Sasha beside him, and continued, "When I heard a body had been spotted in the inlet and it appeared to be Truit's, I felt terrible. I didn't know what happened to him. We still don't, not really. But I wished then, and still wish now, that I knew what was about to happen while he was still on board so I could have prevented his death."

He moved his gaze away from Liam's again and stared at his cup, which he brought up to his mouth before taking a gulp as if he wished it were something a lot harder than coffee.

His anguish appeared genuine, despite Truit's intention to become a competitor.

I looked again at Liam, who continued to watch Palmer. I could imagine what he was thinking—maybe. It was Palmer's boat. Palmer had been in charge. He'd now said he wished he'd known what was happening and could have saved Truit.

But was it true?

And did Liam believe him?

I did—or at least I wanted to.

Still, Palmer seemed the most likely suspect, didn't he?

"And by the way," Gus said, "don't you think it would have been particularly foolish for my brother to aim the *Clem-Wolf* with all of us on it down that particular inlet today if he'd done something to throw Truit off the boat yesterday? He wouldn't know if the body would show up, after all."

I'd wondered that myself. Still, I'd asked him to go that way to follow the mother and baby seal.

Of course, that didn't mean he'd had to do it.

And maybe if he'd been guilty, he wouldn't have known that Truit had washed up on the shore . . .

Okay. I still didn't want to believe it was him, and his heading that way was another good reason not to.

I'd have to ponder the other possibilities more—and figured Liam and his colleagues would too, at least before arresting Palmer.

But I didn't want to believe it was Palmer. And if not him, then who? Not the not-there Gus, of course—unless the Clementos family had decided to do something and had somehow arranged for Gus to be the perpetrator-in-hiding that day.

Hansen? Possibly. He did seem to have a strange attitude.

But if neither of them, then who?

Somehow I'd need to talk to Liam about that, most likely when we were off this boat and alone.

The thought of being alone with Liam sent a flash of heat through me.

Why did it sound good?

And should I really keep pushing to learn more about what had happened to Truit? Even more important, would Liam try to discourage me, or make me stop?

While I was contemplating, Liam asked our tablemates some additional questions, leaning toward them a bit.

"Do either of you have any idea who might have wanted to harm Truit? Someone on the boat yesterday, of course."

Palmer's mind seemed to work similarly to mine on this subject, at least. His still-damp gaze moved from Liam to the other side of the room, where Hansen sat. "That potential partner of his?" Palmer pretty much whispered.

Liam nodded slowly. "A potentially good guess. Anyone else you can suggest we look into?"

"So far, no," Gus said, "but Palmer and I will make a point of talking about it more later, and we'll let you know our ideas after that."

"Good. Thanks." But Liam's mouth quirked and his eyebrows lifted with what I interpreted as skepticism. So he didn't believe them. Or if he did, even a little, he wasn't about to let them know.

Palmer very pointedly looked toward the closed door. "Anyway, we'd better return to the bridge. We'll need to help Steph when we get closer to Juneau."

Liam didn't object as the Clementos brothers stood.

Palmer said, "I feel sure we'll see you again on this boat and off, and if we get any ideas, we'll be sure to let you know."

"But just to reiterate what you should take away from this discussion," Gus said, glaring pointedly down at Liam. "Neither of us had anything to do with what happened to Truit."

"Got it," Liam said. I noticed he didn't say anything like *I know that* or *Of course you didn't*.

Well, there was more investigation to come.

After the two Clementoses left, Liam turned to me. "So what did you talk to Hansen about?"

I gave him a brief rundown of our conversation, including his admission of interest in starting a tour company with Truit, and indicated that Hansen genuinely appeared to be grieving.

"Which doesn't mean he didn't do it," I finished.

"No," Liam said. "It doesn't." He stood. "And therefore, I'm going to talk to suspect number two, Hansen, while we're still on the same deck, assuming he's still there. Care to join me? We can see what he has to say now." We were heading out the door by then, into the galley area.

"Sure," I said, and Sasha and I joined Liam as he headed toward Hansen.

Hansen must have seen us coming, since he rose before we reached him. "Hi." His voice still held a despondent note. "I saw you with the captain and his brother. Did you come over here to tell me something they said?"

When we'd spoken before, he'd been upset and had wanted to learn more about what had happened to his would-be partner. Or at least that was what he'd said. He'd also become teary eyed, as Palmer had.

Interesting that an egotistical guy like Truit could elicit such strong emotions from others when he was dead.

Hansen had wanted me to promise I'd tell him anything useful I learned about what had happened to Truit. I hadn't promised anything like that.

In fact, especially now that Liam was here, I hoped this guy would be the one to make suggestions about what had happened to his intended business partner.

Like they'd fought and Hansen had pushed the other guy over the side, intentionally or not.

Better him than one of the Clementos brothers.

For now, though, I attempted to get the conversation rolling with no accusations or innuendos.

"Hansen, you might have spoken before with Trooper Liam Amaruq." I nodded toward my companion as all three of us sat down at the table Hansen had been occupying. I kind of wondered what my Sasha was thinking as she too sat down, but on the floor beside me. Was she getting bored with her human's ongoing meetings with other people on this boat?

She probably would be happier if I took her aside and fed her.

Or—well, I did dive one hand into my pocket and pull out a beef-flavored biscuit, one of her favorites, and gave it to her. That seemed to make her happy.

Then I continued speaking. I figured it would be a good thing if Hansen confirmed what he'd told me. "I told Liam what you and I discussed before, your hoping to go into the tour business with Truit and that being why you and he took boat tours like this one in an area where you hoped to provide tours someday."

"That's right." He narrowed his eyes as if he was suspicious about what I was saying—like, was I going to accuse him of killing his potential partner right now, in front of a trooper?

"And that you'd said you'd been buddies with Truit and the last thing you wanted was for something to happen to your potential business partner."

"That's right," Hansen said.

"Well, Liam and I saw you sitting here when we walked by with the captain and his brother, and I figured it wouldn't hurt if you told him your feelings about Truit yourself." Or would it hurt him? Was he lying, and if so, could Liam discern that and somehow get it out of him?

Or was he telling the truth—even though I definitely wanted him to be the killer if the only choices were Palmer and him?

For the next five minutes, I rather relived the conversation Hansen and I had had before, since he seemed to reiterate everything I recalled.

But he didn't make it clear whether he was telling the truth or not.

In either event, Liam was patient, asking questions that weren't particularly accusatory but did attempt to elicit attitude from Hansen. I didn't hear anything indicating he'd had any kind of grudge against or dislike for Truit, which didn't help the situation much, at least from my viewpoint.

Liam soon ended the discussion. "You need to go up and finish directing the tour from the top deck, don't you?" he asked me, obviously using that as a means to finish with Hansen—or maybe to get rid of me.

"Absolutely," I said, meaning it. And so, only a minute or so later, Sasha and I went upstairs.

Liam didn't join us immediately, but that didn't stop us. Once we reached the top, I was glad to hear Lettie still talking into the microphone. And the crowd appeared at ease, as before. She was continuing to do a great job.

She saw me. "We've got some more harbor seal mamas and babies around us here and there," she said.

"Delightful!" I exclaimed, and made my way over to the railing along the starboard side.

Sure enough, there were ice floes occupied by black beings, many of them containing two—a moderate-sized mama and a much smaller baby—both just lying there and chilling out.

I reclaimed the microphone and started giving some of my informational spiel about the species, more of it than when we'd been heading into the fjord.

For the moment, at least, I felt normal. Sort of.

And though we were still a distance away, we were heading toward the docking area. I wasn't sure what might be waiting for us there.

A glance toward Liam, who'd now made it to this deck, and his serious expression didn't make me feel better. At least not much.

Somehow, I wanted to talk more with this man and see where his and his department's investigation would go from here.

# Chapter Ten

I actually had fun on the last part of the tour, despite all the things that had happened on—and off—the boat this time. Why? Because I got to point out more wildlife and answer more questions.

Some of what I offered was a repeat of what I'd said before when we were traveling the opposite way along the water— and quite possibly also of what Lettie had included in her narration. So what? It was still enjoyable.

And I told my backup many times how much I appreciated all she'd done when I wasn't on this deck.

What did I have on my mind now? Well, for one thing, why did many of the harbor seals we saw on ice floes hang out there with their new babies?

Because it was safer for them there, I informed my audience. This way they remained far from the predators on land for their first three weeks or so to allow them to mature a bit.

Of course there were other seals out there too. And otters along the shoreline.

I saw a deer in the distance on the shore and pointed it out, although anyone who didn't look quickly wasn't able to see it. We were too far away to see well anyway along the tree-covered hillside, but I told my tourists that it was most likely a Sitka black-tailed deer—partly because it was fairly small for a deer, mostly because there weren't many other kinds of deer in Alaska, although the numbers of mule deer and white-tailed deer were growing.

And then there were a few more brown bears climbing up that hillside from the shore that stayed visible longer.

The several families I'd interfaced with before were up here now too and oohed and aahed and asked a lot of questions, which always made my tours even more pleasant for me and the other passengers.

And we all needed some enjoyment right now after everything else that had occurred on this ride.

Liam remained up here, listening to my talk and looking at what I pointed out—and, I figured, at some of the other people, even though this wasn't the tour from which Truit had disappeared and died.

Hansen was up here as well.

I turned the microphone on so that people on all three decks could hear what I was saying, even those on the bridge. Maybe Palmer and Gus could also have some fun with the tour despite what else might be going on in their heads.

There wasn't as much wildlife to point out as we got into Stephens Passage, although I was delighted to see a humpback whale when we weren't far from our Juneau goal. And some kittiwakes flying nearby too.

I even gave out a few prizes as we headed back to our port.

Sasha seemed rather worn out. Not that she usually reacted much to the wildlife, but today she mostly slept by my feet, following me when I moved to other locations on the deck.

I found out more about what our tourists, or at least some of them, were thinking a while later when we finally pulled up to our dock at the Juneau tour boat landing. I did my usual thing and hurried down, with Sasha, to the bottom deck to help say good-bye to our passengers and invite them to come back for other ClemTours tours.

Judging by the strange looks I got as I invited them, I had a sad but understanding feeling that ClemTours would never again see most of them.

Which made me want even more to help figure out what had happened to Truit—unless the troopers accomplished it right away—and make sure whoever had caused it was dealt with appropriately.

That was another reason I kept looking away from the gangway leading down to the land and toward those appearing on this deck from the stairways. I was watching for Liam, who'd be the right person here now to figure out what—and who—had caused Truit's death.

He was one of the last passengers to reach the bottom deck to disembark, and he was by himself. He'd apparently not hooked up with Palmer or Gus or any members of the crew.

Of course I hadn't been with him, so I didn't know where he'd gone toward the end of the tour. Or whom he'd spoken with, if anyone.

Would I ever see him again? Most likely, if he continued to investigate the death, since I'd been on that last voyage of Truit's. Maybe not, though. Some of Liam's fellow troopers or other official investigators might be the ones I'd have to deal with instead.

He nodded toward me as he said good-bye—but fortunately it was late enough, with few enough passengers left, for me to follow, then catch up with him on the pier along with Sasha.

"I'd really like to talk to you some more about what's going to happen now," I told him.

"I'll bet you would," he replied with the hint of a grin. Now what did he mean by that?

I found out quickly when I saw Palmer, Gus, and Steph exit the boat not far behind me. They turned off toward the right, where a group of uniformed troopers stood. Liam joined them.

Sergeant Peggy Frost, whom I'd met before, was the one in front, and she still appeared to be in charge. She spoke with our bridge crew right away. Of course I'd gotten the impression they expected to be met that way, maybe by her, and wanted to converse with her too.

I could have left but instead found myself and my dog hanging out with the rest of the regular crew as they disembarked—Lettie, Betsy, and the deckhands. All of us were in our usual ClemTours sweatshirts or hoodies, as the air was a bit nippy now, though it was only around five o'clock.

As always, I felt amused by how we all somehow looked different in the same clothing, which came in only two different colors—blue and black. Al was the heaviest, Lettie the slimmest, and Betsy wasn't much bigger despite being in charge of the galley. Rafe's sweatshirt seemed shortest because he was tall.

Only my amusement now was short lived.

"What's going on?" Betsy asked the question that I figured was on all our minds.

"Don't know yet," Rafe said. He was frowning behind his dark beard. Heck, none of us was smiling.

Palmer headed our way, followed by Gus and Steph.

"I'll check with my parents," Palmer said as he stopped in front of us, "but I don't think any of us will be out on a tour tomorrow. The *ClemElk* is still being investigated, and now the *ClemWolf* will be too. We can't use either of them, and I'm fairly sure all the others in our fleet already have tours planned."

"Oh no," Betsy wailed. "Just for the one day, I hope."

I hoped that too. I supposed we all did.

"That's what I gather," Palmer answered. "Although if they find anything they consider suspicious, that could change."

"They won't stop us any longer," Al said firmly. "They can't. Rafe and I have been everywhere on board both of the boats, as usual, and we didn't see anything in the least suspicious. Right?"

He looked at his fellow deckhand. Rafe nodded vehemently.

"Well, I really don't know what's going to happen," Gus said, "but like Palmer said, we'll check with the company management, which just happens to be our parents. I'd suggest all of you give a call to the office first thing tomorrow and see what's going on."

"Sure," Betsy said. "Maybe one of the other boats can use a second galley person."

"Or another assistant to one of the tour guides," Lettie said. I wasn't mad at her. In fact, I hoped she did find a way to keep busy.

Not that any of us had caused the current problem, but—well, I just hoped we all got paid anyway. But I wasn't sure what the ClemTours policy was regarding something like this.

Assuming they even had a policy.

"Okay," I said. "We all have each other's phone numbers, so let's keep in touch. We'll all want to know who's doing what, including which boats will be providing tours tomorrow." Assuming any would.

But surely the authorities wouldn't shut down the entire company while they conducted their investigation. Not unless they found something they considered evidence that someone higher up than one of the Clementos brothers was involved. Or even some evidence that genuinely pointed toward Palmer. Or Gus, though that still didn't make sense. He'd have to have been on the boat to shove Truit over. Although—

My mind was scrambling now, probably because I felt so concerned over the ClemTours company, and not just because I worked for them. I liked them. And I just couldn't see any of them being involved in what had happened to Truit. But—

"You okay, Stacie?" Lettie asked. I realized I'd turned and was staring up at the *ClemWolf,* ignoring all the people around me despite the fact that I'd just suggested we keep in touch.

I turned toward my assistant and smiled. "I'm as fine as I can be without knowing what I'll be doing tomorrow," I told her.

"Well, like you said, let's stay in touch." She looked away from me back toward our coworkers. I hadn't paid attention to the cold breeze before—it was Alaska, after all—but it was waving her short black hair. I realized my own longer brown hair, as usual pulled up with a clip at the back of my head, was also blowing a bit. I figured hanging around out here now wasn't the greatest idea—especially because Sasha's gray-and-white fur was rippling along her back too.

Time to go home. Only—

Well, I still had too many questions. And I still didn't know if I'd ever see Liam again. We'd gotten to know each other a little bit—not at all romantically, at least not yet, even though I found him one heck of a good-looking guy. Smart, too, I gathered from the way he'd jumped into this situation and begun his up-close investigation. And—well, heck yes. I was definitely attracted to him, and it seemed to be increasing despite what had brought us together.

Was he attracted to me? I thought so, or at least hoped so. He appeared to enjoy my company, and not only because I was involved in his investigation.

But the one particularly good thing about knowing him, even a little, was that I might be able to get more info from him about the investigation as it progressed. Maybe it would help to know more about where it was now too.

And so—well, I ignored my own silent self-chastisement and headed toward where he stood near the uniformed troopers.

Fortunately, when I motioned for him to join me off to the side of the paved walkway where everyone stood, inland just a little way from the tour boat, he did so.

"Would you join me for dinner tonight?" I asked him. "You can pretty much pick the restaurant. My treat. I just have some more questions for you."

Those deep brown eyes of his, which had been aimed at me curiously, suddenly appeared amused. And . . . well, sexy.

"Must be some important questions for you to offer to treat me."

"You could say that." But I wasn't about to elaborate now, even though he could undoubtedly guess what I was going to ask. Or at least what the subject would be. Besides me simply wanting to be with him, although I wasn't about to mention that.

"Then, sure," he said. "But like I told you before, I can't talk about everything relating to this investigation. And I won't be able to leave here for another half hour or so."

That didn't thrill me. It didn't appear that Sergeant Peggy Frost or anyone else was making demands or suggestions, and as far as I could tell, some of the official troopers had already directed all the arriving tourists away from the dock area.

"I guess that's okay," I said hesitantly. "Can you tell me why?"

"We're all just going to be updated on the status of the current investigation. Just a brief meeting in the parking lot, from what I understand."

Hmm. Sounded interesting. But I wasn't a cop. I supposed inviting myself along was inappropriate.

Still, maybe I could learn what they talked about when Liam and I met for dinner. At least I could ask.

"Got it," I said.

"But let's decide now where we'll eat," Liam said, "and I'll meet you there as soon as I can. And at least pay for my part of the dinner. Maybe yours too."

Was he attempting to indirectly apologize for not sticking with me now? I doubted it. More likely he was just attempting to be a gallant trooper.

140

Either way, it didn't matter.

"Okay," I said, trying to sound friendly but indifferent. I named a couple of my faves, including a pub and a seafood place. Liam chose the pub, which was fine with me.

And under these circumstances, it might be really good to get there early and order a pint of beer while I waited. Fortunately, I'd been there before with Sasha, so I knew she was welcome.

As my dog and I left the pier area, I wished I knew how long it would take Liam to arrive at the pub. If I had sufficient time, I'd go home and watch TV news for a little while to see if anything was mentioned about the body found off the tour boat. The pub might have TV news on, but I couldn't count on it, and Liam might not want to watch it. And though I had no doubt I'd be able to find something about this situation sometime soon, the idea of waiting didn't strike me as ideal.

Besides, I could feed Sasha at home and leave her there too, so she wouldn't have to put up with the noise of a bunch of humans any longer today.

Okay, there was my answer. I wouldn't spend more than twenty minutes at home, but that was where I headed after fastening Sasha carefully in the back of my SUV.

As I had the evening before, I parked right outside the door to our unit in the development that I liked so much. I didn't need to take Sasha for a walk, since hanging around the pier area had given her the time outside she needed.

Once again I got Sasha's dinner ready as soon as we entered the house. No glass of wine right now, but I again sat down on the fluffy beige living room couch and turned on the TV mounted on the wall across from it. I used the control to flip through channels till I found some local news.

Sure enough, it was as if someone had known what I'd be doing. Yes, the media had at least learned of Truit's death. They wove it into a sordid story about the man who'd gone missing from the tour boat yesterday being found in the water today.

The situation was being investigated, but no good answers had been offered so far. They would keep their viewers up to date as information became available.

Nothing new, but it was useful to know what the world now knew.

Time to leave. "Okay, girl," I said to Sasha, bending to give her warm, fuzzy body a hug. "I won't be back too late." As if she understood that. She'd most likely sleep the whole time I was gone anyway.

I left our apartment then, making sure the door was locked behind me, and started driving to the pub.

My home wasn't far from Franklin Street in downtown Juneau, the area many of its night spots were located. There was no traffic at all until I got into that area, and I assumed many tourists and locals were taking advantage of the good weather and going out for the evening.

Like me.

But I had an ulterior motive, besides having what I hoped would be a good dinner—and a mug of amber beer from our local brewery.

I was fortunate enough to find a parking spot on the street not far from the pub. I checked the time on my phone. It was six forty, just over half an hour since Liam had told me to head to the pub and that he'd meet me there.

I figured he might have arrived first. Well, better that he wait for me than vice versa.

The sidewalk was also nice and dry and not too crowded, so I soon opened the large glass door of the building with green trim that was wall to wall between two other restaurants on Franklin Street. As soon as I'd walked in, I felt inundated but happy as a whole bunch of conversations surrounded me.

And some of those conversations were being held by several couples ahead of me in line. Oops. I hoped Liam had beaten me here and gotten a table.

"Hey, Stacie," came a call louder than the other noise. Sure enough, Liam was wending his way in my direction through the group of people nearby. "Where were you? Good thing I got here a little while ago. Our table's near the back."

"Great," I said, not objecting to his hint of a criticism.

He was still in the casual clothes he'd worn earlier. And I still wore my ClemTours tour guide outfit.

I followed him around the entry crowd and through the occupied tables to the right side at the rear, where our table was clearly identifiable as the only unoccupied space—but we soon fixed that.

We ordered our beer first, then our dinners. What sounded best to me was Irish Pub Salad, which was a bit exaggerated for a salad: lettuce, of course, and dressing, along with hard-boiled eggs, tomatoes, onion, radishes—plus pickled beets and blue cheese. And Liam asked for shepherd's pie.

"Okay," he said, after our lady server left, "why are we here?"

"Oh," I replied, looking at him and batting my eyes. "You mean you didn't just want to go on a romantic date with me?"

"Actually, I did." His response gaze back looked—well, sexy, with his brows raised, his head cocked, and his lips pouting just a little.

"Oh." That caught me off guard and made my body take notice. Oh yeah, I was becoming attracted to this guy.

I was quite glad when our server brought our beers just then and diverted my attention. The ale was quite good too. That helped.

I made myself stay as cool as the beer as I said, "Well, what I wanted was more information about your investigation. Whatever you can tell me. And mostly I'd really like to know how Truit died and who your suspects are in this strange situation." I could guess at least some of them, but I wanted to know if there were any more. Any other possibilities the troopers had come up with so far.

"Ah," he said, taking another long drink of his beer. "And here that was just what I wanted to ask you. You were on that boat. You saw people interact with each other, including Truit. I know we've talked a bit about it before, but who do you really think did it?"

"Then you're sure he was killed and it wasn't an accident?"

"We treat every unknown death as a possible homicide until we know different."

We were at an impasse. But maybe the best way to get him to say more to me was to answer him first. "Okay," I said. "On my tour I just happened to see a small pack of wolves that day around when we were going into that inlet. Maybe it was one of them, somehow getting on board and not liking Truit's scent."

To my surprise, Liam burst out laughing. Those deep brown eyes of his appeared highly amused, assuming I could read this guy at all correctly. "All right," he said finally. "I can't tell you much at this stage of the investigation, but you obviously want to know all you can. You shouldn't really get involved—but you clearly already are. I know I asked you questions before and didn't tell you to keep your nose out of it. And I doubt you'd totally back off if I told you to. So—I want your help, your insight, as much as possible. So let's level with each other, okay?"

"Sure," I said.

But could I trust him?

"Here's what I can tell you," he began—just as our dinner was served.

We soon gave each other tastes of our meals, and then our conversation began.

And what did I get out of it?

Well, unsurprisingly, Liam did particularly suspect Palmer and Hansen. He hadn't ruled out any of the crew members. "Including you," he said.

Guess he was being honest. But I had to admit to myself that I'd sort of threatened Truit, though only jokingly. Sort of.

So far, though his colleagues had interviewed some of the passengers, they hadn't added any but Hansen to the suspect list.

Gus and other Clementoses were on it because of the potential competition, although, since none besides Palmer had been on the boat, they were considered unlikely.

So why didn't I hear anything to make me feel better?

Maybe because, in this situation, there were only a limited number of answers. It certainly wasn't a bear or kittiwake who had shoved Truit off the boat and killed him.

"So now it's your turn," he told me. "Who do you think did it?"

I could really only provide one answer that made sense—although there were, of course, a lot of other possibilities I didn't want to consider.

"It had to be Hansen," I said, and explained yet again my suspicions against the guy—even though he'd teared up when Truit was mentioned.

We were nearly done eating and talking.

"I get it," Liam said. "And of course we'll continue our official investigation till we have all the answers. I'd appreciate it if you'd keep in touch and let me know whatever other ideas come to you, or if any of the other crew members mention anything we should know."

"Fine," I said, mostly meaning it. "I'd like you to do the same, at least as much as you can tell a non-cop what's going on."

"Fine," he returned, and I wondered if he meant it at all.

But the good thing I took away from the meal—the cost of which we split—and the discussion with Liam?

That we would be keeping in touch.

# Chapter Eleven

That night I lay in bed in my apartment for a long time listening to Sasha's gentle snoring, below and to my side. Usually it didn't keep me awake, though if I did awaken, I often heard it. Like now.

But—well, I supposed I shouldn't be surprised I wasn't sleeping much.

As I lay there, I couldn't help thinking about it all.

For one thing, I knew I wouldn't be working the next day despite having been scheduled for a tour. I'd checked my phone when I got home, and Palmer had texted me. No tours out of Juneau tomorrow.

Okay. But that wasn't the major reason I couldn't sleep.

Finding a dead body—or rather, being best buddies with the canine who'd first smelled it and let others know—had certainly affected my sense of well-being.

I took a deep breath as I lay there in my warm pj's with my head resting on a stack of two pillows, ignoring the small nightlight in the corner of my bedroom near the floor, since I didn't need it to find my way to the bathroom.

I tried to relax the way Sasha was, willing myself to fall asleep again—but still thinking.

Yes, I'd been there to help find the body. I resisted bending to pat my smart, sleeping dog for that.

Then there was all the investigation stuff that had come after it, with more to follow. I supposed Liam might not have been kidding when he indicated I was a potential suspect, since I'd been on the *ClemElk* when Truit was pushed off it. I still didn't know what had really happened, but I assumed that was how he'd wound up in the water below.

Hopefully I was just on the list because I'd been on the boat. Liam hadn't indicated there was any supposed evidence against me. Surely he didn't count that joke I'd made about leaving Truit onshore.

Even so, it felt daunting. Scary. And—

Well, I was one determined person. Always had been. Always intended to be. Not my job to figure this out? So what?

For my own sake and for the sake of my employers, the very nice Clementoses, I would do all I could to make sure the mystery of Truit's demise got resolved as soon as possible. I had no interest in being in law enforcement, but as I'd always done if a goal presented itself to me, I would devote myself to achieving it.

And I assumed—or at least hoped—that none of the Clementoses had had anything to do with it.

I sighed and shifted again. And continued thinking.

Other than Hansen, I didn't know any of the tourists who'd taken our tour yesterday, so I had to rely on the troopers to interview them during their investigation.

But then there was Hansen, my suspect-in-chief, whom I'd spoken with since then. If it wasn't him, I had no real idea who it could be.

Maybe another passenger who'd known Truit somehow and had signed up for the tour knowing he'd be on it—and taken advantage of the fact that we were out in the water like that?

Or—

Okay. I shifted under my coverlet. I wasn't going to get anywhere like this. I'd be exhausted tomorrow, when I'd probably have my best opportunity, maybe my only opportunity, to follow up and conduct my own, silly but crucial, amateur investigation.

Sure, I realized it made more sense to continue in my real life and count on Liam to keep me informed.

But he was a professional. He might be kind and tell me some stuff, assuming there was anything he learned that he could pass along to the public. Or he'd drop hints to get me to answer questions he thought I might be able to help with.

Liam. A good-looking, sexy guy. And here I was in bed, thinking about him.

But not in that way, or so I told myself.

I wondered if it would be easier to fall asleep if he were here. His protectiveness as a trooper might help me to relax. And if he were here, we might already have . . .

Enough!

"Go to sleep," I told myself through gritted teeth.

And lo and behold, I did.

After maybe another half hour.

I woke up at my usual time of six o'clock the next morning. No, I hadn't set my phone, but that was when I was used to getting up, so I wasn't surprised.

After showering quickly, I threw on a parka over pants and a shirt and took Sasha out, walking on the sidewalk surrounding the apartment building, letting my dog go onto the grass on both sides to take care of what she needed to. I always left a towel just inside the door so I'd be able to dab her feet and fur when we got home.

I saw another dog walker across the street, but no one else was outside. That was fine, and the reason was clear.

It was colder today than it had been the last couple of days, plus it was raining, though not very hard.

Nevertheless, I told myself it was a good thing I wasn't going out on a boat today. Fewer tourists would come, the boat would rock more, it'd be harder to see the wildlife and point it out—

Okay, trying to kid myself never worked. Though I'd been a tour guide only a short time, I'd given tours plenty of times in the rain, even occasionally in the snow, and I'd always managed to handle things just fine.

No, I wasn't happy that, on top of everything else, I'd miss a day out on the water watching and pointing out the many wonderful animals that showed up as we cruised by.

"So what are we going to do?" I asked Sasha softly as we went back inside.

I had an idea, at least. I fed my dog, then did the same for myself—fruit and sugar-free cereal with low-fat milk. I even made a small pot of coffee.

When I was done, I checked the time. Too early for what I was planning, so I plopped down and put the TV on again. Yes, the news mentioned Truit's death and how an investigation had been started. No, it still didn't indicate that any progress had been made.

One good thing was that I was able to stream a couple of networks, and so I got to watch a show about—what else?—Alaskan wildlife. .

That kept me occupied for a while, even though I was familiar with all the animals they mentioned, focusing on seals and bears and others I saw fairly often.

When the show finished and I checked the time and Googled info on my phone, I figured I was ready to go.

"We're going to the tour office," I told Sasha. She put her pretty, slender muzzle up in the air as if she were attempting to sniff out what I said, and I walked over to where she lay not far from me on the living room floor and patted her head between the ears. Her furry tail wagged.

Soon thereafter we entered my SUV, and I drove to the local ClemTours office, not especially far in downtown Juneau.

Because their tours left from different locations, the company had offices in several Alaska towns, including Skagway and Anchorage. I'd visited both but preferred being involved with the tours nearest Juneau, and fortunately this was where they'd scheduled me to work.

This office was on Egan Drive, a main street in downtown Juneau. It was in a one-story building with a large plate glass window in front, and when someone looked inside or walked through the wooden door, they were regaled by a wall full of posters of glaciers and wood-covered hillsides and, yes, local wildlife.

The idea was to encourage visitors to sign up for tours and keep the boats and workers like me as busy as possible.

But today no one would have an opportunity to see any of those enjoyable sights from the *ClemElk* or *ClemWolf*.

I still hoped that the other ClemTours boats would remain busy. And that some of my fellow crew members and I would have an opportunity to help out on some of those additional tours.

I found a convenient parking space about a block away and got Sasha from the back seat. Despite the imperfect weather—or maybe it was perfect for Alaska at other times of the year—a lot of people cruised the downtown sidewalks on foot, sightseeing and popping in and out of store and restaurant doors. Quite a few exclaimed over how cute my dog was, so we stopped often so Sasha could get a pat and I could make it clear how much I agreed with the compliments.

And mention that I worked for ClemTours and ask if that particular tourist or their group happened to have taken a sightseeing boat tour yet . . . and say that by the way, I was a tour guide.

Okay, that was my usual routine, even though today it made less sense. I didn't know how long the people I talked with would remain in town or if they'd have the possibility of taking a tour with me. I didn't even know if we'd be going out tomorrow. The next day? The day after that?

I usually got a couple of days off a week, and this week I had no idea whether there would be a lot more.

Sasha and I soon reached the shop, and I opened the door for her. She pranced right inside, and I followed, still holding her leash.

I was glad to see that the person behind the long glass counter facing the door that held lots of promotional brochures for the company tours was Ingrid Clementos, parent of Palmer, Gus, and the other tour boat captains and cofounder of ClemTours with her husband Curt. They usually spent their days in the offices, often in different towns unless the weather made that difficult. But they occasionally captained a tour boat like their kids.

Ingrid was short, with silvery hair that surrounded her face in a frame that brought out her pretty features, including a long but attractive chin. She had some wrinkles, though I wasn't sure how old she was—probably in her sixties.

She wore a long-sleeved bright-blue shirt that had on it—what else?—the ClemTours logo.

And she was not alone in the store. Both Palmer and Gus stood behind the counter with her. The three of them had apparently been talking to the *ClemElk* crew, for Steph, Al, Rafe, Betsy, and even Lettie were there.

And yes, all were dressed as if they were about to take a tour boat out. ClemTours shirts on each of them.

I joined them. "Are you all asking about getting an assignment for the next day or two?"

"Hi, Stacie," Ingrid said. "Is that what you're here for too?"

"Do you have any assignments available?" I countered.

"Nope. I'm sure you know the *ClemElk* is the main boat for here, and we borrowed the *ClemWolf* yesterday. The others are all booked for at least the next few days from other ports."

I nodded toward my cohorts. "But if someone wants to make their way to Anchorage or Skagway, can they get a gig while those two boats are beached?"

Not literally beached, of course, but close enough. They'd be full of troopers and investigators, I assumed, and unable to move away from shore for the next day or two.

"Probably. However—" Ingrid pointed toward the door behind her that led to the offices. It was slightly open. Was another member of the Clementos family here? "Someone else visiting here right now would probably say no to that—allowing one or more of you to leave town that easily. Haven't you been told to hang around for now?"

Liam had certainly implied that to me, if not ordered me to stay.

And why wasn't I surprised to see that very trooper come through that door? I wasn't sure what he'd been up to, but I assumed he'd allowed Ingrid to come out here to greet any possible customers while he went through—well, whatever he'd asked to see.

He wore his uniform today, a long-sleeved beige shirt with a thick blue vest over it and long navy pants with a stripe up the side. A badge on the vest identified him as Alaska State Trooper Liam Amaruq.

"Hi, Stacie." He raised his hand in a brief wave. "I figured you'd be here too, since all your coworkers popped in."

I didn't recall talking specifically with him about what I'd be doing today, although we had both mentioned keeping in touch.

Liam was followed out of the office by some other people in uniform, who must also be nosing around here and asking questions.

"Right," I said, too brightly. "Here I am. Now, can you tell all of us when we'll be able to take either the *ClemElk* or *ClemWolf* out again on a tour?"

Before he answered, a couple who appeared to be in their thirties, all bundled up in jackets, came through the door from the sidewalk.

I'd entered through that door, too, with Sasha. It wasn't locked. The investigation didn't require shutting down the entire tour company, apparently.

I was glad about that.

But what could I do to get things going again around here?

Ingrid remained behind the counter and shot a large smile at the newcomers. She gestured for them to join her and began welcoming them to ClemTours, motioning toward the tour brochures on the counter.

As the couple moved toward her, the woman looked down toward my husky. "Hi, sweetie," she said.

Sasha got a ton of attention over the next minute.

"She gets to go along on the tours I give," I told the couple, then realized that might be too much of an invitation. "I won't be a tour guide for a few days, though."

The woman knelt on the floor, hugging Sasha and looking up toward me. "That's a shame," she said. "We're here on a cruise and will be leaving tomorrow afternoon."

"Where do you go next?" Ingrid called over the counter.

"Skagway."

Ah. Good.

"Our company gives other boat tours from there," Ingrid said. "I've got brochures for that too."

The woman stood, and she and the man with her started discussing possibilities with Ingrid.

At least the company wouldn't necessarily lose money from this couple, I thought, nodding.

When I glanced toward Liam, still behind the counter, he was watching me. And smiling.

Did he know what I was thinking? Unlikely, but he might guess the general topic.

I'd noticed that one of the troopers there was Liam's superior officer, Sergeant Peggy Frost, in a uniform similar to Liam's but with a sergeant's insignia. She looked rather impatient as she frowned from one of my cohorts to the next.

What was wrong? What was she thinking?

The potential tour goers soon left, and only then did Sergeant Frost start talking. "Okay," she said, "I know most or all of you have spoken with us already, but we want to talk to each of you again here. First, though, let me tell you some of the rules for the next couple of days."

She didn't say anything surprising to me, at least. No outings on the two tour boats in question. None of us was to leave town unless we were on a ClemTours assignment and we returned, and we were to provide our contact information in case there were even more questions for us than the ones we'd already been asked and those we'd hear now.

"And if any of you get further information on what happened to Mr. Truit, be sure to notify one of us, preferably me. I'll give you each one of my cards. But don't tell anyone else, especially one of your colleagues who's here right now."

Okay. I got it. We were all supposed to suspect one another and not reveal anything potentially helpful to our coworkers.

Soon we were each taken aside, and I assumed the others were asked questions similar to those I got.

And yes, I was paired up with Liam for this. I was a bit surprised, since he must have told his boss and maybe others that he had already quizzed me on my knowledge about Truit's death, which of course was slim.

Had he requested to be the one to interrogate me again?

I certainly didn't mind being in his company, even though we both went into the back office and stood in one of its corners.

The room was small and had piles of boxes with tour brochures taped to the outside, so their contents were obvious. There was a desk and chairs and not much else in here.

When Liam and I positioned ourselves in that corner, Sasha by my side, Gus was in there too, with Sergeant Frost. I couldn't hear what she was saying, but her tone sounded somewhat angry.

I wished I knew what she was thinking.

I was highly aware of Liam's tall, broad body so close to mine, even though nothing about his proximity was inappropriate.

But I realized I was suddenly seeing a lot of this guy. We were talking a lot, trading ideas . . .

I needed to help him get his investigation over with so I could go back to my normal, enjoyable, and solitary—except for my tours and my sweet Sasha—life. That was all. Nothing more personal.

The current question in my mind taking hold, I murmured to Liam, "Has Sergeant Frost learned something that is bothering her?"

"Just the opposite," he responded, also in a whisper. "I'm fairly sure she thinks we should know more by now."

"So what are we supposed to be talking about?"

"I'm sure you can guess. Have you learned or thought of anything you haven't told me? Would you be more comfortable telling someone else?" Those dark-brown eyes of his seemed to attempt to search my mind again. Boy, did they turn me on.

And make me look away. Which I was certain looked suspicious.

But I got an idea. I wanted to know more too, and I doubted Liam would tell me anything under these circumstances.

"I don't really know anything else," I told him, "but I'm wondering if my memory would be stoked if I saw anything you'd found in your investigation about Truit, and maybe Hansen, or—"

"You know I can't tell or show you much."

"Is there any information at your station that you're authorized to show to the media?"

"Well, yes, but—"

"But I'd be likely to see it on TV or in social media or the papers anyway. Look, I love my job and the family who are my bosses. I understand, though, that you have to do your job, and I want to help you figure this all out so you can arrest anyone who's guilty and we can get back to giving tours." It was hard to say all this softly enough that the captain, and another trooper who'd now come in the office with Betsy from the galley, couldn't hear, but I did my darnedest. "Anyway, can I come to your station with you and see what's okay to be made public? It may remind me of something or someone I saw on the boat the day Truit disappeared."

And possibly help me aim Liam and his troopers in a direction other than the Clementoses. That was my goal.

But I recognized I didn't want to do anything to hide any truth I might come up with.

And why did I want to go to the place where these troopers were stationed today? Maybe because I knew I wouldn't be working otherwise, so no need to stay here. My temporary goal remained helping to get Truit's death figured out ASAP so we could all return to normal. I wouldn't learn anymore here, most likely. Even if Palmer or Gus hung around, I doubted either would confess—and I didn't want them to.

But maybe I could learn something more from Liam, or other troopers, or other people at their department, that could help me point them in the right direction faster and get this over with.

Right now I was waiting for Liam's answer. I saw his gaze go past me toward his boss, which wasn't a great idea. I doubted Sergeant Frost would welcome me to their station with open arms.

Unless I could come up with something I could only tell them without my coworkers around.

I pondered what that could be—in a way that wouldn't get me into any trouble. I was glad when Liam said, still in a low voice, "Okay, you can come with me to the station this morning, but only while I stay with you, and for a short while. And only if you promise you'll tell me anything from that tour that comes to mind about who Truit was with, what he said, what happened to him—"

"Got it," I said. "How soon can we go?"

# Chapter Twelve

I was aware that the Alaska State Troopers were connected to the Alaska Department of Public Safety, and that Liam's new division within the Troopers, the Initial Response Section, was a small but important part of the organization.

I'd only been vaguely aware of their location in Juneau but learned the specifics quickly, thanks to Liam.

Our destination now, the Initial Response office, wasn't far from the ClemTours office, so Sasha and I walked there with Liam, who definitely knew where he was going.

He explained, though, that the Initial Response Section here in Juneau had an office separate from that of the Alaska State Troopers, which had a building a distance from downtown.

"We're more in the middle of things here," he said. "Although that's not always necessary, it doesn't hurt—especially since we're the group often brought in first in questionable situations, before it's clear if there's been a crime committed and, if so, what it is."

Made sense to me—a disappearance from a tour boat being a great example of such a "questionable situation."

And I had some more questions.

"How does your group store evidence about a crime like this?" I asked, mostly to get a conversation going. Would he give me a lot of info? I doubted it.

In fact, I remained surprised he'd agreed to let me come along with him to his place of employment—although maybe he wanted to keep an eye on me and make sure I didn't do anything to interfere with the investigation.

Which I didn't really want to do, unless I felt certain that their interest in Palmer as a suspect meant they weren't really attempting to learn the truth.

And I still hoped the truth was that someone other than Palmer, or any other Clementos, was the killer.

"We have a secure system, as most law enforcement agencies do," Liam responded, looking straight at me as if expecting me to argue—or maybe just request access to that system.

Hey, if I'd thought he'd budge, I'd definitely be making that kind of request.

"Of course." What could I do at the moment, though, but acknowledge the information he'd conveyed? "But as I said before, I'd appreciate it if you'd share whatever you can so I can find a way to help you get your answers."

Answers other than a Clementos family member, I continued to hope.

"I'm still assuming you'll share anything you find." That was his response—without acknowledging he'd do anything similar.

We turned a few corners on our walk, stopped now and then to let Sasha sniff gravel-covered areas between the sidewalk and the roadway, and wound up in an area that had buildings on a hillside overlooking the street. One building, on the right side and up the hill, was constructed of red bricks and had a sloped roof.

Liam led me up a sidewalk beside the rising driveway that turned a bit to keep the incline from being too steep, probably a good idea when the weather was bad.

My suspicions about the building were quickly confirmed. Part of the roof overhung the glass surface at the front, and a sign over the door said Alaska State Troopers Initial Response Section.

"Ah," I said. "This must be our destination."

"You got it." Liam walked ahead of Sasha and me to open the door.

There was a greeting area just inside, with a long wooden counter that had a couple of uniformed officers seated behind it. Their outfits were similar to Liam's: long-sleeved beige shirts with that blue vest over it and long navy pants with a stripe up the side.

"Hi, Liam," said the African American man who was closest. He remained seated on a tall chair, and so did the woman who looked like a teenager beside him. "And who are your companion and her companion?"

I smiled and didn't wait for Liam to respond. "This is Sasha, and I'm Stacie Calder."

Both officers first wore what I interpreted as welcoming expressions but then shot glances at Liam as if they were puzzled.

"Stacie is one of my contacts in the Sheldon Truit investigation," Liam told them, and the puzzlement seemed to disappear—maybe.

But I had a strong sense that they might still want to know why I was here with Liam.

"You'll need to sign in," Liam told me, and motioned for me to go up to the desk, which I did, Sasha remaining, as always, at my side. The officer behind the desk shoved a metal pen with a rounded tip in my direction, then pointed to a tablet computer sitting on the desk closer to me.

And as I filled out my name, address, and reason for being there, I had no problem eavesdropping on the brief conversation Liam held with his colleagues.

I learned nothing new. Nothing helpful. Except that apparently some troopers were asking questions at other places where Truit had worked recently—other tour companies through which he'd gotten temporary jobs.

Plus a relative of Truit's was on her way here today—a sister who lived in Anchorage.

The autopsy hadn't been completed, so they weren't releasing Truit's body yet. But the sister, like me, apparently wanted to know where their investigation had taken them so far.

And unlike me, she probably had the right to know.

When I was finished playing with the tablet, I turned around and saw that Liam had gone to the reception room's front door.

I also saw through its glass that a woman was approaching from outside.

It could have been anyone, but the timing told me it was Truit's sister. She was dressed much like Truit had been when I'd last seem him, plus this woman's face, which somewhat resembled his, looked highly upset. And it appeared that Liam was going outside to greet her.

To prevent me from meeting her?

Or was I just being paranoid?

Either way, I figured it was a good time to take Sasha out for a brief walk before I had an opportunity to quiz Liam more about the investigation here at his headquarters. And so I got my sweet, obedient pup to stay at my side as I headed for that door.

"Hey," called the woman officer from behind me.

I turned briefly. "Sorry. My dog needs to go outside. We'll be right back." And then we continued on for the remainder of the short distance—just as Liam stepped out that door.

Well, so did we. He looked surprised as we showed up on the walkway beside him. The woman who'd been approaching stopped and regarded us quizzically—although she focused mainly on Sasha.

Oh, good. Possibly another dog lover. Maybe she'd be willing to talk to my pup—and me.

"Hi," I said to her. "This is Sasha. Are you, by any chance, Sheldon Truit's sister?"

I noticed Liam's furious glare. Well, he and his cohorts had been the ones to mention she was on her way—assuming my guess was right.

It was.

"Yes," she said hoarsely. "I'm Arla Truit. Are you one of the officers here who's investigating his . . . his death?" Tears rose in her brown eyes, and I thought they looked a bit like Truit's. She wore a knit cap similar to his, although her straight blond hair showed at the bottom. Her slacks were black, and she wore a puffy vinyl jacket over them—as he had. I'd never considered her brother especially good looking, yet this woman's appearance seemed striking to me.

Before I could answer her, she knelt on the cement and held her arms out toward Sasha, who understood the gesture. Sweet dog that she was, she pulled her way toward Ms. Truit and let her pet her while the woman allowed her tears to flow.

Liam took a step in their direction, glaring at me. I figured his message was that I should stay back, but I ignored it.

In moments I was kneeling beside her. "I'm so sorry," I said—and I was, for her, even though I hadn't been best buddies with her brother. "No, I'm not a trooper. I'm Stacie Calder, and I just happened to be on the boat. Are you aware—"

"That Sheldon fell off a tour boat?" She looked at me. "Yes, that's what I was told. But he was never klutzy. I'm glad the police are looking into it, because—because I'll bet he was pushed." She stopped talking, and her expression hardened behind her tears. "You were on that boat?"

"Yes, and I wish I knew what happened to him. In fact, I'm hoping to help the troopers investigate it." I couldn't help glancing at Liam again. He didn't say anything, but his expression had turned even more irritated.

"And you didn't do it?" She stood, and now she too was glaring.

"Of course not." *But did you?* I wondered. Oh, I suspected I'd have noticed her if she'd been on the boat, since she resembled Truit. I doubted she'd been a tourist that day. But I'd no idea how caring her relationship with her brother had been—and whether she'd had any reason to hire someone else to do him in.

Did she want him out of the way so she could start a tour boat company herself—with Hansen or otherwise? Or had she and Truit planned to be partners until he kicked her out, so that she wanted revenge? Or—

I almost laughed aloud at myself. I must be getting desperate. Or at least my imagination was working overtime.

Wasn't it?

Why was she here today—to be interviewed about where she'd been at the time of Truit's death and what their relationship had been?

Darned if I knew—but I was going to quiz Liam about that.

"Let's go back in." Liam's tone was stern, so Sasha and I headed for the door again. The other two followed us.

When we got inside, I saw that Sergeant Peggy Frost had arrived here too. She was waiting near the desk, frowning. "I heard all three of you were here. I want to talk to you. Let's go to my office."

I wondered why, and my heart rate quickened. Was she about to arrest either of us civilians? Or did she just want to bawl us out?

And was I somehow in the same category as Truit's sister in the sergeant's mind? If so, were we just intruders—or something more?

Time to find out. Arla went first, Sasha and me following and Liam bringing up the rear—and I had the sense he was making damned sure neither of us fled when his superior officer wanted to talk to us.

I tried to ignore the amused expressions on the faces of the two officers who'd greeted us.

Sergeant Frost's office was the farthest down a narrow hallway lined with doors. She opened her own door and stood there, gesturing for us to enter. And all of us did, including Liam.

The place appeared all Alaskan—with wallpaper consisting of views of snow-covered mountain slopes. I saw something on those slopes and realized it was hikers with poles, apparently scaling the mountains.

Was this sergeant a hiker? Or did she just want the notion of being able to tackle anything, including seemingly impossible ascents, to keep her company while she was here?

"Please sit down." She gestured toward the orange upholstered chairs facing her long, low, and perfectly clean desk. A computer sat on a compact table off to the side.

We all complied. Who wouldn't obey an officer in charge of a law enforcement office that was probably investigating all of us? Arla and me, at least. Not Liam, of course. But he listened to his commanding officer. A good thing, as far as I was concerned, particularly because she was a female officer.

Not that this female non-officer named Stacie had any intentions of giving him orders. Unless I thought of some that might help these troopers reach the right conclusion about Truit's death—assuming I was correct, of course, and no Clementos, especially Palmer, had been involved.

As I sat, I gestured toward Sasha, and she obediently lay down on the deep-toned plank floor beside me. Liam pulled his chair back so that he sat near the door, behind both Arla and me.

"Okay," Peggy finally said.

Yes, I had started thinking of her by her first name, as I did most people. Was that okay with this law enforcement group? I hadn't heard otherwise—but neither had I tried to address her that way to her face.

She continued, "Ms. Truit, I know why you're here, of course. The coroner has not released your brother's body, and the investigation into what happened to him is continuing. I'll let you know when we reach any conclusions and take anyone responsible into custody, if that's appropriate."

"It's got to be." Tears began flowing down Arla's cheeks. "My brother was not only a good guy, he was careful. He wouldn't have jumped off that boat, and he wouldn't have fallen either—not without being pushed. Please, please figure out who killed him and why."

She dipped her face into her hands, and her body shook as she continued weeping. Her sadness was so obvious that even Sasha stood and went over to her, laying her muzzle on the woman's lap. Arla reached down to pat her with one hand, still crying into the other.

That grief certainly looked genuine, and the fact that she was pleading with the authorities to find who'd murdered her brother and arrest that person made it seem as if any suspicions against her were absurd.

But I didn't dump them. Everyone I'd wondered about remained on my list, at least for now.

I couldn't yet determine why I'd been included in the meeting where Arla was being informed of what was going on with her brother. But why not?

Peggy didn't directly respond to Arla's sorrow or pleas, though I was certain she'd heard them. Would they make a

difference in her actions or in what she wanted those reporting to her to do? I doubted it.

"And Ms. Calder," Peggy said. My turn now. "I asked you
to come in here even though it may not have been appropriate for you to hear our update about our investigation into
Mr. Truit's death. But I know you're involved in that investigation, maybe as an insider within the tour boat company.
Could you enlighten me further?"

I found it interesting that she moved her gaze from me to
Liam and back again, which suggested she at least had some
idea how I was involved, even if she didn't necessarily grasp
the full reason. She must have at least heard Liam's take on it.

And what was that reason? I actually wasn't certain, other
than the fact that my habitual determination made me want
to look into absolutely everything that might provide answers
eventually—or even better, right away. As an insider at the
tour company? Sure.

I decided to be as honest as possible.

It probably wouldn't do me much good to lie anyway,
since I'd talked to Liam enough for him to understand my
motivations.

I therefore leaned forward toward the desk and looked
Peggy as straight into her hazel eyes as I could, hoping I
looked earnest. Which I was.

"I realize I'm reaching outside my duties as a tour guide,
but I really love the company I work for, ClemTours."

Peggy said nothing, and I didn't hear Liam move or comment or anything from behind me.

And so I continued. "I was on the boat when Mr. Truit
disappeared." I glanced toward Arla beside me, cocking my

head and attempting to show her I was sympathetic. As far as I knew, Truit hadn't deserved to die, even if he'd wanted to go into competition with my employers. "I believe I was the first to realize I hadn't seen him for a while and start looking for him. We were already on our way back to port here in Juneau by then, and no one knew what had happened. The next day, oddly, we followed a mother seal and her pup into the inlet, then went a bit farther when we spotted some bears. My dog barked to alert us that something was wrong." I decided not to mention the scent in Truit's sister's presence, but I bent over and petted Sasha between the ears, even though her head was on the floor, cushioned by her front paws. "That's when we saw Truit on the shore."

I paused, trying to decide what to say next.

"Okay, we get all that," Peggy pushed. "But what are you doing? Why are you here, at our offices?"

This time I heard Liam stir behind me, and I wondered if he was going to step in and tell her I'd started trying to help. Or criticize me for being too snoopy.

But he said nothing, so I pressed forward. "I'm here because, well, I've been trying to figure out who might have been involved if Mr. Truit didn't jump or fall off the boat." I ignored Arla's indignant gasp and continued fast so she couldn't interrupt me. "I know neither of those has been ruled out, but I gather you troopers are looking into the possibility this was a homicide." Yes, I knew the more official word for murder. "I've spoken with people I knew were on board. And I've talked to Liam and think he recognizes that I'll tell him if I find anything that actually might lead to an answer. I want to learn anything that's going on that you can reveal to a citizen so—till you've got it solved—I can use that information to help me figure out what and who to look into next."

I didn't mention that I didn't want the person or people in question to be any of my bosses or that this was the main reason I was snooping into the situation—but of course Liam knew that. Insider on the tour? Yes.

I stopped talking at last, still looking closely at Peggy. She, in turn, had continued to look at me. "I see," she said. "I figured you were an amateur, and you are. A nosy one. And I gather you don't have any great new insights or, even better, evidence against someone that we can look into."

"No," I admitted. "I don't." I didn't comment on her calling me an amateur, since it was true.

She stood and bent in my direction. "And you realize, I assume, that you are not authorized to do any of this and that you might hamper the real investigation." Those hazel eyes were now glaring as if she wanted to use them to grab and shake me.

I didn't respond verbally, but I looked down as if I were repenting—which I wasn't. And as long as I didn't get in their way, hopefully she couldn't, or wouldn't, attempt to stop me.

I almost crowed aloud when the opposite occurred. "I never thought I'd say something like this," she said, "but in some ways you're in a better position than those of us conducting the official investigation. As long as you promise to stay out of our way, to stop if you see any indication of danger against you, and to reveal anything you find right away to Liam, our officer who's primarily in charge of the investigation, I'll look the other way."

She looked toward Arla. "Same goes for you, in a way," she continued. "If you can get in touch with friends and family members here and see if anyone has any ideas about who could have wanted to harm your brother and you let us know, that would be most helpful."

Interesting. I hadn't thought official investigators would ever encourage civilian assistance.

But then, this was a new division outside the general organization. Who knew what they could do—and how they could accomplish it? Maybe going outside the box was part of why the Initial Response Section was formed.

"Sounds fine with me," I said, standing and turning toward Liam. "I guess you'll be my official contact."

He nodded. "Yes, I will."

"Mine too?" Arla asked.

"That's right," Peggy responded. "He'll give you his contact information. And so you all know, the initial investigation of the *ClemElk* has been completed. It will be able to start giving tours again tomorrow."

*Yay!* I mentally shouted. I'd once more be able to point out all the wonderful wildlife this area of Alaska offered the world.

And as I wandered the boat, I could talk to people. Most of them would be newcomers—but who knew? Some might have friendships or relationships with some of the tourists who'd been on board that fateful day.

The crew members were likely to be the same.

"In case you're wondering," Peggy continued, "Liam will also be on your tour tomorrow and will continue to accompany the *ClemElk* for as long as it makes sense."

Why did I like that idea so much? I was still looking at the guy and tried to interpret his smile at me.

Well, he'd do his job and hopefully find some answers, with my help, and possibly Arla's too.

And if I got to know him a little better?

That was fine with me. And maybe together we would figure out what really happened to Sheldon Truit.

# Chapter Thirteen

I was glad when Arla asked to speak with Peggy in private, even though my mind swam with many possibilities of what she might want to discuss. She probably at least wanted an update regarding what the authorities had found so far while looking into what had happened to her brother and figured the sergeant in charge here would be the best resource.

I, on the other hand, was relying on Liam. After all, he'd been on this case nearly from the beginning—since late on the same day Truit vanished from the boat, only a couple of days ago. It felt a lot longer.

I was glad when Liam invited Sasha and me to accompany him out of the room, leaving the two other women alone, and follow him down the hall and into his office behind one of those hallway doors.

His office was about half the size of Peggy's, and he had only two chairs facing his not-so-clear desk. Fortunately, there was enough room for Sasha to lie beside the one on the right, where I sat down.

The walls weren't the artistic Alaskan vision of the sergeant's room but plain beige plaster. There were three large photographs on them, and I had to smile. This man and I had something in common besides checking into what had happened to Sheldon Truit. The pictures had been taken from a boat, maybe in Tracy Arm, and one featured several harbor seals—including a mother with her baby. In the background was a tall, icy glacier.

Another showed two bears on the shore somewhere. And one more photo showed a humpback whale, breaching.

The guy apparently enjoyed being here in this unique and amazing state, as I did. And he must enjoy watching its wildlife too.

That gave me another reason both to like him and to be wary of what my emotions did around him. I wasn't looking for a relationship. I'd had several before that had gone nowhere. And I didn't think an officer of the law would have much interest in someone who was involved in a case he was working on. But if he did—well, yeah. I wouldn't mind giving another relationship a try if it was someone like Liam.

Not that I knew what law enforcement offices generally looked like, but these pictures seemed unusual. And appealing, at least to me.

I was surprised when my cell phone rang as soon as I sat down. I pulled it from my purse and glanced at it. The screen identified Maria Dobbs—one of the other ClemTours tour guides and a buddy of mine. She was stationed in Skagway now. I suspected she'd heard what had happened on the *ClemElk* and wanted to talk to me about it. And though I hadn't wanted to discuss this with anyone before, talking to her about it might help my state of mind. But I pushed the button to send her to voice mail. I'd call her back later, when I was alone.

Right now I began my conversation with Liam. "So tell me more about this Initial Response Section. You've told me a bit, how you were selected to check out the report of a missing person before anyone could say something happened to him, but aren't there other departments in the state troopers who are considered to be the experts at conducting investigations?"

"Yes, of course, but as I said before, our group is sort of experimental. We're looking into things that might not be crimes or other issues troopers generally get involved with, and sometimes they turn out to be non-issues, so we drop them, which can save time and expense. But in situations like this, we eventually turn them over to the appropriate section—then continue to not only give the info we have but also help out as needed. And right now, considering the interesting but so far unfinished facts of this case, we're still the main investigators. Since I was first assigned to look into it, I'm the top investigator and recorder of whatever goes on."

"Got it." I felt comfortable with his being in charge. So far, he'd been professional yet easy to talk to. I believed I could run things by him and get a reasonable response, as long as he wouldn't be violating the department's rules if he spoke with me.

He put his hands behind his head and leaned back. I also liked the sense of informality he often gave, like now. "So you'll be giving your tour tomorrow again. Do you feel comfortable doing that?"

"You mean because there could be a murderer on the boat too? Well, I was on board the day Truit disappeared. I didn't know to be worried then, nor was I concerned at first on the day he was found. And I know it's not my job to figure it all out. But—"

"But you like your employers and want to do all you can to get them cleared. I know that." Liam bent toward me with his hands down, his gaze stabbing at me, that informality gone. "If they're innocent, I'll want them cleared too. My job isn't just to help find out what happened but also to make sure the guilty pay for it—and only the guilty. So, in case you're wondering—yes, I'll be taking your tour tomorrow too. You and I can split up and do our respective jobs and talk to people and learn what we can. But you know what?"

I'd been feeling so good as he described exactly what I'd hoped for, including his being on the boat. With me, even though we wouldn't be together much. But—did I know *what* what?

"No, tell me," I said.

He was standing now, glaring down at me in a way that also made Sasha stand to protect me, as her name said she would. "You will be really, really careful, since whoever did it has murdered before and undoubtedly would again to protect himself."

"Or herself," I said. Not that I really had a woman as a suspect, but I figured Liam was still fixated on Palmer, who would never hurt me. Unless, of course, he was guilty and I found proof and he knew it . . .

No. That wouldn't happen. I knew the guy. I liked the guy. Our silly attempts at flirtation had meant nothing, but I enjoyed his friendliness, and I trusted him. Palmer couldn't be the killer.

I hoped.

"Of course I'll be careful," I continued. "Still. Again. And while we're on the boat, you and I should remain in constant touch so I can provide you with any information I come across, and vice versa." Well, I had to try.

Liam shook his head gently and smiled as he lowered himself back into his chair. "First part, yes. You tell me. Second part, it depends on what it is and whether I'm authorized to provide that information to you or anyone else."

"Got it," I muttered, trying to scowl, but I really did get it. And I couldn't help but appreciate that, in doing his job right, this guy was likely to find the truth—and hopefully do so while keeping Palmer and all other Clementos family members from being treated like major suspects.

But I couldn't count on that. Especially when it came to Palmer.

"Anyhow," I said, "I guess Sasha and I ought to get on our way home." It wasn't too late in the day, but I didn't have a tour to give, so I supposed I could relax. Assuming I could recall what relaxation was.

"See you tomorrow," Liam said.

"Right." As I left, I noticed that Peggy's office door was open. I popped my head in and said good-bye to her and Arla. I again expressed my sympathy to Arla and nodded toward the sergeant to acknowledge that I knew she and her staff would do all they could to solve the crime. Then I departed the building, Sasha at my side. I fastened her in the back seat of my SUV, got into the driver's seat, and pulled out of my parking space.

And was delighted to see a bald eagle soar above us as we headed home.

*　*　*

I walked Sasha after we parked. I needed a walk to allow my mind to relax a bit, given all it had been dealing with even just today. And Sasha obviously enjoyed her sniffs along the grassy areas between the sidewalk and the road as well as meeting up with a few other dogs along the way.

When we finally settled in our unit, Sasha grabbed a drink from her bowl of water, and I got mine from a glass bottle in the fridge that I filled with filtered water from the sink and reused after washing it. She lay down for a nap on her plush oval dog bed on the gray-carpeted floor while I sat down on my fluffy and equally comfortable living room couch. I pulled out my phone and checked for the message from Maria. "Please call as soon as you can," she said.

But I called the ClemTours office first and was delighted when Ingrid confirmed that the *ClemElk* was providing a tour the next day and my services were definitely needed. I assured her I'd be there.

Next, I returned Maria's call. She answered immediately, which was a bit surprising, since it was still a weekday afternoon and I assumed she might be out on one of the ClemTours boats conducting a tour.

"Please tell me all you know about what happened, Stacie," she said, without beginning with her usual hello. "I've seen stuff on the news, but I want to know what's real, and our bosses just won't talk about it."

"Hi, Maria," I returned. "And things are a mess, as you've undoubtedly heard."

"Tell me. I only had a short tour this morning. I've been in touch with Robin and Mark last night and today, and we're all so concerned—"

Robin Perez and Mark Sordan were also ClemTours tour guides. Maria was currently assigned to the *ClemSeal*, Robin to the *ClemMoose*, and Mark to the *ClemBison*. All of them worked out of Skagway.

"Maybe I'd better talk to you all together," I said, wondering how I'd do that. On some kind of online meeting?

"Good idea," Maria said. "Tonight? We can do a video conference call, okay? I'll set it up. Too bad we're not in the same town so we could meet for dinner. But tell me the basics now."

Which I did—conveying only that one of the passengers on the *ClemElk* had gone missing a couple of days ago and I had tried unsuccessfully to find him. The news had reported that his body was found by our tour boat the next day, making it sound quite sordid but not giving details like who had seen him first. I looked down at Sasha as I spoke and rubbed her gently with my slippered foot.

"Wow," Maria said. "I want to hear more. Can I try to set it up for around eight o'clock? We should all be free then."

"Fine," I agreed, then hung up. And grabbed some of my favorite books on wildlife from the small bookcase off to the side of the living room. I needed to do something to keep my attention, and finding information about and seeing photos of delightful Alaskan animals always did that.

Eventually, early evening rolled around. I walked Sasha again and fed her dinner. Then I fed myself too—another frozen dinner from a company reputed to sell healthful meals, a steamed chicken and pasta dish with veggies. Definitely tasty. Healthful? Who knew?

I checked my computer and saw that Maria had indeed set up a video meeting. I watched a bit of TV news to keep my mind occupied until eight o'clock.

I did all the right stuff online, pressing the links until I entered the chat room, complete with pictures of each of us as well as sound.

Like me, each of them had set up some kind of back-ground—Maria's image indicated a bookcase behind her, Robin's a blank wall with a window covered by draperies, and Mark's just a blank green screen. Me? I used a false pic-ture from my computer that showed the sea with dolphins in it.

"Hi, everyone," Maria said, starting the meeting. We all greeted everyone else in turn. It was good to see them. Though we all had essentially the same job, we didn't get together much, especially since I mostly stayed in Juneau and the oth-ers mostly worked from Skagway. But when we got together, it was always fun trading stories of the wildlife we saw—and the crazy, fun passengers who were our tourists.

Until now.

Maria did as I'd anticipated and kind of turned things over to me. I observed the others before I started talking. Maria was twenty-seven, with closely cut blond hair and dark rimmed glasses. Tonight she wore a pink velour robe, so I knew she was at home—no surprise.

Robin was the oldest, in her fifties. Her hair was starkly black, and I figured it had help staying that way. It was wavy and framed a face that seemed to have deeper wrinkles tonight than I was used to seeing.

Then there was Mark, a bit of a clown, with fuzzy brown hair on his head and on his face too. I'd heard him give tours where he joked nearly as much as he pointed out the wildlife in and around the water. Of course he was popular. A nice guy. But right now he was frowning like everyone else.

"Okay," I finally said. "It's good seeing all of you." I paused. "And I hope all your tours are going well and that you never experience what I just have."

I told them about being out on the water two days ago and finding out that the Clementoses were irritated that this guy named Sheldon Truit was giving them a hard time, taking tours while saying he wanted to start his own competing boat tour company.

"He probably took tours on your boats too," I added.

"Truit? Yes," Robin said. "I met him when he worked for ClemTours as a deckhand when I conducted tours out of Juneau and later saw him now and then taking tours on our boats."

"Me too," said Maria. And even Mark indicated he thought he might have met him.

I told them that the guy who might have become Truit's partner was also on the tour that day.

"Hansen?" Robin asked. "I met him, too, when he took tours with Truit along."

Interesting. But neither of the others indicated they'd met Hansen.

Next, I described how I'd discovered that Truit had disappeared and a section of the state troopers was called in to check out what had happened.

Then I told everyone how we'd gone out on a tour the next day—on the *ClemWolf* while the *ClemElk* was being examined—still not knowing Truit's whereabouts till my dear Sasha barked at the shoreline in an inlet in Tracy Arm.

I didn't go into a lot of detail about the little I knew regarding the investigation, and I certainly didn't mention Liam. I did say I was glad to be going back to the *ClemElk* and giving another tour tomorrow. But I didn't tell my fellow tour guides that that wasn't all I'd be doing on board.

I'd be attempting to find evidence to clear Palmer in particular and all the Clementoses in general.

They asked questions. I gave the few answers I could.

Then sweet Maria focused on me. "Are you doing okay, Stacie? This all has to have been damn hard."

*Okay, tears*, I thought. *Stay out of my eyes.* I admitted that it was hard but reassured them that I was fine. And then I said, "I know there wasn't anything I could have done to prevent this—but now you're all aware of it. No one has been named or arrested or anything. I hope this was one horrible event that will never be repeated—but I have to tell you all to please, please be careful. Keep an eye on your tourists—and even the crew, just in case. And report it to your captain right away if you see anything amiss, okay?"

And hopefully each Clementos captain would know enough now to call in Liam's group right away if there was a problem.

"Okay," Maria said, and the others repeated it too.

"You take good care of yourself," Mark all but shouted, his hands on his hips now visible on his screen.

"And if there's anything we can do to help you now," Robin said, "just let us know. And we need to figure out a time to join up in one town or the other and grab dinner—and drinks—one of these days. Maybe tomorrow. There's a slight possibility Maria or I, and maybe both of us, will be in Juneau for some tours."

"Great!" I said. "If so, let me know. I'd love to see you."

We soon ended the virtual meeting—and I wondered if my colleagues were getting together in another one to discuss the situation . . . and me. And my involvement. And the unexpected horrors of being a tour guide.

Not wanting to think about it anymore, I decided to take Sasha out for another walk. The sky wasn't dark yet, of course, so we got along just fine.

As we returned to the house, my phone rang in my pocket. One of my fellow tour guides wanting a follow-up? Or, better yet, to virtually hug me in sympathy?

No. It was Liam. I blinked when I saw his name and stopped walking, allowing Sasha to sniff a lawn close to our entry.

What did Liam want at this hour?

To talk about tomorrow, it turned out. Which wasn't really surprising. "I'd like for us to get together for breakfast, if that's okay with you."

Interesting. That sounded nice and safe, whereas dinner tonight could have led to something else . . .

No way. But I was still fine with the idea of breakfast.

As a date?

"I want to talk about how we'll handle things on the boat a bit more before we board," he continued, doing away with any thought on my part that this would be just for fun.

"Fine with me," I said, and we made arrangements to meet early the next morning at a fast-food place not far from the port.

Again, not exactly the setup for a hot rendezvous.

"Good night," Liam finally said. "See you tomorrow."

"Right," I returned, to stay on the same page.

We hung up, and in a minute I unlocked the door for Sasha and me. I managed to watch a bit more TV news, and then we went to bed.

Only to rise a little earlier than usual, then follow my usual morning routine till it was time to meet Liam.

I loaded Sasha in my blue SUV, and we soon arrived at the designated fast-food place.

I saw Liam sitting in the driver's seat of his similar black SUV, waiting for us. He exited his car as Sasha and I did mine. He was in civilian clothes again today—a button-down brown shirt over slacks and under a warm jacket.

"Good morning," I called, and he reciprocated.

We both took slightly diagonal paths through the parking lot to the restaurant door, although I was slower, since Sasha found the scent of the ground to be interesting.

We'd purposely chosen one of the dog-friendly restaurants in Juneau and were soon inside. There wasn't a line, so all three of us stood at the counter while the two of us who were humans ordered individually and Liam and I each paid for our own. Nope, no inkling of a date. It was a fast-food place, so Liam and I took our cups of coffee with us, and we found a table in a corner in the back. Liam went back to the front to wait for our food.

I'd ordered an egg sandwich. He'd ordered hotcakes. And soon, Sasha lying at my feet, Liam and I were talking.

We said nothing that I considered new and exciting, though. We were each going to act as we normally would. I'd be a tour guide. Liam would be a tourist. We'd both observe the passengers. And the crew. I'd concentrate on the latter as much as he would, although he'd be looking for indications of guilt and I'd hope to be able to point out to him indications of innocence, since I trusted my coworkers. I'd no reason not to . . . I hoped.

"Can you see a list of passengers in advance?" he asked, watching me as I enjoyed my sandwich.

"Once we reach the boat, probably. Steph will have a list."

"Good."

Was that it? I didn't mind being in Liam's company, but why were we together for this breakfast?

And then he told me. Watching me closely as he took a bite of his pancakes, he said, "Look, I wanted your company this morning before we got on the boat, partly for fun and partly to talk again about my official investigation, and your unofficial one."

Interesting.

But before I could say anything, he continued, "I know it's probably a mistake to allow a civilian to continue to snoop around in a situation like this, let alone encourage it. But we discussed this before. Your presence at the time of the victim's disappearance and your knowing some people who could be involved, being the tour owners' employee but not a family member—well, as you saw, even my sergeant is okay with your helping to investigate a bit, for now at least. But please report anything you learn to me. And most important, you'd better be damn careful."

"Of course." At least I'd try to be careful. But I realized he was kind of recognizing me as an official amateur sleuth. Stupid, but it sounded good.

"Okay then. My superiors have told me to concentrate on the boat's crew members today. They're the only obvious ones who could take the heat off your captain, if I can find any indication someone else could have had something against Truit."

Interesting. "Do you want me to do the same?"

"Sure. And if you see anyone else who was on the boat the day Truit disappeared, let me know. We'll both watch them carefully too."

"So that's the reason you're coming along this time?" I asked.

"Right. And I'm assigned to keep coming on your tours pretty much all the time for now, unless the crime is solved."

I didn't mind seeing him. But the idea of someone being on my boat, watching and dissecting all of us and—

*Us.* I had to ask, of course. "And the crew members you'll be keeping an eye on—does that include me?"

"What do you think?" he asked softly . . . and slowly grinned.

# Chapter Fourteen

Okay, enough fast food. Enough conversation—and enough unspoken accusations. I finished eating fairly quickly, as did Liam. We stood, and so did Sasha.

"See you soon at the pier," I said, and got my coffee cup refilled at the counter. Then my dog and I headed out the door without looking back. I'd no doubt Liam was following, but only into the parking lot.

I drove Sasha and me to the port area and parked, same as usual. Then we walked to the dock where the *ClemElk* was still located, taking time for Sasha to sniff and do whatever.

Lots of other boats were lined up at the nearby docks, including the *ClemWolf.* No troopers around this time. Only Steph stood by the gangplank where we would get on, also as usual. The sound of the water beneath us as it hit the shore and the dock poles was familiar too. I liked it a lot.

"Hi, Steph," I said excitedly. Despite my covert reason for being on board—snooping—I'd also do my job and what I enjoyed most: acting as a tour guide and pointing out the local wildlife to our paying guests. Still . . . well, I had to ask. "Would you mind if I took a peek at the passenger list?" If she said I could, I'd try to study it fast. But doubted I'd see anything—anyone—useful.

The somewhat older crew member, in her ClemTours hoodie as I was, cocked her head as she looked at me. "You've never asked that before." At least she wasn't accusing me of what I was actually doing—helping the authorities poke around.

Still, I decided to provide her with a reasonable explanation. I glanced down at the ground, then back up at her pale-brown eyes. "I'm a bit nervous right now. I wouldn't be surprised if you are too. I'm just wondering if any of our customers today were also on the boat . . . well, you know."

"Yes, I do," she said softly, her expression sad and uneasy.

Would Liam check her out today as a possible suspect? Well, if he was considering me, including Steph wouldn't be a surprise. We were all on his list, I figured.

But as far as who was on Steph's list—well, two couples in their thirties arrived at the dock before I got her answer. When they gave their names, Steph checked those names off and told them they could board.

"They didn't look familiar," I said to her softly.

"Not to me either." Looking around as if expecting to be chastised, she handed me the printed list. "The only tourist I know of who's coming that was on the *ClemElk* that day is that Hansen Horwitz. But he comes so often, that's no surprise."

No, it wasn't, I thought as I took the proffered pages. Fortunately, despite the previous possibility that we'd not be able to provide our tour today, the list was nearly as long as usual. The Clementos in charge must have been able to contact the tourists who'd signed up previously and let them know that the tour would proceed.

Yes, Hansen was on the list. He remained at the top of my unwritten list of suspects—not particularly because he liked coming on our tours, although I now recognized he'd been studying what we did for future reference. He'd known Truit and had been his potential partner, and he'd admitted it. The significant part was that we knew he'd known Truit. And he'd been on the *ClemElk* that important day.

Of course he'd said since that he was holding his own private investigation to try to learn who'd hurt his potential partner, but that could be baloney.

If—when—I saw him today, though, I'd try to act more sympathetic than I had before, hopefully to get him to admit something.

He had to remain my favorite suspect unless I somehow discovered that another of our passengers had had it in for Truit.

Anyway, I carefully scanned the list of names. Surprise, surprise, his was the only one I found familiar—besides Liam Amaruq's. "Just in case I didn't think of someone, I'd like to check this list against the one from . . . that day. Do you keep it on your computer?"

"Yes, and you can certainly look." She paused. "I've provided it to the troopers, and I also looked at it myself at the ClemTours office this morning. I didn't see anyone I'd consider of interest."

Really? So I wasn't the only ClemTours employee attempting to find answers? I shouldn't be surprised, I supposed. We all had good reason to have the truth come out—especially if it didn't involve our bosses. Or ourselves.

"Then I won't either. And it's probably none of my business to try to figure out 'whodunit.'" True, but that hadn't caused me to back off when Liam and I discussed it. Even so, I hardly had the time or inclination to check out all the passengers from that day and figure out anything they'd had against Truit. And most of those I'd spoken with were couples or families with kids—none of them likely to shove a man off the boat, even if they knew him. Let the authorities follow up on that. "But . . . well, I'm particularly concerned about what the officials think of Palmer under these circumstances. I like our shipboard boss. I believe him when he says he didn't do it. And if I can find good evidence to get the troopers pointing their noses in another direction, I'd like to do that." Maybe I wasn't supposed to admit that to anyone except perhaps Liam, let alone another potential suspect, but I figured it wouldn't hurt.

Unless the guilty party was Steph and I found something to that effect, and she came after me . . .

Okay. Yes, I was paranoid about all this.

But that wouldn't stop me.

A few more tourists came our direction and started to line up. "I think it's time for Sasha and me to get on board. Thanks, and I'll see you there later." I smiled and raised my hand in a good-bye gesture, then my pup and I started up the gangway.

First deck. A few tourists were already there, ordering things from Betsy at the galley. I'd do so too later, when things weren't busy. Not that I'd any reason to suspect Betsy, but I intended to talk to all our crew members while we were out today.

That included deckhands Rafe and Al, whom I didn't see just then. I figured they were busy somewhere on board, getting things ready to shove off.

As I stood there, Lettie joined me from the ramp. "Good morning, Stacie," she said, her voice bright and her face smiling. My young assistant wore a black ClemTours hoodie today, and her dark pixie cut looked newly trimmed. "I'm so glad to be here today."

"Me too," I said. "And so's Sasha." I bent over slightly to pet my pup between the ears. "I just hope—"

I didn't finish, but Lettie knew what I meant. Her face melted into a shocked expression. "Oh, I'm sure, whatever happened before, it had to be a one-time occurrence." I was about to verbally agree with her, hoping it was true despite being unsure, when she finished with, "Right?"

"Of course," I said, wishing I felt more certain. But no need to make her worry any more.

Nor would I mention that I'd be talking with her later, asking questions so I could definitely remove her from my suspect list—and tell Liam so. Plus, I wondered if she had any ideas about what had happened and who had caused it.

"Are you coming right up to our deck?" Lettie asked.

"I'll be there soon. I have some questions for Palmer first." Like, *How can I protect you from the troopers?* Better yet, first, *Are you really innocent?* I believed the answer to the latter to be affirmative. But in actuality I'd ask him neither question . . . directly.

"Okay. I'll greet our passengers up there and start amusing them."

"Great. Thanks."

Lettie headed for the forward steps, and I let her go first, even though I also intended to use them to go up to the middle deck. But I wanted Sasha and me to head up there on our own.

Which we did, a minute or so later.

The middle deck didn't have many people on it, as usual. Not now, at least, when the passengers were just boarding and would most likely either stay on the first deck for a while to hang out and get something to drink and a snack or go up to the top deck to stake out where they'd hang out when we left the shore and started our tour.

I checked my watch. The boarding would continue for another half hour or so before we pulled away from the port. Captain Palmer would need to get ready before we left, but he should have at least a little time to talk to me now. And I could possibly resume a discussion later, when we were on our way toward Tracy Arm and Steph was steering the *ClemElk*.

Yes, now was a good time to start a conversation. Jostling Sasha's leash, I directed her to accompany me to the bridge. I looked through the glass. Only Palmer was inside the enclosed area, watching ahead through the window. No Gus today. I figured he was still on the *ClemWolf*. And Steph remained on the pier, ushering tourists in.

I knocked gently on the glass, and Palmer turned. As usual, he wore his ClemTours uniform. His expression, as he pivoted, appeared stern. He seemed to relax a little, though, when he saw it was me. He gave a gesture toward the door at the side, inviting me in.

Sasha and I complied right away. "Good morning," I said. "It feels good to be back on the *ClemElk*."

"And to be preparing for one of our tours." Palmer seemed quite happy now. I wondered what he'd thought when he first heard the knock on the window. That someone was here to arrest him?

Not me, certainly.

"I just hope things go smoothly, and I don't just mean the calmness of the water," I said.

He actually laughed. And nodded. "I'm with you, Stacie."

I definitely hoped so.

Okay, I had to start what I intended to do today—learn all I could from everyone who'd been on board the fateful day of Truit's disappearance. Palmer had to be number one on that list because the authorities wanted to zero in on him as being guilty—which undoubtedly was of concern to him.

I edged my way beside him right near the helm and looked out at the pier through the front window, as he'd been doing before. "I just—well, you know I've been talking to Officer Liam Amaruq. He's one of the special Initial Response group, and he's probably going to be coming with us until the case is resolved."

"Yeah," Palmer said. "I'm aware of that." Once again he didn't sound or look happy, and he stood next to me, looking ahead of the boat once more. I saw his hands tighten on the controls.

"In case you're wondering," I said softly, "I'm still making it clear to him and anyone else I talk to that I know you had nothing to do with what happened to Truit."

He turned quickly and looked me in the eye, as if wanting to make sure I wasn't lying. Well, I wasn't.

Maybe he saw it there and maybe he didn't. But all he said was, "Thanks, Stacie. And you're right. I had nothing to do with it."

Good. And I'd already decided I believed him.

Still, I'd taken on an additional purpose here today. "I just wish I had some idea who did do it." I took a step toward him behind the wheel, feeling the boat sway gently on the water beneath me. "Do you have any idea? I'm sure you've been thinking about this too. Who do you think did it?"

Some voices sounded from behind us, and he turned.

Drat. The timing sucked.

I turned too and saw a family with three kids circling the deck beyond the glass enclosure as if checking it out. One of the kids had broken away and was running between the rows of seats.

I hoped the parents would get that boy under control— for his own safety and everyone else's. We didn't need anyone else to go overboard.

And I wasn't at all happy now at the interruption. Would Palmer answer me? Would I have to ask him again?

He was watching the performance on the deck too. His expression appeared rueful. "We might have a very interesting trip this time. Guess we'll all have to keep an eye on that little rascal."

"I will when I'm on the same deck as him." I paused. "But—"

Palmer motioned for me to follow him to the couple of chairs near the other entrance to the enclosed bridge area. "Come here, Stacie." He sat down. So did I, and so did Sasha, who'd stayed on the floor beside me. "You know I can't talk long here. I need to prepare for our departure. But I want to respond to what you asked, because I think it's important—especially if you're keeping in touch with Officer Liam, as you indicated."

I prevented myself from cringing. It was, after all, the truth. I didn't confirm or deny it but just said, "I think it's important too. I want to make sure the truth comes out and you're no longer a suspect." Boy, did I hope that would be the case—that the truth would let Palmer off the hook.

"Me too. First off, I know you're aware that Truit used to work for ClemTours, so I'd known him even before he started taking tours to study what we do more. Did I like him? Not especially, but I didn't dislike him at that time either. But even though I didn't appreciate what he was up to lately, I want to assure you that I had nothing to do with Truit disappearing or winding up off the boat. Just in case you had any doubts."

"Of course I didn't." Well, that was an appropriate fib. I certainly hadn't wanted to have any doubts, but some had surfaced within me—before. Now, I felt positive. But that could change if I found any evidence otherwise.

His sincere expression made me feel more comfortable believing him. Still, I'd feel a lot more comfortable once the apparent murder was solved and I knew who'd done it.

"Anyway," he said, "the answer to your question is that I really don't know who did it. My best guess would be Hansen Horwitz, since they knew each other and maybe their attempt at starting a business went bad before it got anywhere. But I've talked to Hansen before that day and after, and he seems like a nice guy, sincere about wondering who could have done that to his friend and potential partner. He could be a good actor, of course. Or not. I just don't know."

"He's listed to take this tour today," I informed the captain, in case he didn't know. "I guess one or both of us"—and Liam—"can talk to him some more about it."

"Fine with me," Palmer said. "Now I'd better go ahead with my preparations here. Will you be sure to tell me if you hear anything helpful about who might have been involved?"

"Of course," I lied. "If you'll do the same."

"Of course," he repeated. "And pop in here anytime to talk when we're not busy changing course or anything."

*Anything* could mean, well, anything, but I appreciated his offer and figured I could interpret *anytime* to mean at any point when the boat wasn't heading into Tracy Arm or an inlet or whatever. Even then, I'd obey if he or Steph told me to leave.

"See you later," I said to the captain. "Sasha, come," I said to my dog, and we left the bridge enclosure.

So now what? I figured it was time for Sasha and me to head for our favorite deck. But I'd be giving the tour for hours and could question Lettie between wildlife sightings. Yes, I intended to quiz my assistant, too, for her opinion of what had happened and who'd done it. Right now, though, it made more sense to talk to someone I'd see less after we left.

One of the deckhands? That would be a good idea if I could find one and he wasn't too busy. Another possibility was Betsy in the galley. She might be fairly busy now serving arriving passengers. But I could always use a cup of coffee. And when she was between customers, maybe I could lean over the counter and have a conversation with her.

And so Sasha and I headed back downstairs. A string of arriving passengers passed us on their way up.

First thing—no, first person—I saw was Hansen, sitting at the far end of a row of tables with a cup of coffee in front of him. Of course he was another person I intended to spend time questioning whenever I got a chance, but when I glanced toward the galley counter, I didn't see any tourists lined up there. I did see Betsy scrubbing one end of it. Very nice. Sanitation was a good thing on any boat, especially in the galley.

It also meant she might be able to talk with me somewhat privately. I'd just keep my voice low, and hopefully she would too.

As I wound my way around tables and tourists, Sasha at my side, I noticed Hansen watching me. I wondered what he was thinking. Hey, I'd have to be careful around him in case he was the killer. If I pressed him too hard to admit it, I might wind up being the next to be tossed overboard.

Of course, that could be the case if anyone I quizzed was the guilty party—and my suspicion would be activated whenever I spoke with anyone I knew had been on the *ClemElk* that fateful day.

Including Betsy? Well, I couldn't let her off my list any more than I could the deckhands, but why would a nice, popular lady in charge of the galley on this tour boat do such a thing to some passenger—assuming she was strong enough to do so to a man?

I'd have to ask her—subtly, of course. Maybe she'd heard of what Truit was up to and wanted to protect our captain.

But she and Palmer had never seemed that close.

Anyway, I headed toward the counter where Betsy was scrubbing. "It's so great to be back on the *ClemElk* just like it was a normal day," I said.

She looked at me through her glasses, her pale-brown eyes squinting just a little. Her garb today was a blue, long-sleeved ClemTours T-shirt. And her smile dominated her face. "It sure is. I wish nothing bad had happened, but—well, since we're allowed to get back to our regular routine, maybe they've learned what happened to that Truit guy and figure it doesn't really affect our tours or any of us."

"Hope so," I said. "Although I think they still believe the guy was murdered. Intentionally shoved off the boat somehow. And they may still be looking for whoever did it."

Her eyes widened. "Really? Who do they think it was? And how do you know this?"

"Well, the state trooper guy who first started looking into the situation keeps in touch with me. We even went to dinner together." I smiled as if it had been a date so she wouldn't think I was collaborating with Liam in any way. "I have the impression he and others still think our captain did it."

"Oh, the guy who questioned us, who you hung out with on the *ClemWolf*?"

I nodded. "And I've been keeping my nose in the situation, trying to figure it out so I can point them to someone else if I learn anything. I definitely don't think it was Palmer." I leaned over the now-clean counter. Would it still be sanitary if I touched it? I tried not to. But I wanted to talk confidentially with Betsy. "I know you asked who they think it was, but what are your thoughts about it? Do you suspect anyone? And if so—who? And why?"

Betsy shook her head. "I'm just not into stuff like that. I definitely don't think it was Palmer, of course, but I haven't even considered who it might be."

"Well," I said, "I'd appreciate it if you'd keep your eyes and ears open on this trip. If you get any ideas, please let me know. Unless you'd rather tell my new buddy Liam, the trooper. He's coming along on this tour too."

"Really?" Betsy looked surprised. "He's going to be investigating all of us?"

"Maybe," I said. "Anyway, feel free to let me know if anything pops out at you, okay?"

"Okay," she said, just as a couple of guys came over to the other side of the counter, obviously wanting to place an order.

"Talk to you later," I said. "I'll want coffee soon, but not right now." I motioned for Sasha to join me as I walked away.

So where was Betsy now on my list of possible helpers—or guilty persons?

Not very high on either. But she was still on it.

So was everyone else around here.

I wanted to go up to the top deck but decided to stop for a minute and begin speaking with Hansen.

The big guy was sitting up straight at the table, a large paper cup of coffee clutched in his right hand. His eyes followed me from the moment I left the galley till I reached him. I couldn't help glancing somewhat jealously at his coffee. I was ready for some.

"Good morning, Stacie." He sounded as if we were buddies and not just acquaintances who might have a similar goal.

Which made me smile. Maybe the conversations I hoped to have with this guy wouldn't be so bad after all.

"Good morning, Hansen," I responded enthusiastically, pulling out the chair across from him as Sasha moved up to the table and rested her head on it. I patted that head. If Hansen had eaten something that smelled good, it wasn't apparent to me. But I did decide that, depending on how the first part of our visit went, I would go get that coffee from Betsy after all, and also get Sasha some toast. And maybe nibble on it myself first. "So you're taking another tour today. You must really enjoy them." Or he was coming along for some other reason. If so, I wanted to learn what it was.

Wasn't this his third tour this week? And I'd seen him on board before. He certainly was doing a lot of research for his own tour company, assuming that was still his intent.

"I definitely do," he said. "And—well, right now I have an ulterior motive for being here, as I'm sure you can figure—especially since I know you think I could be guilty."

I nodded. Wow, was getting him to talk today going to be this easy? "Of course. And though I'm giving my tour today as usual, I also feel I've got an ulterior motive for now."

I noticed that Sasha was no longer interested in smells at the table. She'd lain down on the floor, which was a good thing for now. But we wouldn't stay here long, since I needed to get up to the top deck. I wanted to finish this conversation with Hansen—and most likely have another one later.

"Oh yeah." He reached for his coffee with his puffy fingers. He wore a bright-green sweatshirt that said Juneau, Alaska and had a black grizzly bear shape on it. "You want to clear your boss Palmer from being a suspect in what happened to Truit, right?"

"Right," I said. I recalled that Palmer had said he considered Hansen sincere when he said he was innocent, but that didn't mean it was true. "I'd really like to do that. But I don't necessarily want to assume it was you."

"Really?" He leaned toward me, his hazel eyes appearing sad. "I didn't get that impression before. But no matter what you really think, I didn't do it."

"Then you think Palmer did?"

"Not necessarily. I'd rather it not be him either."

Interesting. Okay, it did seem he was willing to talk today, without admitting his guilt if he had done it. But that fit with my goal of the moment: getting others who could have done it to tell me who they thought had done it and why.

Before I responded, I saw that Liam had come onto the boat and approached from behind Hansen. I didn't react to him. I'd get to say hi again later.

For now, I continued my discussion with Hansen. "I'm glad to hear you don't think it was Palmer—" I stopped when he opened his mouth. That wasn't exactly what he'd said, after all. "Or at least you'd rather it wasn't him. So who else do you think killed Truit? Anyone you'd prefer suspecting, for a good reason?"

Hansen's mouth rolled up into a larger smile on his pudgy face. "Oh, I've got a good answer for that. Who do I think did it? Who do I want to have done it?"

"That's right," I said, still avoiding looking at Liam.

"That's easy. My answer is . . . you."

# Chapter Fifteen

"What!" I exclaimed. "Why on earth would you think I'd have killed Truit? How you could imagine I had the knowledge of how and where to toss him overboard, let alone the strength? Or the motive? I barely knew the guy."

Okay, I guess if I'd really wanted to kill someone and pondered all those issues carefully, maybe I could have figured them out. At least all but the strength to dump the guy. After all, I'd been on this tour enough to get to know what inlets aren't visited much and all. But I hadn't. And competition with my employers wasn't motive enough for me.

I really did want to know why this man suspected me—or at least said he did.

"Yes, why?" asked Liam, who'd now joined us—sliding onto the chair across from where Sasha now lay. I still wasn't used to seeing him in civilian clothes, but I appreciated how he looked.

But that was completely irrelevant, especially now.

"Oh, I think you know." Hansen's voice was soft, but it somehow rang with challenge.

"No," I said. "I don't."

But he didn't continue. He just looked at me, grinning.

Okay. I'd considered being subtle in my questioning, maybe not with Hansen but with the crew members, including even Palmer. I figured it would help to know everyone else's suspicions. And Liam had wanted me to do it, since I worked with the individuals and knew them at least a bit, certainly better than he did. Maybe they would be more likely to share their suspicions about others with me—or even say something suspicious about themselves that I could pass along to Liam.

With Hansen, though, subtlety wasn't an issue. He knew he must be at the top of everyone's suspect lists.

Maybe he even knew who did it, assuming it wasn't him.

Was he simply attempting to annoy me by accusing me like that?

Surely he wasn't serious, was he?

And he'd said it in front of Liam. I didn't think he'd known Liam had been there initially, so he might not have been attempting to accuse me in front of anyone, let alone a law enforcement officer who could follow up on it.

Okay. I wanted to know everything. Why accuse me? Had Hansen in fact known there was an important audience? Was he treating this like a game? Or was he somehow serious?

Yes, my mind was spinning—and all of this was taking up time.

Time in which he hadn't yet answered my question—or Liam's.

Time in which he simply grinned at me with his big, happy face that I had an urge to slap.

But I stayed calm. And I was determined to get Hansen to respond.

I heard more voices around us now. Additional tourists had boarded, and some remained on this deck.

I didn't want any of them to hear what was going on at this table. But this conversation had to continue here and now.

Leaning closer to Hansen across the table, I saw Liam also lean closer to both of us. As softly as I could speak and still be heard, I asked Hansen, "Are you just accusing everyone and anyone associated with this boat to try to get suspicion off you? Or do you think there's any credible reason to accuse me? And in case you're wondering, no, I didn't do it."

"You'd say that anyway." Hansen glared at me. "And I'm glad you know how it feels now to be accused like that when you're innocent—if you are. I definitely am."

He paused, so to encourage him to go on, I said, "Of course. But still, why me?"

"Oh, you have a reasonable motive. More reasonable than me, since I wanted to go into business with the guy who got killed."

"So what motive is that?"

I wished Liam would participate, but I knew he wanted me to try to get what I could from my fellow crew members as well as this particular suspect.

Hansen leaned back just a little and regarded me with a scornful smile. "Because you're trying so hard to protect your bosses, especially Palmer," he said. "And you heard that Truit and I intended to start a competing company. And you were on this boat with probably no one paying attention to you when you weren't giving a tour. And—"

"And I don't really hear anything that would make me want to kill someone. Argue with him, maybe. But nothing fatal."

"Well, what if you did start arguing with him and he attacked you? Wouldn't you try to protect yourself?"

I glanced at Liam, whose face was bland and interested. Damn, why didn't he jump in to help me?

"Yes," I finally said through gritted teeth. "But if something bad happened, like the person who attacked me falling off the ship, I'd tell someone. And I wouldn't be guilty of murder. It would be self-defense."

"Well, who's to say that didn't happen with me? Assuming—incorrectly, of course—that I was the one who knocked him off the ship."

"Were you?" I demanded immediately.

"Of course not. I already told you I'm innocent." He shot his irritated gaze to Liam. "And you should believe me and keep looking for someone else before whoever it is disappears."

"Right," Liam said, finally jumping in. "Let me ask you this, though. Let's assume, for now—" He looked at me. Was that a wink? It was so fast I could have imagined it. But it was with the eye farthest from Hansen, so if it had happened, Hansen probably couldn't see it. "—that Stacie is innocent. Who's number two on your list? And three and four, for that matter."

Hansen leaned back and put his hands behind his head. His stretching that way emphasized the grizzly bear shape on his green shirt. I wondered what a bear would think of someone as bulky as him for a meal . . .

My thoughts were getting out of hand, and I reined them in. I didn't want anything to happen to Hansen or anyone else.

One death related to my tour boat was more than enough.

"Well, you're not going to like this either," he said, those eyes still on me. "But maybe you'll like it better than my suspecting you."

He stopped, obviously wanting me to prod him to continue.

"Okay," I said. "What are your answers?"

"Just one," he replied. But he said nothing more till I goaded him further.

"So who is that?" I glared at him, as if that would make him act faster.

"I said you won't like it."

"Tell me." Although with a response like that, I had a pretty good idea who he was talking about.

"Whether or not I like the idea, your buddy and boss, Palmer Clementos." This time Hansen's look was also a glare—a challenging one, as if he was daring me to deny it or give him a hard time about it.

I leaned back a little. I understood why he said that— to possibly take suspicion away from himself and encourage Liam and me and others, if he told anyone else, to look long and hard at possibly the most obvious suspect in this situation.

"Of course," I responded in a mocking tone. "Who else would you point to, since you need to get yourself out of the crosshairs? But I'm not going to buy it now any more than I did before. And if you want to suggest someone else and give a good reason for it, then maybe I'll stop being certain it was you."

"You're certain?" His voice was raised a bit now, which wasn't a good thing. A few people sitting at nearby tables glanced in our direction.

"No," I said, "I'm not, or I wouldn't be asking you these questions. But I'm hoping to find a way to prove that Palmer, and all the other Clementoses, are innocent. I like my job. And I like them as bosses."

"Then who else, logically, could it be?" Hansen demanded. "Some tourist who was a stranger to all of us?"

"Could be," I said. "If so, he or she probably wasn't a stranger to Truit." I paused. "I know you talked to Truit while we were out in the water. Did you also see him talking to anyone else much? A passenger or one of the crew?"

I glanced toward Liam, who was quiet again and staring at Hansen, waiting for his answer.

"Unfortunately, no," he said. "Though I've been trying to replay most of that trip in my mind and just don't remember anyone like that. If I could—well, I'd tell you." He looked at Liam. "That way maybe everyone would leave me alone. That's why I'm here for this trip, just to see if I recall anything or anyone helpful and to watch for anyone who looks familiar or anything that'll get suspicion off me." He stood then and looked down at us. "In case you haven't figured it out by now, I'm innocent." And then he bent, grabbed his coffee, and stomped off toward the stairs.

I rose too, and that got Sasha to stand. Liam continued to sit there, though. "Well, that wasn't especially helpful," I told him.

"Maybe it was. Maybe he'll think of something or someone to tell us about."

"Right. Anyway, I need to go to the top deck. You coming?"

"Not now," he said. "It's better if we're not together much, and I want to talk to Steph when she comes on board."

"Okay." I took a step away and paused, looking back. "She's on my radar, too, for a conversation later."

"Good. You're doing what we talked about, and so am I. See you later, during your tour. If nothing else goes right on this trip, I at least want to see the wildlife."

I gave a brief laugh and started moving away with Sasha.

By now the boat was filled with passengers. Delightful! A lot of those on this deck moved around the perimeter, looking out the windows. It was a bit early to snack much, especially since everyone had probably just had breakfast. I eavesdropped a bit as I walked by and enjoyed listening to couples and friends mention the wildlife they hoped to see. I figured most had done their homework, since I heard references to seals, whales, otters, bears and birds—the animals we were likely to catch sight of.

I also noticed some families near the windows, the parents holding their kids up to see. There'd be a lot more interesting views in the future. I was tempted to stop and tell them so, but I did want to get up to the top deck. And they probably anticipated it anyway.

Sasha and I reached the stairs and started up—and I directed her to get off at the middle deck with me for just a minute. Yes, some passengers were there, also mostly at the windows. I did a small circle with my pup, again listening a bit. Mostly, though, I looked toward the enclosed bridge. Palmer was still there. I didn't see Steph, but it was drawing closer to our time to leave, so I figured she'd be here soon. Since Liam had indicated he wanted to talk with her, maybe he'd come here when the boat started moving.

Then Sasha and I went toward the forward stairs, where we had to wait, since quite a few passengers—also going up to the top deck—already filled them.

"Looks like we'll have a good crowd," said a voice to my rear. I turned back and saw that Al had joined me and was also waiting.

I glanced around and didn't see his fellow deckhand Rafe. Al was taller than me but shorter and heavier than Rafe. He of course wore the standard ClemTours uniform sweatshirt—a black one this time. His dark hair looked rather scruffy, and I assumed he hadn't shaved today, because his facial hair looked scruffy too.

"It sure does look like we'll be full," I agreed. "So we should all keep busy." Which meant I might not have a lot of time to talk with him or Rafe later.

Now wasn't a bad time, though, for a conversation with at least him.

We were still on the second deck, although the crowd on the stairway was starting to get smaller. Still, I took a step closer to Al and said softly, "Hey, do you have a minute? There's something I'd like to ask you."

His light-brown eyes looked confused for a moment—unsurprising, since I rarely talked to him alone. I had reason to only if I wanted him to check on how well a window had closed or move Sasha's pad or look into something relating to the boat's configuration or cleanliness. He was in his twenties and probably muscular under that sweatshirt from all the physical stuff he did.

He looked down at the watch on his wrist, then back up again. "Okay, but not for long. I'll need to look at a few things and make sure they're okay before we leave, and that'll be soon."

"It won't take long." I motioned for him to follow Sasha and me. I found a spot near some windows toward the aft of the boat and stood at an angle so it was unlikely Palmer would see us both if he happened to look in this direction from the bridge. Not that I shouldn't be talking to one of our deckhands, but I didn't want to incite Palmer's curiosity.

"So what's up, and why so secret?" Al didn't look happy as he stopped there, looking down at me. And I supposed I had been a bit obvious about not wanting Palmer to notice us.

"It's just—well, here we are on the *ClemElk* again. I love being here, but after . . . since we had a passenger die, and it's being investigated by the authorities as possibly not an accident, I've been thinking a lot about what happened and who might have been involved. It may be kind of dumb on my part, since I'm not in law enforcement or anything like that, but I'd really like to help figure out what happened, especially since the authorities appear to think it's our captain, Palmer, who did it. I don't want to make a big deal about what I'm doing, but I'm asking my fellow crew members who they think did it. So . . . who do you think did it, Al?"

He glared at me. "What, do you want me to admit to something I didn't do to save our captain?"

"No, no, no, that's not what I said. But who—"

"Do I think did it? Other than Palmer, of course? Well, from what I heard, he'd met Truit initially 'cause the guy used to work for ClemTours. And he'd taken some tours on this and other ClemTours boats. He even looked a bit familiar to me, though I wasn't around when he worked here. And he said now he wanted to start his own company using what he'd learned to compete with ClemTours. I'd just as soon it not be Palmer, since I want to keep my job, but I don't know who else it was. And I've been trying not to think about it, or at least not much. So—can I go and do that job right now?"

He didn't wait for me to dismiss him but just turned and stomped away.

That hadn't gone well. Did he really think Palmer had done it? Did he have any other reason to think so? Or did he give a damn at all about who was really guilty?

The answer to that last question certainly seemed to be no—unless finding the bad guy helped Al keep his job here.

But his attitude wasn't great. And his body was strong. And he certainly knew this boat well.

I hadn't seriously considered him before, but I started to wonder if Al had been the one to toss Truit off the boat.

But if so, why?

As I got Sasha to rise and accompany me to the aft stairs, I realized I'd have to mention this to Liam. I couldn't question Al further, since I'd no doubt he'd refuse to talk to me, but maybe Liam could find a nice, friendly way to chat with him.

And get him to admit to the murder?

Well, I doubted he would do that. Even if he'd done it.

Sasha and I finally reached our goal: the top deck. And boy, was it crowded—a really good thing! Lettie stood at the front holding the microphone, but she wasn't talking, at least not right now. But she saw us and waved. Of course, the forward area was where we were headed, though it took a while for us to make our way through the crowd—especially since, as often happened, my adorable Sasha got a whole lot of attention.

Not many seats in the middle were occupied, though some had jackets or other paraphernalia tossed there to save them. Most people stood near the open sides of this deck, even though there wasn't much exciting to look at now.

But I was where I wanted to be. About to do what I loved to do—tell people about the natural sights and about the wildlife that was visible from where we were. Yes!

And it felt so good that, at least for now, I could forget about Truit and think about good stuff . . .

As if I would forget about Truit and what had happened. But at least that wouldn't be at the forefront of my mind much longer.

When Sasha and I reached Lettie, she spoke into the microphone. "Hey, everyone, I'd like you to meet our wonderful tour guide, Stacie Calder. She's not only a delightful, informative speaker, but she's a naturalist too. She majored in wildlife conservation and management at the University of Arizona a while back and has turned that background into being one superb ClemTours tour guide. Stacie—" She handed me the microphone, and I flipped the switch so what I said could be heard on the other decks too.

"Hi, everyone. Welcome to our tour," I said into the mic as Sasha settled down at my feet. Good dog, as usual. I resisted bending to hug her and continued. "We're just starting off now on our journey to Tracy Arm—to see the amazing sights and wildlife there and on the way. Right now we're heading down the Stephens Passage."

And as I spoke, our boat began to vibrate. Perfect timing. Yes, we were just starting off.

I looked at my crowd. Most were appropriately dressed for Alaskan weather. I assumed the temp outside right now was in the high forties and it would climb into the fifties soon. And this deck was open enough that we got a breeze as we proceeded forward—chilly at times.

But our passengers had been warned. I saw lots of parkas and heavy jackets, mostly unzipped, although a few were fastened tightly and high enough to obscure some faces. Then there were long-sleeved sweatshirts and hoodies, and of course I was among those wearing the latter, as usual. This wasn't one of the days where I had felt compelled to bring a jacket too.

"Now, I can't say exactly what wildlife we'll see, since none of the animals is so in love with being observed that they promise to show up on each trip. Or at least none has ever told me they were. But we'll definitely see some. I can promise you that. And we'll see a delightful shoreline and some glaciers. And most likely some other tour boats too. Meanwhile, stay safe, don't get too near the railings, parents take care of your kids, and we'll all have a great time."

I paused again. Most of the passengers were now watching me. Some had sat down on the chairs in the middle.

That was when Palmer spoke through the boat's public address system to welcome people and give his instructions.

I noticed that Rafe was off to the side toward the aft, undoubtedly watching to make sure the passengers were all happy and that none of the chairs or anything else needed to be moved.

And Al? Far as I could tell, he wasn't on this deck. Would he avoid me now? I wouldn't be surprised.

But if I wanted to talk to him more, I'd come up with a good reason to need a deckhand's help at a time and a place where I wasn't seeing Rafe. Right now, though, I was glad I saw him.

I spoke for a few more minutes and noticed Liam appear at the upper part of the steps. I wondered who he'd been talking to. Steph, maybe, since she had to be on board now. Had he learned anything useful yet?

Not that it was my obligation to get helpful info, but I felt bad that I hadn't. I'd taken on this chore, and like everything else I ever did, I wanted to do it well.

I spoke for a few more minutes about the fun I had touring this area so often and how I was always delighted and amazed at the Alaskan sights and wildlife and the tourists who came to see it.

Soon, though, I didn't have more to say until we reached our goal of Tracy Arm, unless some interesting wildlife appeared on our way.

"It does take a while to get there," I told my audience. "So right now, just settle in and watch out the openings along this deck. Either Lettie or I will tell you if we see any wildlife to view, and you can always let either one of us know if anything exciting comes into your sight or if you have any questions. Meantime, enjoy your ride."

I handed the microphone back to Lettie. I had my other goal in mind.

I'd watched as Liam made his way across the deck. He was now looking out the opening on the starboard side.

Rafe was on the port side, and I headed toward him, Sasha on her leash following quickly behind me.

Rafe was talking to one of the passengers, and I wasn't sure he had noticed me till I was right in front of him.

"Hi," I said, then looked at the passenger, a twentysomething woman wearing a pull-on knit hat and a huge smile. "Have you been in Alaska long?"

"No," she said, bending to pat Sasha's head. "My husband and I just got here yesterday. And I knew even before I got here that I wanted to take a tour like this."

"Well, let me know if there's anything I can do to make it even more enjoyable." I watched as the woman patted Sasha again, then edged toward Rafe with my dog at my side. "This looks like a good bunch of passengers," I said to the tall man with the short, dark beard—and frown. I gestured for him to join me at the side railing. "Can I ask you something?" I wasn't sure where we could go here to keep our discussion private, but I'd at least speak as quietly as possible.

But Rafe clearly chose to ignore me. "No thanks." He didn't move, and his voice was loud. I sighed.

"Can we go farther aft?" I suggested. "I really want to—"

"Ask me the same damned questions you asked Al?" he spit out. "He told me about 'em. Forget it." He slipped past me toward the stairway.

I considered following, but I doubted I'd get his cooperation even if I caught up with him in a good location. He certainly wasn't as friendly now as he used to be.

Well, I wouldn't give up—but I wouldn't push him for now. I sighed, preparing to head forward again and hang out with Lettie.

Maybe I could even talk with her while we were en route to our destination—sometime when neither of us was using the microphone.

But before Sasha and I walked to the prow, I was joined by Liam. "So have you talked to anyone who's given the answer to our questions?" he asked. "If so, I gather it wasn't that guy."

"No," I said, "it wasn't. And I haven't learned much more information either." I stared into his brown eyes, hoping I could see answers there. "And you? What do you know now?"

"That I'm really looking forward to your talk about the wildlife we see. And"—he raised his hand as I started to push him to give more information—"I've had some interesting talks with people, but nothing that hints of final answers either. But more to come. You?"

"Oh, yeah," I said. But then I shook my head and glanced around. No one was nearby, fortunately. I still spoke softly. "Are all your cases as weird as this?"

"No. But if there weren't an apparent homicide involved"—he kept his voice low too—"I'd find this a rather enjoyable investigation."

Because he got to be on a tour boat talking to a bunch of people?

Because I was there?

Not the latter, certainly. But I couldn't ask, because a family with a child came up to us and started asking me questions about the animals we'd likely see. And so, with an apologetic shrug toward Liam, I started to answer. That was why I was there.

# Chapter Sixteen

B y the time I'd finished talking with the family, Liam had left.

Well, that was fine. We couldn't talk much here anyway with all the people around. And we apparently didn't have anything much to tell each other.

Besides, that family was followed by another with teenage kids, who asked questions as we stood near the window area with the boat heading at a good speed toward Tracy Arm. Maura and Mike, the two teens, who wore open parkas and both had braces on their teeth and pale-brown hair, wanted to know how I'd decided to study wildlife conservation management. Ah, that was always fun to discuss. I told them I'd grown up in Los Angeles and had spent as much spare time as I could visiting the LA Zoo because I'd loved to watch all kinds of animals. "They took good care of the many different species," I said, "and taught me enough that I was sure I wanted to see as many as possible in the wild someday. And that meant I decided to study about them too."

I gestured for them to follow Sasha and me, since I'd decided it was time to head forward again to hang out with

Lettie and the microphone, plus see the view straight ahead from the prow as well as off the sides.

When we got there, I answered a few more questions, and then Lettie and I were left alone for a while—with Sasha, of course. Good. I made sure the microphone was turned off and did my current extra non-job by asking Lettie how she was doing after all the excitement relating to the last *ClemElk* trip we'd taken.

"Fine," she said. "And you?" Her deep-brown eyes appeared caring beneath her black brows. Her ClemTours sweatshirt today was blue, and my young assistant, with her pixie haircut, looked like an eager kid, even though she was taller than me.

"I'm okay," I assured her, "but I'll be a lot better once the truth is determined regarding what happened to Truit." Then I asked what I needed to, keeping my voice quite quiet. "Do you have any idea who might have pushed him off the boat? Did you see him talking to anyone before he disappeared, or arguing or anything?"

Surprise—her answer was no. "I know the cops are still looking for answers, and I keep racking my brain to picture wherever I might have seen him on board. I do recall seeing him talking to other passengers, I think, but I couldn't tell you who."

"I get it," I said. "That trooper Liam Amaruq is on board again today, and he's asked me the same questions. I'd like to help him find the right solution, since I gather they still think Palmer may have done it, and—"

"Oh, that's not possible." Lettie looked shocked. "Our boss is such a good man. Yes, I did hear rumors that the man who was killed was trying to start a company competing with ClemTours, but that wouldn't give Palmer a reason to kill him. Especially not with all the other competing companies there are."

"I agree," I said, and paused. Okay, it wouldn't hurt to ask—in jest, of course. "And I suppose you had no reason to kill him either." I grinned to show I was kidding, although I was interested in her answer.

Her deep-brown eyes widened, although she cracked a small smile in return. "Hmm. Let me see." She put her index finger on her chin for a couple of seconds, then said, "Nope."

"Got it."

A group of three senior women came up to us just then and began asking questions.

Well, I'd now spoken with nearly all of our crew. I still had a couple more to try, including Rafe again, but it didn't look like I'd have anything useful to report to Liam later.

But what mattered just then was that someone spotted some black-legged kittiwakes on the cliffs off the port side of the boat. I was delighted to have the opportunity to point them out to others and used the microphone to let passengers on all decks know they were there and describe how they resembled sea gulls.

We spotted a few more types of birds as we neared the turn toward Tracy Arm, including pigeon guillemots and arctic terns. I described each of them and their habitats and breeding habits, such as how the guillemots' plumage was different when they were breeding and how the terns were known for their vast migration.

And then there we were, in the Tracy Arm fjord. Our route would take us toward the north and south Sawyer glaciers at the end of the fjord.

And we would see more wildlife as we continued.

This was what I came for. It was why I chose to be a tour guide here in Alaska, working for ClemTours.

The company had to continue. Its family members had to go on, running the boats and keeping their business sound.

Palmer Clementos had to continue captaining the *Clem-Elk*, like he was today.

But as I spoke into the microphone, describing what we were seeing and would see, I hoped my imagination wasn't taking over logic.

Had Palmer actually been involved in Truit's . . . no, I simply didn't believe it.

And that, fortunately, was when we started seeing ice floes with harbor seals on them, including mothers and babies.

Everyone on this deck was clearly infatuated, including me. My attention was soon fully occupied in talking and answering questions. Lettie's too. She was my backup, my friend, my helper, and I relied on her to let me know of other seals I hadn't yet noticed.

Fortunately, this boat, like all the others in our fleet, was relatively quiet and didn't seem to upset any animals we saw.

Oh, and then a couple of bears showed up on the shore nearest us, climbing toward the cliffs. Pointing them out was wonderful too.

Plus a bald eagle soared above us. What a perfect tour we were having today! And as always, we approached the glaciers, returning to the middle of the waters and occasionally entering inlets to see if we could spot more animals—which reminded me too much of Truit, even though we avoided that particular inlet. We hung out near the glaciers for over an hour, watching for wildlife and often seeing it.

But all good things come to an end. And though it felt much too soon, we started motoring back through the fjord toward the passage that would return us to Juneau.

I could take a little time off now. Where was Liam? Would Steph have a minute to talk?

I told Lettie I wanted to go grab a fresh cup of coffee and maybe visit the restroom. She was fine with taking over.

Both of those goals were real, but I'd see what else I could accomplish—like checking on both the people I was wondering about.

Unfortunately, Steph appeared to be in charge of running the boat when Sasha and I got to the middle deck. Turned out Hansen was now seated in the middle seats there—and Rafe was with him.

What did that murder suspect and the deckhand have to talk about? Was Hansen actually doing what Liam and I were and casually conducting an inquisition of people who might have met Truit or at least known what he was planning in the tour business? Maybe I could check with Hansen later. And if that was the case, was Rafe talking to him when he wouldn't talk to me?

But going over to say hi now probably wouldn't get me anywhere, so Sasha and I instead started down toward the lowest deck.

Yes, Liam was there, sitting at a table alone, drinking coffee and playing with his satellite phone. I headed in his direction, Sasha and me both moving around groups of passengers. When Liam saw me, he motioned for me to sit down beside him. As I did, he leaned over and said, "I've arranged for a dinner get-together with the Clementos family members who're in town plus any other tour guides like you. Will you join us?"

"Sure." Sounded like it could be enjoyable. Or at least I hoped it would be. And I was a bit surprised the Clementoses had agreed. Of course, Liam might have phrased it in such a way that they couldn't refuse. "Is your plan just to have fun, or are you going to be quizzing them about . . . you know?"

"*You know*, of course. But subtly. Maybe. And we'll have fun too." His grin looked teasing, but I knew what it meant. Surely that family might point fingers at other people in the interest of protecting all of them—right?

The get-together could be a great idea. Even if no one had answers, folks might be looking for someone to blame in order to protect Palmer. Had they gotten together to trade info before?

If nothing else, I'd possibly get a chance to see one or two of my fellow tour guides who happened to be in town, if the information Robin had provided yesterday was right. I did think the *ClemWolf* and *ClemMoose* were around Juneau today.

For now, I thought about just hanging out with Liam for a short while on this deck. Why not? I'd go get my fresh cup of coffee, then return to this table. Maybe we could talk—although I figured he'd rather listen to anything I'd learned, which wasn't really much, than pass along anything that had been revealed to him.

The atmosphere was pleasant here, warmer than on the top deck. Plus there wasn't as much stress on me to narrate a tour or address questions. Not that I minded that stress. It was who I was.

Even so, continuing my break for a short while sounded good.

"Stay," I told Sasha, who'd been sitting beside me, as I rose to approach the galley. Only I hadn't completely risen when I saw Hansen appear at the doorway from the aft stairs, look around the deck, and head in our direction. Interesting. If he actually was coming here, I'd hang around to see what was on his mind.

Liam looked up quizzically when I sat back down again, and I nodded in Hansen's direction. Liam raised his dark brows but didn't say anything either.

Sure enough, Hansen joined us, sitting down at our table. Had he come to this deck to get something to eat or drink? Or had he been looking for one or both of us for some reason?

I soon gathered that the latter was true. He scanned the deck as if searching for someone or something. Then he leaned over a bit and moved his thick shoulders forward, appearing to huddle us together over the table so he could speak.

When I'd last talked with him, it had been on this deck and he had accused me of murdering Truit. What was on his mind now?

He finally began to say what was on his mind. "Can't stay here long. I don't really want to be seen with either of you. But we've talked about asking questions of anyone we know was on this boat . . . that day. I haven't done much, but I had a strange conversation with one of the deckhands a little while ago—Rafe?"

He looked at me as if he wanted me to confirm the deckhand's name, and I nodded. "That's one of them."

"Yeah, Rafe, then. It wasn't Al. Anyway, he came over to me while I was looking out the window on deck two and started talking while he pretended to wash the inside of the glass. He said he'd heard I'd been hoping to open another tour company with the guy who went overboard. I said I had, and then he told me he'd become interested in doing it too, so we should talk sometime. He handed me a piece of paper with his phone number on it, then walked away and started ignoring me like we'd never talked."

"So . . ." Liam said. "Did you get the impression he might have also asked Truit about it?"

"Couldn't tell, but maybe. And . . . well, maybe something happened and Truit wasn't nice about it and Rafe got mad or—well, I don't really know, but you said you wanted to know anything that could show that someone else besides me and the captain talked to Truit and maybe had something against him." He'd started shifting his gaze between us to see our reactions.

What he said could be true, or he could have made it up to add to our suspect list. And since Rafe had made it clear he didn't want to talk to me, I really had no idea which was correct.

Before I thought of how to respond, Hansen stood and said, "Gotta go. I made sure before that the guy had gone up to the top deck, but in case he comes down here, I don't want him to see me with you." He bent and patted Sasha on the head, then looked back at Liam. "Oh, and something he said about this boat . . . can't remember exactly what it was, but I got the impression he wasn't the only one who'd been interested." And then he hurried away.

I watched him for a minute, then turned back to Liam. "So what do you think? Is he telling the truth or just making things up to try to get us to take him off our radar? And someone else—who?"

"Wish I knew," Liam said. "But I doubt we'll get him to say any more on this outing. Maybe I'll have him brought in for further questioning."

"Good idea, but I'll bet you won't want me there to hear it."

"You got it," he said with a sharp nod.

Which irritated me. I was cooperating with what he'd asked. He should keep me in the loop.

I mentally shrugged aside the fact that he'd invited me to the dinner tonight. He'd said he'd invited any other ClemTours tour guides who were in town too.

"I need to get back to the top deck," I told him, and this time Sasha and I rose. We headed to the galley counter first, where Betsy was brewing some fresh coffee, her back toward me. No one else was ordering anything at the moment. "Are you brewing that just for me?" I called.

She turned and smiled. "I did notice you were sitting there with that trooper." She didn't mention anyone else, so I didn't know if she'd seen Hansen with us or not. "As always, I enjoy when your tour narration can be heard down here, even though I can't always peek out and look at what you're talking about. But I really like being on this tour boat. I just love Alaskan tours."

"Me too," I said.

A middle-aged guy came up to the counter to my left, and Betsy went to wait on him. In a few minutes she brought me my new cup of coffee. I once more appreciated the running tab paid by ClemTours, took the cup and thanked her.

I soon noted that Hansen sat alone now on the middle deck. At the bridge, Palmer was in charge again, but he and Steph were having a conversation. It didn't look like a good time to talk to her either. I hadn't had a chance to ask Liam if she'd told him anything helpful, but that could come later.

Back up on the top deck, I saw that most passengers there were looking out the opening on the port side. Who was there? Birds? Something else?

After taking Sasha to her special, secluded pad, I headed toward the cluster of tourists and found a spot to look out. There were a couple more bears on the nearest cliff side. I was glad. The passengers today were definitely getting their money's worth.

We soon joined Lettie at the prow, and then I told her to go have fun for the rest of our journey, which wouldn't last much longer.

Soon we had docked, and people started saying good-bye to Sasha and me and thanking me before heading for the stairs. I felt happy. I felt relieved. This had been pretty much a regular tour. Of course I had found the opportunity to ask questions of some of the people I knew on board, though I hadn't learned anything particularly helpful—unless Hansen's info meant that Rafe had been involved in what had happened to Truit. I doubted it.

But at least on this fun journey, nothing bad had happened.

Now I had dinner with Liam and some of my bosses and fellow tour guides to look forward to.

Sasha and I waited on the bottom deck for a while as people descended the gangway—including Hansen. He didn't look at me. I wondered when and if I'd see him again and whether his sort-of accusation of Rafe had merit.

After the passengers had mostly gone ashore, I wondered where Liam was. I hadn't seen him depart, and I didn't know exactly what the plans were for tonight, only that there would be a get-together sometime and somewhere that I wouldn't want to miss.

But I didn't especially want to go looking for him.

The very idea reminded me of when I'd lost track of Truit a few days ago and had combed the ship attempting to find him. I shuddered slightly and pulled gently on Sasha's leash. Time to debark. And not look for Liam.

Steph stood by the gangway, saying good-bye to our guests as they left. I still hadn't had a chance to talk to her, but maybe I wouldn't need to make a special effort tomorrow or whenever, depending on what Liam had learned.

"See you tomorrow," I said as Sasha and I reached the way down.

"See you then. You're off the day after that, right?"

That would be Saturday, my next day off. "Yep," I said, "though I always miss our tours on those days."

"Me too. But I've also got Saturday off this week."

Though she was a little older, Steph seemed to have plenty of energy. Plus she really cared about her job, and therefore our employers.

Could she kill to protect them . . . ?

Yes, I'd definitely be interested to hear Liam's opinion.

Liam. He'd suddenly appeared at the base of the stairway and was headed in my direction. Since I didn't fully know our plans for tonight, I decided to wait for him.

As he reached us, Steph said to him, "Enjoy yourself this evening." Interesting. She must know about the dinner plans, but apparently she'd not been invited.

Why just the Clementoses and the tour guides? I supposed Liam would let us know. Or not. He was the official law enforcement guy on the case, and I didn't know if state troopers ever had to explain themselves to their suspects.

And at least some of us were suspects.

As far as I knew, that still primarily meant Palmer. But was I genuinely on the list? Maybe, although Liam had sounded as if he was joking. I hoped so.

Damn Hansen for suggesting it too!

Soon Sasha and I were accompanying Liam as he went down the ramp to the shore. "So," he said, "did you have an interesting and productive day?"

"Yes to both, although if you're asking whether I've now solved your crime by talking to my associates, the answer is no to at least the productive part." We'd reached the bottom and stepped over the crack onto the pier. "How about you?"

We got out of the way in case more people had yet to disembark but remained standing there. "Similar answer. Maybe we'll get more answers tonight."

I looked up into his face. He was scowling, so I assumed he felt frustrated. I had a lot of questions. First was, "How was your talk with Steph? I wasn't able to get her alone."

"Not productive. She feels loyal to her boss and spoke in a way that makes it clear she thinks he's innocent. But would she have pushed someone off the boat to protect her job and boss and his family? Couldn't tell. And she didn't suggest anyone else."

So I still might find a chat with her productive. Or not.

"So what are the plans for tonight?"

His strong facial features suddenly unlocked into a smile. "We're all meeting at the ClemTours offices. I'm having food brought in. Very casual. And sure, I'll try to get people talking then. Maybe it'll be easier in a situation like that."

"So you think Palmer will confess or his family will protect—or accuse—him?"

"We'll see. But my intent is to do as we've been doing on the *ClemElk*: ask them all who they think it is and why."

"And you think they'll tell you anything helpful?"

"We'll find out, won't we?"

Apparently all the passengers were off the boat now. Palmer exited along with Steph, and behind them were Betsy and then Al and Rafe, who began closing up the entrance.

They were much more likely to have answers than Palmer's family members or any of my fellow tour guides.

But they hadn't been helpful. And I doubted the rest of this evening would be any better.

Except—as we walked in the direction of the parking lot, Liam said, "Why don't I pick you up at your place so you can tell me about the result of your conversations with those fellow crew members you were able to talk to today?"

"Good idea," I replied. "We'll at least have some privacy then. But just so you know, I didn't learn anything potentially

useful other than what Hansen said, and you heard that too."
At least some of it.

"Well, I'd like a more specific rundown. So, see you there
in about half an hour, okay?"

"Sounds fine," I said. "But I'd like you to park someplace
not close to the office so we can walk in separately. I don't
want my employers to know—any more than they already
do—that I'm cooperating with you."

# Chapter Seventeen

A bout forty-five minutes later I walked into the Clem-Tours offices by myself. No Liam, and not even Sasha with me. I'd fed her and left her at home to relax.

I kind of wished I could relax as well, but I wanted even more to see what went on tonight.

Liam had dropped me off a block or two around the corner so we wouldn't be seen together. Even though what I was primarily doing by snooping around and asking questions was attempting to clear Palmer, I probably shouldn't be seen helping one of the troopers who might ultimately arrest him if no better answers were found.

I didn't want to put my job at any further risk than it already was.

Liam had indicated he was paying for this meal himself, since not even the unusual Initial Response Section had a lot of extra funds to achieve its goals. Apparently Liam was committed to getting this murder solved correctly, no matter how he had to do it—even if it meant spending money of his own. I suspected our meal wouldn't be a huge, expensive feast, though.

I reached the place quickly and glanced inside the large plate glass windows. My two fellow tour guides were just inside, so I opened the door quickly.

Maria and Robin must have come directly from their respective tour boats. Or maybe both of them, like me, had chosen not to change out of their uniforms. After all, we'd all known this tour office would be our goal for the evening. Besides, our uniforms were comfortable, fun looking, and geared toward Alaska weather.

"Stacie!" Maria exclaimed as I entered. She ran toward me and gave me a big hug, then stepped back and looked at me through her glasses, her smile lighting her entire face beneath her short blond hair. "So good to see you. After our conversation yesterday, I was hoping you'd be here when I agreed to come tonight."

"And I was hoping to see you too," I told her. I stepped back just a little to look at Robin. Our older colleague was smiling too, her wavy deep-brunette hair framing her wrinkled face perfectly, as usual. "Hi, Robin," I said.

"Hello, Stacie." No hugs from her, but I thought we were both happy enough to see one another.

We weren't alone in the entry area. The company owners, Curt and Ingrid, stood behind the counter, and Palmer and Gus were off to the side. Their daughter Kate approached the door I'd just entered, and I saw Liam coming through it.

"Hello, Officer," Kate said. I liked to think of her as Kake, since all the Clementos siblings were named for Alaskan towns, but they'd taken some liberties with this one, so apparently Kate was her real name. She was younger than her two brothers here and also captained one of the tour boats, the *ClemMoose*. All three of them wore hoodies like me, less formal than the jackets they wore on board. Kate's was beige. Like her brothers, she had light-brown hair, but hers was long, below her shoulder, with attractive waves in it. And yes, like them, she also had brown eyes.

Liam said hello in return, smiled, and attempted to move around her, but she got in his way. What was she up to?

That became clear in a moment. "It's very nice of you to buy us all dinner," she said. "In fact, it's already been delivered. But I'd really like to know why. Are you expecting one of us to admit to the murder you're investigating? Or to give you lots of info about our brother Palmer so you can glom onto it as evidence and arrest him? You and your fellow troopers have already asked us a lot of questions, and I don't think we really came up with answers."

Liam stopped as everyone in the room stared at both of them, obviously waiting for his answer. "Oh, good," he said. "I'm glad the food has arrived. And the answer is no, I'm not going to point fingers at any of you tonight, although the possibility isn't completely off the table. But I do have some questions I'd like for all of you to answer, so I figured a group setting, like having a dinner here, would be a good start." He then smiled and sidled around her, walking up to the counter. "So," he said to Ingrid, "where will we be eating?"

"Follow me, everyone," the older lady said, waving her hand in the air so that her arm brushed her silver hair, and then she headed toward the door behind the counter that led into their office area. Her sweatshirt was charcoal gray.

"Be with you in a minute," Curt said. "I'll lock the door behind us." I thought again how much the guy looked like his sons except for his long but well-trimmed gray beard.

The rest of us followed Ingrid around the counter and into the small office I'd seen before. There wasn't room for us to eat in there, so I wasn't surprised when she opened another door at the back of the room and it led into a warehouse area. There were shelves around the perimeter that held boxes of different sizes, and I figured they might contain various things needed on the tour boats. The center of the room was filled with several rows of tables with chairs around them. Ah, our dinner location. The room was cool but not overly chilly.

A few plastic bags sat on the tables, and Ingrid immediately started reaching into one, pulling out boxes of food. She began asking each of us, "Who wants a chicken sandwich? Beef? Tuna salad?" She'd apparently helped Liam with the order or had at least peeked into the boxes to figure out what was there.

And I wasn't surprised that our meal consisted of sandwiches—probably good ones, but not overly expensive.

Soon we were all seated and had our food in front of us. Palmer helped his dad get soft drinks or water for us.

I was at the same table as my fellow tour guides. Liam sat with the senior Clementoses, and the siblings were at a third table.

Once we were all settled, Liam rose. He held up his bottle of water as if proposing a toast. "Here's to getting the answer to our mystery," he said. "Preferably one that doesn't involve any of you or your family members."

There were plenty of *Hear, hear*s after that. And then Liam told everyone in essence what he'd told me—that he was hoping to hear about any suspicions anyone here might have as to other people who'd known Truit and might have had something against him.

There was a brief discussion about Truit's apparent desire to form a company competing with ClemTours. Nothing new there. Nor did anyone here have suggestions about anyone else who was trying to get into the business or keep their tour company going in this area or otherwise potentially disliked Truit. Hansen Horwitz's name was mentioned, but he was the only one.

Meanwhile, everyone ate with apparent gusto. I had fun chatting in person with my fellow tour guides. I was especially fond of Maria and enjoyed her banter about some of her most recent outings and how passengers had reacted to the wildlife. It didn't sound as if she or Robin had seen any different creatures from those I'd spotted, which was both good and bad. I always enjoyed seeing someone new, but I was delighted that I had been able to visit with all the kinds of animals my colleagues had.

"Maybe we should take an outing of our own," Maria said. "A smaller boat, if we can all take the same day off, and see if we can find anything different."

"Yeah, right," Robin retorted. "We each only get days off when the other tour guides are available. Tourists come here every day and want their tours to be special, and that means not only seeing the wildlife but hearing what the animals are and their backgrounds."

"Can't argue with that," I agreed. "But it would be fun to do something on our own sometime—if we can ever figure that out."

"Yeah, you're both right," Maria said. "Maybe someday."

I was glad to hear that both of them would be in the Juneau area for another three or four days, at least, as would the boats they were working on. Most of the ClemTours boats were scheduled to be in the same location each week, like the *ClemElk* being based in Juneau, but the Clementoses never seemed reluctant to move one or more for a day or two now and then. I was glad they had done so this time. Maybe I could join Maria and Robin for dinner on our own one of these evenings.

Liam was still standing as he ate his sandwich. Nearby members of the Clementos family were talking to him, but I couldn't hear what they said. I didn't gather that they were answering his questions about who besides Palmer, or maybe Hansen, might have had something against Truit.

At one point, Kate stood and looked at Liam. "That's what this dinner is all about? I mean, aren't you troopers conducting a real investigation into the killing? Something silly like asking the questions you just did isn't likely to get results, is it?"

She drew her gaze from Liam then and looked at others in the room, as if attempting to see who agreed with her. Several of her kinfolk began nodding.

"I agree," Curt said. "I was wondering as you spoke—are you trying to get one of us, like my son Palmer, to step up and admit something untrue, maybe to protect our tour company or another one of us? Well, we won't."

"Well," Liam said, "the idea is not just to get you to point out right here who the guilty party is—although I certainly wouldn't mind it if it were true. But I doubt it. And I wanted to get you thinking. You've good reason to think about it—to get all suspicions off Palmer. If anything occurs to you tonight or any other time, the sooner the better; just let me know and give me details of your suspicions, and we'll see if we can get this resolved in a way you'll all be happier with. Okay?" He looked around, then sat down at the nearest table and took another bite of his sandwich.

"That sounds all right," Curt agreed. "We can do that. But none of us would kill that guy over something so stupid. Yeah, we have competition. And yeah, now and then our own employees joke about starting another company to compete with us. Joke. Got it? We listen and laugh about it. We do all we can to make sure they like their jobs. Right, Stacie?"

Yikes. I hadn't been expecting that. And why ask me instead of Maria or Robin? But I played along. "Who, me? Like my job well enough not to want to start a competing company? Well, let me think." I made a fist and touched my forehead, then looked down at the floor. "Hell yeah," I finished as I looked up again.

Everyone laughed at me. No one disagreed with Curt.

We all continued eating.

It didn't take long for everyone to finish. I saw Liam rise from the next table, and Palmer joined him.

Palmer was the one to speak. "Look, everyone. I want to thank Liam for this meal and for his request that we all think even harder about Truit, what we knew about him, and anything we saw or heard from anyone who might have disliked him. I know I disliked him, not necessarily just because he wanted to start a competing company but because he enjoyed goading me about it. And yes, maybe he'd have stopped if I'd just ignored him, but I didn't. Not completely. But I also didn't kill him. I think you all know that. And . . . well, I'd appreciate it if you'd do as Liam requested and think about all those possibilities. Somehow, someone will come up with the right answer and not only get me off the hook but also provide justice to Truit. He might not have been my favorite person, but he didn't deserve to be murdered."

I wasn't surprised when his family members began applauding. What Palmer had said and how he'd said it seemed spot-on—and highly appropriate for an innocent man to say.

I wondered how long Truit had worked for ClemTours and if all the Clementoses had worked with him. I gathered it had probably been one or two seasons. I hadn't gotten the sense he'd left on bad terms, so maybe he hadn't mentioned his interest in starting a competing company then. Maybe he'd waited till he'd also worked with other companies before making his final decision. But I didn't see any of the Clementoses wanting to kill him because of it.

I hoped not, at least.

Liam, still standing, joined in the applause, as did I and my fellow tour guides. I still wasn't sure why we were here, but tour guides were, in fact, used to observing things carefully. Those "things" mostly included the scenery in the areas where we sailed and especially the wildlife we saw, but seeing our passengers and their interactions sometimes came into play too.

I traded glances with Maria, who sat there with her brows raised beneath her glasses as if she was considering what she'd heard, and also with Robin, who had a hint of a smile on her face as if she, too, was pondering Palmer's words.

Liam finished by thanking Palmer and everyone else, who, it seemed, all thanked him back. He passed out some business cards that had the Alaska State Troopers logo on them as well as the name of his group, the Initial Response Section. I took one too, though I had his contact info.

Ingrid started with the cleanup soon after that, and everyone helped her. Soon the room no longer appeared to have been the location of tonight's dinner.

We all started toward the entry room once more, then said good-bye to one another. I noticed Palmer shaking Liam's hand appreciatively. I only hoped that Liam's approach, which I was using too, would wind up getting us the right answer—and soon.

"So, I'll be in town for another week, or so I was told," Maria said as we stood near the door. It was dark outside, and lights from other businesses shone through the picture windows. I saw Liam leave and then Kate. "Let's keep in touch and see if we can get together another evening. What's your schedule, Robin?"

She shrugged. "I think I'm here for another few days. So yes, let's keep in touch."

"Great," I said. "I'm working tomorrow but have Saturday off, so if either or both of you can get together then, that would be best for me, even late in the day."

"So far that's fine with me," Maria said.

"Maybe me too," Robin responded, without sounding especially excited.

Well, getting together with one of them, preferably Maria, would be fine with me. But I wouldn't count on it.

They left together. I chatted briefly with Ingrid, saying how proud I was to be working for ClemTours and how I wanted everything to go well for all of them and myself too. Too many compliments, I figured, but it took up some time and was definitely true.

Soon, though, I said, "I'd better go. Great seeing you, and as always, I'm looking forward to tomorrow on the *ClemElk*."

"Great seeing you too, dear," Ingrid said, and Curt also came over to say good-bye.

I finally left. And, seeing none of the others outside, I had no problem joining up with Liam around the corner.

As I got into his car, I said, "I had an enjoyable time tonight, and it seemed the others did too, even though no one stepped right up and set you looking at a possible suspect they'd thought of."

He shrugged. "Not yet, at least. But I have to say, this investigation is a challenge. My fellow troopers are going to want to get this over with as fast as possible, and I'm not sure I can convince them the guilty party isn't Palmer. And—" He put the car into gear and pulled away from the curb. Without looking at me, he continued, "I can't be certain of his innocence either."

"I can," I said, then changed the subject. Sort of, at least. "Why don't you come in and join me for a drink at my place?" Then I could quiz him about what the people he'd questioned, besides those tonight, had told him.

Evidently nothing had been too helpful, though, or he wouldn't still be pushing so hard.

Sure enough, a short while later, as we sat in my living room on my comfortable couch after taking Sasha for a brief walk, I held up my bottle of beer and said, "Here's to getting the answer about Truit fast!"

"I'll drink to that," Liam said, "though I have my doubts."

I took a long gulp and looked beside me, where Liam sat watching me. "And I guess that means your colleagues may want to wrap this up soon by bringing Palmer in," I said.

"Maybe." And Liam took a long drink too.

His eyes were on mine, and mine were on his. It felt inevitable that we would both put our glasses down on the coffee table and draw closer.

And kiss in empathy. Or attraction . . .

Definitely both, on my part.

As we sat there, his arms drew tight around me, and I hugged him close too. And those warm lips on mine . . . wow.

I had an urge to grab his hand, get him to follow me into the bedroom. I knew it was inappropriate, a bad idea, something I'd regret later—maybe.

But it wasn't going to happen anyway. Oh, we did make out there for a while. I enjoyed it. And got all heated and even more inclined to have sex with him.

But eventually he stopped and moved back a little. And looked me in the eyes. And smiled.

"A nice end to the evening," he said, and I could only agree. He stood then, so I did too. He took me into his arms, and we kissed again. And again. But then he stopped, backed away a step, and bent down to chug what was left of his beer.

"I'd better go," he said. "Oh, and I won't be on your boat tomorrow. The next day, maybe."

"But that's my day off," I grumped. "The day after that?"

"I'll try."

We shared another hot kiss while Sasha rubbed against my legs as if she wanted me to give her my attention now instead of Liam.

Which I did—since that's when Liam left.

With no definite plans for when we'd see each other again.

I waited a short while, watching some national TV news that wouldn't mention the Truit situation, then took Sasha out for another walk.

I did manage to get some sleep that night despite my mind churning on dinner and whether the Clementoses would think of anything helpful. Unlikely, unless it was Palmer who'd done it, since how would they know about Truit's contacts?

And of course, I kept virtually reliving those kisses . . .

I woke up with more resolve the next morning. Okay, I wouldn't see Liam on board the *ClemElk*. That meant I was in charge of this investigation. For today. On the boat.

I didn't let myself think much about how unlikely it was that I'd learn anything useful.

Everything seemed normal as Sasha and I headed to the dock. I parked, Sasha and I walked for a few minutes, and then we embarked on the *ClemElk* as a few passengers did too, including a couple taking photos of the boat with their phone cameras.

Steph again stood on the lower deck, checking names off on her list. "Good morning, you two," she said to me, then squinted at the piece of paper she held. "I don't see either of you on here."

"No?" I said. "Then maybe we'd better leave." I pretended to pull Sasha's leash off to the side so we could turn around.

"You know what?" Steph asked. "I think I'll let you board anyway."

"Sounds good to me," I said with a smile. Steph played this kind of game rarely, but I always found it amusing. In any case, she was in a good mood today. Maybe I could find a way to get her off on her own—maybe a short coffee break right around here. The only place we could easily go was this deck, at least to grab our drinks. I stepped closer to Steph, since no tourists were right behind me then, and said, "Would love to meet you for coffee or whatever later this morning."

"To talk about—you know?" Her tone was wry and her brows were raised.

"Sure," I said, "as well as a few other things."

"Like what happened at that meeting last night? I'd love to find out."

"Sure. I'll be glad to give you a rundown." And I would be. Steph deserved to know.

"Great," she said. "We can work out a time later. And it hopefully will be private. I don't see that trooper Liam on the list today."

"So it should be a good time for privacy in public around here," I agreed, then had to ask, "But is Hansen on the boat today?"

"Yeah, he is," Steph said.

Since another couple of families had just walked up the gangway, I raised my hand in a wave. "See you later," I said. So I'd have at least two people to talk to about potential suspects who theoretically could be suspects themselves.

Yeah, I'd make it a point to talk to Hansen again. Why was he coming on so many tours? Still casing the joint, figuring out how to run a tour boat like this?

Still looking for people who might be more suspect than him in Truit's murder?

That made sense, assuming he hadn't done it. In any case, I'd try to find out more about Hansen's reason for being here. I'd talk to Steph despite the fact that she'd spoken with Liam.

And would I get Rafe to talk to me too? Well, I'd at least give it another try.

# Chapter Eighteen

Sasha and I made our way up the two flights of steps. On the top deck I looked around. Not too many tourists were there yet, nor was Lettie. I checked my watch. It was a little early. I approached a group of people standing near the starboard side, looking toward the direction we'd go when the boat started off. They all wore jackets or parkas, which wasn't surprising. Today was a bit chilly. But hey, we were in Alaska. And I was used to May weather, so I felt okay in my usual hoodie.

"Hi," I said, and introduced Sasha and me. They were two related families—two sets of parents in their thirties with five kids between them ranging from about seven through the teens—who'd come to Alaska on vacation, as most of our passengers did, and they seemed excited to be meeting their tour guide so quickly.

Which only made me feel even happier about today's outing.

The deck filled with more passengers, including Hansen. Well, great. I'd find a way to go talk with him. Again. Probably as we navigated the channel toward Tracy Arm.

And how would I survive without Liam on board? Just fine.

Of course, I wished I'd have cell phone service for the whole trip in case I learned something I wanted to discuss with him. I didn't have one of those satellite communicators like he had, and I most likely wouldn't want to use the ship's official equipment—though it was available to all the crew on a limited basis—to reach Liam, depending on why I needed to talk with him.

Oh, well. It wasn't like the tour would go on forever.

And I doubted I'd learn today what had happened to Truit, since no one had given any helpful answers so far.

Liam and his gang would continue looking for the solution in the way law enforcement people did and hopefully come up with something that solved the crime. Something that didn't focus on the Clementoses.

Lettie appeared on our deck just then. Sasha and I excused ourselves from the tourists, and I promised I'd be around not only to give the tour later but to answer any questions they had.

Sasha's way of excusing herself? Butting gently against a couple of the kids to request a final pet before moving away.

As I maneuvered around arriving passengers with Sasha and approached Lettie, who was making her way toward the prow, I saw Hansen sit down. He had a cup of coffee in one hand and a doughnut in the other, and I figured it was a good thing he'd come up here before we got going, since the boat's shaking might mean he had to hold on to the stair rail with no free hands.

"Morning, Stacie," Lettie said with a large smile. "Are we going to have a good tour today?" She stood near where the microphone was mounted, but there was nothing either of us needed to say to the crowd yet.

"What do you think?" I countered.

"Of course!"

Although I had to agree, I was also charmed by my assistant's optimism—and hoped we both were right.

I got on the microphone a short while later, since this deck was now fairly full and we were scheduled to leave in about five minutes. "Hi, everyone," I said. "Welcome." I gave my usual introduction—what we were up to, where we'd go, how to be careful, and my hopes that we'd see lots of wildlife.

A short while later, the deck began vibrating beneath my feet. Time to depart.

I handed the microphone to Lettie, and she took over for now, letting everyone know how to watch for other tour boats as well as other vessels as we left our port. She grew quiet when Palmer gave his usual welcome to the crowd over the public address system.

Me? I aimed myself toward the row of chairs where Hansen sat, Sasha at my side, and we sat down near him. "Another tour?" I asked, as if I didn't know the answer. "What are you looking for today? Brown bears?"

"You," he said, glaring at me with his puffy eyes. "I still suspect you. I also want to know where your inquiries stand. And when and if I can stop worrying about getting arrested."

"I'm innocent, as I'm sure you really know. My inquiries haven't stopped, and I don't have any knowledge about if or when the authorities will arrest you. Unless, of course, you have some answers that'll send them headed in a different direction." Yes, I still considered him the most likely suspect.

"Have you, or better yet your buddy, that trooper, looked into Rafe and his interest in starting a tour company?"

"It's still on the table," I said. It was certainly on my table, if the guy would talk to me. And I assumed it was on Liam's, unless he or one of his colleagues had been able to interview that deckhand and he'd convinced them he wasn't guilty.

"Well, get it off the table"—Hansen stood and glared—"and get your act together. You and the trooper. Surely someone on this boat that day will at least admit to wanting to join Truit, like I did, and get something going. He sometimes even hinted at having a large following but didn't tell me who else on this boat or elsewhere he was talking about. And since you think that makes me a suspect, you should have others in the same position."

The guy tromped away. What he said had been interesting, though I figured he might have made it up. Or not. He'd hinted at it before but hadn't stated it so clearly.

Someone else on this boat? Like Rafe, whom Hansen had already accused? Or who?

Well, he hadn't said anything particularly helpful or worthy of an attempt to contact Liam.

And so I rejoined Lettie and anticipated our usual, but always unique, tour of the day.

First, though, I put Lettie in charge again and went down the stairs with Sasha. We strolled the middle deck, which, as usual, didn't have too many passengers hanging around. When we got to the enclosed bridge area, I was happy to see Palmer at the helm, and I smiled as Steph and I traded glances. She cocked her head sharply in response, and I had the impression that she was telling me to go downstairs. We'd mentioned scheduling a time to talk before, and now was fine with me. I hoped that was what she intended.

Just in case, Sasha and I went down the stairway to the bottom deck. Betsy looked busy at the galley, but she saw me and set a cup of coffee on the counter. "Yours, Stacie," she said.

I thanked her, picked it up, and got a table as far aft as I could. The deck had plenty of passengers on it, but I still managed to find a place to sit, Sasha at my side.

Steph soon arrived at the base of the steps. She approached the galley counter, and though it took a few minutes, Betsy soon handed her a drink too.

After getting her drink, Steph headed directly toward Sasha and me and sat down. Holding the sleeve of her large, lidless paper cup, she took a swig from it. Her drink looked and smelled like mocha to me. Her ClemTours dressy jacket today was beige, as usual.

Yes, Steph was older than me, judging by her graying short brown hair and the additional faint wrinkles that lined her face, but I had the sense she was not only smart but also young at heart. And she seemed to like her job here a lot, as well as her employers.

"Don't have much time," she told me now, "but I did want to talk with you. I'm aware you've been questioning all of us who were on board the day Truit died. That you've been sharing what you've learned with that trooper Liam, who interrogated me too. Are you and he buddies?"

A recollection of our kisses last night swept through my mind, but though that had been fun, it didn't mean anything.

Even if I hoped it would. "No, but I told him I'd try to find out the truth to help clear our boss-buddy Palmer."

"Amen," Steph said. "Well, here's my story, pretty much as I told Liam." She proceeded to let me know that yes, Palmer had been irritated with Truit, not just because the guy had let it be known that he intended to start a competing company but because Palmer had also had Truit as a hand on some of the ClemTours boats a few years ago and the guy had always been attempting to steal things, like money from the galley and information from the tour guides as well as other crew members and even Captain Palmer himself.

Really? That was new to me. And it would provide more reason for Palmer, and for the other Clementoses, to hate the guy. Still, kill him because he was a thief? Well, I'd have to consider it . . .

. . . and let Liam know.

Steph continued, "And when Truit started coming back on the *ClemElk* as a passenger now and then and making it clear he was getting ready to start his own company, scavenging information here even harder, asking questions of Palmer, talking to crew members for info and as potential employees of his—well, yes, Palmer got damned mad. Told the guy off. But didn't forbid him from coming on board."

"Too bad he didn't," I said. I felt sure now that I'd seen him before, but I hadn't paid any more attention to him than I had other tourists. Maybe less, since, as far as I knew, he hadn't asked me any questions.

"I agree," Steph said. "Still, Palmer let me know he purposely gave disinformation to the guy, wrong tour targets and more. But Truit apparently recognized that and just laughed at him. Anyway, Liam now knows all that too, since we talked about it as well as my certainty that Palmer may have despised the guy but he wouldn't have killed him."

"Got it," I said when she was finished. "I didn't know the details before, but I'm glad you trust Palmer too. Now, who do you think might have done it?"

Steph shook her head and took another sip of her mocha. "If I knew, I'd have told Liam. But I did tell him two things in particular: it wasn't me, and I'm sure it wasn't Palmer either."

"I agree," I said—and I did, at least about the Palmer part. And though I didn't completely exonerate anyone, I felt fairly sure of Steph's innocence too.

"Gotta get back to assisting that very Palmer now," Steph said with a teasing look.

"And I need to return to the top deck. But I'm really glad we had a chance to talk." Which I was, even though all I could do was check one more person off my list of those I'd wanted to talk to. And a very interesting talk it had been. Unproductive, yes, as far as narrowing the possibilities down to one suspect, but all my similar talks with those I knew had been on the *ClemElk* that day had been pretty much unproductive too.

Now, though, I wondered if Palmer or his relatives had been even angrier with Truit than I'd thought.

We'd nearly reached Tracy Arm by the time Sasha and I joined Lettie at the prow of the top deck.

"Who did you talk to this time?" my assistant asked. She clearly recognized what I was still up to.

"Steph," I said. "And no, she didn't point out the guilty person we're looking for, nor did she confess to anything herself, except for caring for the people she knows here."

"Me too," Lettie said, smiling as she handed the microphone back to me.

In a short while we were surrounded by the glories of Tracy Arm. Yes, we'd seen some scenery and wildlife on our way here, as always. But now—

It was fantastic! Well, that was my opinion of nearly every day on tour. Most of the wildlife we saw in the fjord was similar to what we'd seen yesterday and even before: Alaskan birds, harbor seals including mamas with babies, brown bears onshore, some otters, and even a couple of wolves.

Our passengers seemed enthralled, which was a good thing. They took lots of pictures, mostly on their phones, but a few with cameras too. Even Hansen was up here now, also staring off the deck.

I turned the microphone on so it reached the other decks, pointed out all I saw, let everyone know when passengers told me about a few other animals I hadn't mentioned, and just had a great time. I hoped everyone did, of course.

But as always, eventually our time in Tracy Arm ended and the boat started in the other direction along the fjord. Lettie had taken a break for half an hour or so, and with no other wildlife besides what we'd already seen to talk about, I wandered the top deck with Sasha and let people ask me questions and give my husky lots of attention.

When Lettie returned to our deck, I met her at the prow and told her the little that had gone on since she'd left. "I think Sasha and I will go downstairs for a little while now too." And we started moving away.

First stop was Sasha's pad at the stern.

Next, we reached the bottom deck, and I visited the restroom.

And when we approached the galley counter, I was interested to see that Rafe was there too.

What the heck. Fortunately, not many of the passengers were nearby at that moment. I edged our way up to the deckhand, who turned and stared at me.

"Hi, Rafe. How are you doing today?" I tried to sound upbeat and perky and didn't even hint that I still wanted to get him to step away so we'd have a hint of privacy and talk with me.

But he knew.

"I was doing just fine till you got here," he snapped, though he kept his voice low. I was used to seeing his frown emphasized by the downward tilt of his beard, but I still found it both amusing and unnerving.

"Sorry," I said. "But if we could just talk for a minute, I wouldn't feel like I needed to bother you again."

"Yeah. Sure. Well, okay. Let's get it over with."

I was amazed that he actually moved away from the counter a short distance, and Sasha and I followed.

Before I could start the conversation the way I hoped to, he said, "Look, I know what you want to talk about." I figured he did and hoped to lighten the discussion to the friendliness we'd had before all this happened—but he didn't let me. "No," he growled, "I didn't kill that guy Truit. I don't know who did. That's what you asked Al, wasn't it?" He still didn't let me get a word in. "And in case you're interested, I've no intention of starting my own tour company, with or without Truit—even though I discussed it with him just for fun. But yeah, his very outspoken goal seemed to be why he and our captain didn't get along. Now leave me alone." He turned and stomped off.

Well, okay. He was right. That was what I'd asked his fellow deckhand, and it was what I wanted to know from Rafe too. I now had the answers I was looking for from him, true or not.

He was the last one I'd been trying to talk to too.

Sure, I wanted to help bring the truth to light. I'd promised both myself and Liam I would try. But unless I got some additional ideas of how to search for it, I wasn't sure what else I could do.

I felt an emptiness inside—and realized part of it was hunger. Well, good place to be for that. I made my way back over to the counter, Sasha at my side.

Of course Betsy had seen me, and now she handed me my usual cup of coffee. I asked if she happened to have an apple or something else I could eat.

"No fresh fruit left this trip," she said, looking at me through her glasses, her smile plastered on as if she was used to saying that. "But how about some cookies or a sweet roll or something more? A sandwich?"

I pondered for only a second. I'd get my usual lunchtime sandwich in a while but wanted something sweeter first. "Chocolate-chip cookies, please," I said, and of course she had some.

As she handed them to me in a sealed wrapper, she said, "You're still at it, aren't you?" She didn't need to explain what *it* was, since I'd also spoken with her the way I had with Rafe, although much more pleasantly.

"Yeah," I responded. "But I think I'm winding down from it. I've tried but haven't learned anything useful."

"Sorry," she said, and handed me another package of cookies. "I think you may need this."

I figured I must appear as sad and frustrated as I'd felt before, but now I was a lot happier. "Thanks," I said, and Sasha and I walked away.

Well, the good thing was that since I'd already talked to everyone I'd promised to question, I didn't have to worry about that for the rest of this trip. So, shoving it all to the back of my mind as much as I could, I had a delightful time completing my tour narration, talking about Alaskan wildlife in general and pointing out the wonderful creatures we saw on our way back.

The boat started rocking more than usual as we approached Juneau, and the sky was darker than it had been at this hour recently, thanks to a covering of clouds. It was Alaska, and I wasn't surprised when the rainfall started— not very heavily, fortunately. But it meant that Rafe and Al had to cover the most vulnerable parts of the lookout area on the top deck with see-through plastic as the water started blowing in.

At least it was spring, and though it was characteristically chilly, it wasn't cold enough for a snowfall. Boat tours, even return trips, didn't go as well in the snow as they did when it was clear or rainy, like now.

It didn't take too long to get back to the dock despite the imperfect weather. Sasha and I hung out with Palmer and Steph near the gangway, saying good-bye as our tourists exited, as always.

And that was that for my job and other obligations until my next tour day. Even so, after exiting the *ClemElk* and hurrying—with my poor, damp Sasha—toward our car, I had a couple of phone calls to make. I wanted to let Liam know whom I'd talked to on this outing and how those conversations had gone. After my discussion with Maria the other day, I wanted to call her as well and see if she could join me for dinner. I knew she was in port, since I saw the *ClemWolf* docked near us. Tomorrow she was taking my place on the *ClemElk*, and the *ClemWolf* would remain in port as the extra boat again.

I pressed in Maria's number first. "Hi, Stacie," she said almost immediately. I wondered where she was.

"Hi," I said. "We just pulled in, and I wondered if you could join me for dinner."

"Oh, I'm so sorry." She did sound rueful. "I've got other plans tonight. How about tomorrow?"

"Sure," I said. We quickly made tentative arrangements for when and where, assuming the *ClemElk* would dock around the same time tomorrow.

Me? Who knew where I'd be on my day off?

Sasha and I had finally reached my car. The parking lot was only partly filled now. I quickly unlocked the vehicle and helped my pup in after taking some towels from the area behind the back seat and putting them where Sasha would sit. Of course I had towels in my SUV. This was Alaska, and Sasha was nearly always with me.

In a few moments I was able to get into the driver's seat and close my door. I could wait till I was home to call Liam, but I decided to do it now and get it out of the way.

And if he happened to have no other plans for dinner . . .

He answered right away. "Hi, Stacie. You're back on land?"

"Yep. It's that time." He knew full well what the *ClemElk*'s schedule was.

"I know. And I want to hear all about how things went today, who you talked to and all. Care to grab dinner with me?"

Of course I cared. We made plans. And I drove Sasha home and waited till Liam came to pick me up.

# Chapter Nineteen

We decided to eat at DelishAFish, a relatively new restaurant in downtown Juneau that specialized in—you guessed it.

It had stopped raining, so we took Sasha for a brief walk again before we left—after I fed her, of course. When we returned, I got her settled down in the kitchen, and then Liam and I walked to his car, which was parked at the curb about a block away.

When we were both in the front seat, he said, "So tell me what exciting things you learned today."

"If that's why you wanted to have dinner with me," I said, "you're going to be sorely disappointed."

Liam was in casual attire tonight, so he must have had time to go home and change clothes. He wore a waterproof parka so black it made his short, dark hair appear lighter. His slacks were also black, and he looked good in the outfit. Of course he'd looked good in everything I'd seen him wear. And that thought made me wonder, as I had before, what he'd look like without—

"I won't be disappointed eating dinner with you," he said, making me feel all warm and fuzzy. I cast that aside as he pulled out from the curb when traffic slowed a bit. "And I assumed you wouldn't have anything new—but I could always hope."

"As I did."

For now, we chatted in general about the weather and the wildlife I'd seen on today's tour and how much Liam had missed being on the boat, though he'd spent the day doing his job, talking to his fellow troopers and learning what was going on in the investigation. "Not much," he said, "but I'll tell you more later."

He soon parked outside the long restaurant, which resembled a diner, and we went inside. Yes, it smelled like seafood, which I generally enjoyed.

It wasn't especially crowded, though there were other patrons. We were shown right away to a table not far from the entrance.

I ordered beer and salmon, and Liam ordered beer and halibut. I sat across from him at our two-person table and enjoyed watching his craggy, masculine face as he watched me right back. Maybe he was just observing me as a trooper did, not because he felt any attraction—but I thought I knew better after those kisses we'd shared. I kept telling myself I should tone down my attraction for him, but so far I hadn't succeeded.

Yes, I scolded myself at times, and I had good reason to now. Even if I found him sexy and wanted to get to know him better, we had only one common interest but for different reasons. And once Truit's killer was found, or the wrong person was arrested, or the cops stopped looking because the case had grown cold or whatever, I doubted I'd ever see this trooper again.

Although his company was enjoyable and the food was really good, this evening out wasn't especially meaningful. Liam let me know that the troopers hadn't yet officially settled on a suspect. They hadn't discovered suitable evidence, even after checking into the other tour companies Truit had worked for recently. There was no indication of any animosity there toward him—or that's what I gathered. Liam couldn't reveal a whole lot.

I, on the other hand, said a lot about having spoken with Hansen and Steph and Rafe today. And having learned nothing new.

"Tomorrow's my day off," I said, although I believed he knew it. "I've talked to everyone from my boat who was on the *ClemElk* that day at least once now. I don't think I'd learn any more anyway."

"Probably not."

We chatted about our lives in Alaska for the rest of our meal. Liam was originally from Anchorage, so he was a native Alaskan. I enjoyed his company and his descriptions of climbing glaciers now and then, and I in turn talked about how my love of wildlife had always been part of who I was and how taking on a career like mine had been a natural thing.

As we finished, I had to ask, "Will you be taking any more tours on the *ClemElk*?"

"Don't know yet. Why? Did you miss me today?"

The answer was yes, I realized. But so what? Even if we developed a relationship, which we wouldn't, this guy was hardly going to spend a lot more time on my tour boat. Were the troopers paying for his presence there? I didn't know, but even if he was taking the tours for free because searching for evidence in a crime didn't require payment, he probably had other things to do with his time.

"About as much as you missed me by not coming on the tour," I responded, grinning at my own silliness.

"Then gee, I'd better take another tour or two. Soon."

Wow. That knocked me for a loop inside. His expression consisted of a smile, sure, but somehow he appeared serious.

Or maybe I wanted him to be.

I decided to act as if I knew he was kidding. "Of course. I'll look forward to it. Maybe you should join us as a crew member. Let's see. Have you ever given tours? Or maybe you should become a deckhand."

"Sure. Any of the above."

We both laughed. And finished eating.

He insisted on paying, as if this were a date. Well, what the heck? I let him. It wasn't as if we'd start seeing each other more socially. And if we did, I'd insist on paying my share.

When he drove me home, he offered to walk Sasha with me, and I offered him some more beer. The answers to both were yes.

In a while we were sitting in my living room again, Sasha at our feet. I proposed a toast. "To getting answers. Soon." We clicked beer bottles I'd gotten from my fridge and each took a swig.

And, looking each other straight in the eyes, we stood.

Hmm. I knew what was coming. Or at least I hoped so. Very soon we were in each other's arms, kissing. And then I led him to my bedroom.

Bad idea? Well, it would be a once-in-a-lifetime experience with him. Or . . . well, maybe there could be more. Maybe we would start seeing each other more after all.

Especially since this very skillful, very attractive, very hot guy stayed the night . . . and we had some fun.

It was probably a good thing he had to get to work early the next morning, though, since I didn't.

"Thanks for everything," he said at my front door after we'd walked Sasha and had a simple breakfast of cereal and coffee.

"Thank *you*," I said. "You paid for our dinner and drove me back and forth and—"

"And that wasn't all we did." His grin down at me was damned sexy, and I swallowed the urge to invite him to stay for one more—

Well, he couldn't anyway.

"Are you available for dinner tonight?"

Really? This was potentially going to turn into a relationship?

But—

"Sorry, no," I said. "I have dinner plans with Maria. You met her. She's one of the other ClemTour guides." I figured I'd let him know I wasn't going on a date, just in case there was a possibility of more between us.

"Well, plan to join me for dinner tomorrow, then. Okay?"

That was Sunday. I'd be working then. And I hadn't made any additional plans for after we docked.

"Sure. I'll look forward to it." And I would. It dawned on me then that since this was Saturday, maybe Liam had it off too. This was the weekend, after all. "What will you be up to today?" I asked.

"I've got a few meetings to attend regarding the case. And I'd better get on my way."

Liam opened the door. My dog got a snuggly pat on the head. I got a kiss that was a whole lot more than snuggly. And then Liam left.

Sasha and I went back into the living room, and I sat on the sofa, pondering. What was I going to do today?

Sometimes on my days off I took tours on other Clem-Tours boats, but I just didn't feel like doing that today. I also occasionally pretended I was a newcomer to Juneau and visited tourist sites, like the Glacier Gardens Rainforest just outside town. Better yet, I'd visit my winter employer and its inhabitants at Juneau Wildlife World.

I sometimes spent time taking Sasha on long walks. And I often got online and dug into websites of interest, mostly about Alaskan wildlife, both to make sure I remained up to date and knowledgeable and just to have the kind of fun I always enjoyed.

Today, though, I pondered what I could do to prod my pretext of having something to do with solving crimes and researching potential suspects in one particular murder . . .

"Okay," I finally said to Sasha. "Let's do a combo." I first of all donned a non-ClemTours sweatshirt and was soon strapping Sasha into the back seat of my SUV. We drove downtown and took a nice, enjoyable, somewhat chilly walk along the city streets, observing businesses and tourists as I kind of pretended I was a newbie to the area, just looking around. It took up time, provided some exercise, and made my large, fuzzy pup happy to stroll the sidewalks and enjoy the attention of people who stopped to pet her. I kept my eyes open for wildlife here, since bears and porcupines occasionally showed up in town, but I didn't see any.

We returned home in time for lunch. I gave Sasha some healthy dog treats I'd bought and made myself a tuna salad sandwich. Then I was ready for what I'd decided to do this afternoon: look up Alaskan wildlife on the computer yet again and maybe attempt to find some sources besides my usual ones in case there was a different slant on the descriptions, types, and numbers of animals I already knew.

I kept a glass of ice water near me at my desk in my bedroom and started perusing the usual sites, such as the Alaska Department of Fish and Game, the U.S. Fish & Wildlife Service–Alaska Region, the Alaska Wildlife Conservation Center, and the Alaska Wildlife Alliance. I conducted a further Google search of Alaskan wildlife and made a note in my computer files of sites I hadn't seen or spent much time on before.

But then my mind started wandering . . .

Okay, it had already been wandering. One of the reasons I'd decided to spend the afternoon on my computer was because there was something else important to me that I wanted to research online.

Truit's death.

I'd checked the news now and then, but time was passing, and I wanted to see if the matter was still prominent several days after the fact and what the media had to say about it—if anything—at this point.

And so I Googled that too.

There were a lot of articles and references from the first couple of days after Truit was found this past Tuesday. There wasn't much on his having gone missing first, and not too many days had passed since his body showed up on the shore, since today was only Saturday. But the troopers working on the case, including Liam, had clearly not wanted to be interviewed, so most of the media stories involved speculation and interviews of Truit's friends and family, though not Arla, and nothing especially illuminating.

I was glad word hadn't gotten out that snoopy tour guide me was doing a bumbling job of talking to people known to have been in Truit's presence the day he'd disappeared off the *ClemElk*.

And yes, some of the speculations, disguised to seem like genuine news, had to do with the guy's disagreements with the Clementoses.

But there was nothing especially helpful. Certainly nothing as interesting as my discussions with those who'd been on the *ClemElk* that day.

But I did spend a lot of time looking—enough that most of the day had passed by the time I was ready to take a break. Time to take Sasha out for another walk and feed her. And wait till I heard from Maria that the *ClemElk* had docked and she was ready to join me for dinner.

I received that call around six o'clock. I had returned to the computer before then, so I appreciated the distraction. "Hi, Maria," I said when I answered the phone. "How was your tour today?" I was still somewhat surprised she'd been in Juneau this long. She usually gave her tours out of Skagway on one of the ClemTours boats.

"Wonderful, as always. I'll tell you about it later. We're still on for dinner, aren't we?"

I assured her we were. "Do you want to come to my house?" Hey, I enjoyed cooking sometimes, when I had time and energy, though this wasn't one of those occasions. But I could always go pick up some takeout food.

"Sounds good to me," she said. "How about if I bring a pizza?"

She'd read my mind, kind of. I hadn't planned on pizza, but that sounded fine. "Good idea." We briefly discussed what toppings we each liked, and Maria said she'd be here soon. She'd visited my home before, so she knew where it was. I'd popped in at hers in Skagway when I was there on ClemTours business too. We had a lot in common, after all, not the least of which was a fascination with Alaskan wildlife.

She also knew my beer preferences and insisted on bringing brew too, even though I still had some.

While waiting, I walked Sasha yet again in the chilly evening air. We came upon several other dogs, as usual, in this mostly residential area. That was how I mostly met my neighbors—as our dogs traded sniffs.

Soon it was nearly time for Maria to arrive, so we went back home to wait while Sasha had her dinner. The doorbell to my ground level unit rang just as Sasha began eating, and she of course barked and joined me as I went to the door. She greeted Maria with a sniff— aimed especially at the flat pizza box our visitor held—and a tail wag, then returned to the kitchen.

"What, she doesn't want pizza?" Maria asked, smiling and stepping inside.

"Oh, she's eating what she assumes will be her appetizer right now." Not that I'd really allow her to eat pizza—except maybe a taste of bare crust.

"Got it. Will you take this, please? I need to go back and get our beer."

I took the box from her and headed into the kitchen, leaving the front door open. She soon returned with a six-pack of my favorite amber Alaskan beer. I noted that she still wore her blue ClemTours hoodie.

"So," I said, after we each got slices of pizza and a bottle of beer and sat down at my kitchen table, "tell me about today's tour."

And she did. It sounded as full of sightings as mine had been yesterday and on most recent days, with views of delightful harbor seals and kittiwakes and bears and more, as well as the glaciers of Tracy Arm.

I had to ask, as I was certain she expected me to, "Was there any chicanery on the *ClemElk* today—any passenger disappearances or anything?"

"Nope, although one of the passengers was a guy named Hansen Horwitz. He chatted with me for a while, said he'd been taking the tour almost every day lately. As we talked some more, he indicated he'd talked with you too. Said that you were aware he'd been discussing opening a new tour company with the guy who'd died—Truit. I was surprised at that and about his admission, since I know the authorities haven't yet arrested anyone even though it looks like Truit was purposely killed, right? I know you've been trying to help the cops find out what happened, especially that one state trooper—Liam, isn't it? The one who held a dinner at the ClemTours offices?"

"That's right." Interesting. I'd thought about questioning Maria some more about the situation, as subtly as I could, and she was the one who'd brought it up. Well, I might as well take advantage of it. "Did Hansen say anything else that was interesting?"

Looking at me over her glasses, Maria took a big bite of pizza. We'd agreed on pepperoni, green peppers, and mushrooms, and I was enjoying it a lot. Maria seemed to be too.

"Only that he didn't kill Truit. But he still was considering starting his own tour company and asked if I'd like to be a tour guide on it. I said no, even though I'd thought now and then about what it would be like to own a tour company. I even considered asking if he was looking for another partner. But of course I didn't."

Really? Did I need to start considering Maria a suspect?

As far as I knew, she hadn't been around Juneau, on a boat or otherwise, on that fateful day, so I wouldn't add her to the list. Unless she'd been somehow collaborating distantly with . . . who?

I just didn't see that as a viable suspicion.

What was more interesting was that Hansen had asked Maria to potentially become a tour guide if he ever did start his own company. He hadn't invited me. Maybe he hated me. Or maybe I reminded him too much of what had happened to the guy he'd wanted as a partner.

Or maybe he thought I'd learn too much if I considered becoming a tour guide for him. I just might pretend to do it if he asked, hoping to get more information.

"That's good," I said. "But did he talk about anyone else he wanted to hire? Anyone else who was hoping to start his own tour company? Anything else interesting?"

"Not really, although we were sitting in the galley when we talked and Betsy must have heard what was going on. She kept rolling her eyes in apparent amusement, and when I talked to her later, she said that was the kind of conversation Hansen apparently loved having with people. But would he have been able to start his own tour company, even with Truit? She doubted it. She'd looked into it herself a while back and figured it would take too much investment and effort."

Now that really was interesting. Betsy hadn't mentioned that when we'd talked. Maybe I hadn't phrased my questions right.

But even showing some interest that way didn't mean Betsy had killed a guy who'd gone farther in his research and efforts to possibly start a competing company.

Still . . . well, I'd bet that, despite what I'd been told, everyone on the *ClemElk* I'd talked with might have considered starting their own company at one time or other, then dropped the idea.

Would that make them more likely to kill someone else who had the same idea and seemed to be working harder toward accomplishing it, or at least talking it up a lot?

Okay, I really didn't want to think about that any more tonight. It was what I'd been thinking about pretty much nonstop for days now, and here I was with a friend I didn't see as often as I liked.

I therefore changed the subject to something we both enjoyed: Alaskan wildlife. What else?

For the rest of our evening together, we traded stories about unusual animals we'd seen or situations we'd been in, sharing with each other how our passengers reacted when they saw bears, wolves, and more—like porpoises and humpback whales.

I could tell when Maria felt frustrated by something her passengers had done or asked her or talked among themselves about. She'd taken up the habit of running her fingers through her short blond hair. I wondered why but didn't choose to ask.

I just hoped I didn't start doing it too, through my longer brown hair, just because I'd seen her . . .

Eventually my sweet Sasha, who'd been sleeping against the wall as these two humans talked and laughed and didn't feed her treats, stood up and came over to me.

"Walk time?" Maria asked.

"Looks that way," I agreed.

That turned out to be the beginning of the end of the evening. Maria joined us on the brief walk, but when we returned to my house, she finished her last slice of pizza and the bottle of beer she'd been imbibing, then said, "I'd better go. I'm back on the *ClemWolf* tomorrow, and I'd like to get a good night's sleep. Much as I love it, I find it exhausting at times to have our passengers' attention so much when what they really enjoy is watching the wildlife and glaciers and all I'm describing."

"Sounds familiar," I said, and soon Sasha and I were walking my buddy back to our front door.

"Can we get together again before I head back to Skagway?" she asked.

She'd surprisingly be here for another week, and so we made tentative plans to find another evening for dinner and schmoozing over seals and more.

She left, and then Sasha and I were alone. That was our usual nighttime situation. I'd always been fine with it before.

Before last night. And Liam.

I considered calling him, but I really had nothing to talk with him about. And we did have tentative plans to meet for dinner again tomorrow.

Plus I was going out on the *ClemElk* again tomorrow. I needed to rest my mind tonight so it would be ready to spew out all kinds of fun info on the tour.

And so I started getting ready for bed. But I didn't get farther than reaching my bedroom before my phone rang.

It was Liam. He'd apparently read my mind from—well, wherever he was.

We didn't talk long. He said he was just confirming our plans for tomorrow night, since I wouldn't be easily accessible tomorrow to do so.

"Yes, I've got you on my calendar," I said. The one inside my head, since I hadn't jotted it on my phone or computer or anywhere. But I wasn't about to forget it.

"Good." We decided on another restaurant, though I considered cooking for us. But then he'd be here at my place for a prolonged period . . .

I could only hope he would be anyway.

Before we hung up, I had to ask. "Anything new today on . . . you know?"

I pictured him smiling as he said, "Yes, I do know. But the answer is no. See you tomorrow."

"Good night," I responded. And wondered how hard it would be for me to fall asleep tonight now that Liam was back on my mind.

Assuming he'd left it before.

Somehow I managed. I realized that when I woke the next morning and hurried to get ready for my upcoming day on the *ClemElk*.

# Chapter Twenty

Today felt like the old days. I took Sasha out for a walk and fed her, ate my own breakfast, and then drove us to the parking lot near the pier. We were greeted by Steph when we got on board. I grabbed some coffee from Betsy before Sasha and I headed to the top deck.

Lettie soon joined us, and our passengers began to arrive.

"Do you want to talk first?" my young assistant asked as we stood at the forward area near the microphones.

"Nope," I told her. "I like how you do it."

"Thanks," she responded with a smile, but her expression quickly morphed into something more serious. "Are you going to be asking anyone more questions today? I mean—well, I haven't heard how the investigation is going regarding . . . you know."

I did know, of course. And I wondered why Lettie had even brought it up. Was she concerned about it?

Surely she didn't consider herself a suspect . . . did she? Or was she just worried about what was going on with our captain?

I didn't have a chance to ask, since a hand-holding, smiling senior couple joined us then and started asking questions about what we were likely to see. Other passengers—tall and short, young and old—crowded around as if they wanted to learn the answers, so I spoke loudly enough for them to hear.

Soon our boat started vibrating as it pulled away from the pier. We began our cruise along Stephens Passage toward Tracy Arm. Palmer presented his welcome and rules. We saw a humpback whale breaching way ahead of us, and Lettie, then in charge of our tour, pointed it out to our passengers, who stood along the outside rail and oohed and aahed and called out, as our passengers tended to do. We also saw a large cruise ship behind us and, of course, other tour boats.

Me? After my initial introduction, I stayed quiet, Sasha at my side, and grinned a lot.

Before we entered Tracy Arm, Sasha and I headed back down to the lowest deck, but I got a chance to wave at Captain Palmer and Steph on our way. And yes, I saw Hansen standing at the side looking through the window. Again?

I didn't stop to say hi to any of them but continued down, took Sasha to her water bowl, had Betsy refresh my coffee, and then headed back to the top deck, where it was my turn to point out seals and ice floes and birds and bears and glaciers.

I talked between sightings to more avid groups of passengers. And eventually, after a really good day of viewings and enthusiasm, it was time to leave Tracy Arm and head along Stephens Passage back to Juneau. I did spend a little time then talking to Palmer while Steph steered the boat.

He seemed in good humor, so I figured no one had tried to arrest him yet.

But I'd be a lot happier about the situation when I heard that someone had actually been taken into custody.

Then—back in port. Saying good-bye to the debarking passengers. Another tour day had passed, one like the old days before the disastrous death of Truit.

Oh, if only all the rest of my *ClemElk* tour days could be like this, including having a free Palmer at the helm.

Tonight, though, I was meeting Liam for dinner. We hadn't decided when, so after I said bye to Palmer and Steph, who stood there with me near the gangway, Sasha and I disembarked and I called him as we walked in the chilly air toward where my car was parked.

He answered right away. Good. He apparently wasn't in a meeting that might delay his ability to get together. Or at least that was my assumption.

It turned out to be true. "You're ashore?" he asked. "When can you join me for dinner?"

"Anytime," I said. It was around six o'clock, and Sasha and I were free for the evening—except for the dinner company I'd been anticipating.

"Good. How about if I bring dinner to your house instead of going to the place we were talking about?"

Mixed emotions flitted through my brain as I watched a group of tourists pass us, also apparently headed for the parking lot. Maria had brought pizza to my place yesterday, so I'd prefer something different. But pizza was one of the easiest carryout foods.

And having Liam come to my place to eat—well, that brought a lot of immediate ideas to my mind.

"Sounds good," I told him. "What do you have in mind?"

I braced myself for him to say pizza, but what he said was, "I'll stop at Jay's Restaurant and pick up some of their seafood paella, if that's all right with you."

I'd heard of Jay's but not their seafood paella. "Sounds delicious," I said. "I'll look forward to it." *And you.* But I didn't add that.

We hung up, and Sasha and I soon reached my car. I drove home immediately so we could be there waiting when Liam arrived.

He got there maybe half an hour after we did, holding a large paper shopping bag. I couldn't help smiling. That was certainly better for the environment than plastic, and I liked anything that helped wildlife stay safer.

"Come in," I told him as he slipped past me at the door. Sasha was waiting for him—and held her nose in the air as Liam entered with that food-filled bag, even though she'd just eaten dinner. I picked up a nice, spicy scent as well. "Mmm," I said. "Smells good to me too."

"You've never had it before? I love it and hope you will too."

Interesting. He'd used the word *love* while talking about food, and that sort of triggered an emotion in me. Love? Well, not yet, certainly. But I definitely found this guy sexy. And more. Still, though I'd occasionally dated seriously, my only true loves had been dogs and other animals I'd met before and during my naturalist and tour guide careers. And yes, some kinds of food, beer, and red wine.

"I'm looking forward to trying it," I said.

Of course Liam knew where he was going as he carried the food inside, so we were soon sitting at my kitchen table with some of the microwave-warmed paella—plus a cabernet I especially enjoyed.

Dinner was delicious. And of course I thought the company delicious too.

We talked about today's tour first—the seals and kittiwakes and brown bears and more I'd been able to discuss with our passengers.

"I can understand why you're so enthused about what you do," Liam said.

Which triggered what I'd wanted to ask him since he'd arrived. "And I want to keep doing it," I said, "with the same captain. And our crew, if possible." That surely made it clear again that I hoped he and his fellow troopers weren't zeroing in on Palmer as Truit's downfall. Literally. From the boat. I took a quick sip of wine as punctuation and put my glass back carefully on the table.

"I understand," he said, also drinking some wine before taking another bite of the delicious meal he'd brought. Yes, I was enjoying it.

And I enjoyed the company, as did Sasha, who lay at Liam's feet rather than mine. I wasn't jealous. I knew she was silently begging. But I'd already told Liam not to give my pup anything from the table. Besides, I wasn't sure whether the seafood and Sasha would agree with each other.

But at the moment, Liam didn't respond further. He understood my concern but wasn't saying anything else?

He wouldn't stay silent if I could help it.

"So how is the investigation coming along?" I asked, attempting to sound nonchalant. "What did you do today?"

After swearing me to silence, he actually gave me a run-down of sorts of a meeting he'd been to with his colleagues that included a recap of all evidence found so far, though there wasn't much.

Truit's cause of death had been drowning. He'd had some bruising that could have been caused as he fell into the water or was hit by the boat or was washed against the shoreline.

"But there were also bruises around his throat, so there's at least speculation that he was choked by whoever shoved him overboard." The way Liam looked up with his deep brown eyes and pursed his lips indicated he was likely one of those doing the speculating. "And—well, the location of some of his bruises indicated he might also have been kicked first."

Poor Truit. I might not have liked the guy very much, but he hadn't deserved to die, and certainly hadn't deserved to suffer first.

"That's a shame." My whisper sounded raspy even to me, and I quickly looked down and speared a shrimp with my fork, lifting it to my mouth. It tasted good but didn't really soothe me.

"Yeah, it is." Liam took another bite too, and our eyes locked. I wondered what was on his mind. But he told me before I could decide whether to ask. "I have some pictures I want to show you after dinner, mostly to get your opinion about them but also to see if you can identify something that was in Truit's pocket. I mean, it's clear enough what it is, but I'd like to know if you've seen something similar before, like on your boat."

Now I was really curious. "What's that?"

"I'll show you in a bit. And really, even if you have seen something like it, that won't actually help solve the case."

"Then why—"

"Why bother showing it to you and asking?" He sounded, and looked, rather exasperated. "Look, like I told you, I'm allowed to ask you questions, but I'm not supposed to say much of anything to you about the case, let alone something like this. But . . . well, not much time has passed and the investigation will take as long as it takes, and our higher-ups are getting rather frustrated that we haven't a better handle on a good suspect."

Really? They weren't actually zeroing in on Palmer?

I tried not to smile as I took another sip of that delicious, dry red wine.

Still—while that might be good for now, it didn't really mean Palmer was off the hook. Or at least I didn't get that impression from Liam. "Do you have a plan about how to continue?" I asked.

"Sure. But in a situation like this one . . . never mind. We'll solve it. Soon." His turn to take not just a sip of wine but a deep swig, and I could see his frustration.

Time for me to refill our wineglasses, and we talked about things we liked to eat and drink for the rest of the meal. I hoped staying away from discussing what was really on our minds would help him relax.

When we were done eating, we took Sasha for a walk around my neighborhood in the somewhat waning daylight. I was really curious about what Liam intended to show me, but it could wait for a while.

We went into my living room on our return. "Would you like some more wine?" I asked to be polite, rather than urging him to dig out his phone and show me those pictures.

"Could I have a bottle of water instead?"

Good idea, I thought. Neither of us needed to get drunk.

On some level, though, I hoped Liam's reason for staying sober wasn't that he intended to drive home real soon.

Did I want him to stay the night? I wasn't sure—but I wasn't necessarily against it either.

I got a couple of bottles from my refrigerator and sat beside Liam on the sofa on my return.

"So how about—" I began.

"Let me show you those pictures now, okay?" he asked, after taking a gulp of water.

"Sure."

He pulled out his phone and got into the gallery of pictures on it. In a minute he began scrolling through them, his side snug against mine as he pointed things out. "Here's what was found in Truit's pockets," he said.

Nothing too unusual. A wallet. A cell phone. Some keys. Some change. I figured all those photos would remain in a computerized file that the cops could access if they had any questions. But nothing prompted any ideas of what could have happened to Truit—or who could have caused it.

Neither did the last of the pictures, the one Liam apparently hoped I'd have some thoughts about. And I did. I really liked what he showed me, since I was used to eating it. Them, rather.

Truit had apparently had, in a pocket, a package of two chocolate-chip cookies wrapped in plastic, with the brand name ChocAlaska Cookies on the label. They looked a bit wilted—probably soggy, if the package hadn't held up in the water.

And yes, they looked familiar. They were available in some grocery stores, I believed, but they were also sold sometimes in the *ClemElk* galley and on the other ClemTours boats too. The cookies I'd gotten the other day on board had been different, though—packaged with no label.

"Those are good," I told Liam. "I sometimes eat them in the afternoon on the boat, after I've had lunch."

"Then Truit might have gotten his on the *ClemElk*?" Liam asked.

"Sure," I said. "But even if he did, I don't see the significance. I don't see anything on them or the packaging that points to who pushed him overboard."

"Neither do I," Liam said, shaking his head. "I was kind of hoping we'd get some clues from something Truit had with him, but it seems what was photographed might be interesting but not especially helpful."

I had an idea, though probably not an original one. Liam might have shown me this picture because it was on his mind too, though he hadn't suggested it. "How about if I check at the galley tomorrow and see if Betsy recalls Truit buying them? If he didn't but was given the package by someone else, I suppose that could be another indication of who he'd talked to that day. But they're sold enough that Betsy might not remember who got them that day."

"Maybe not, but I'm curious. Not enough so that I'd interrogate her about it, but if she says anything interesting, I hope you'll let me know. Or anyone else, for that matter. If you see anyone, crew or passengers, eating that kind of cookie, I'd like to hear about it."

"Sure," I said.

That was the last picture. Liam didn't stand to leave, so I turned on the TV and we watched a little news. And snuggled up together. And wound up kissing. And touching. And . . .

Liam stayed the night. And yes, we had some fun.

Morning came too fast, although we did make plans to get together later that day. Though we hadn't done this often before, we now had a routine: walking Sasha, a light breakfast of cereal and coffee, and a kiss good-bye as Liam left first, Sasha and I soon following.

Which signaled the beginning of our usual workday routine: parking my car, walking to the pier, and boarding the *ClemElk*.

I was greeted by Steph on the lower deck when Sasha and I arrived. Apparently several groups of tourists had boarded early and were already there. At least some were getting drinks and food from Betsy, so the galley area was crowded.

That was okay. This would not have been a great time to talk with her anyway. I did walk close to the counter with Sasha, though, scanning the small racks containing packaged snacks that sat on it.

Cookies and sweet rolls, yes. But those ChocAlaska ones? I didn't see any. That didn't mean they weren't there, but asking Betsy later if she still carried them and, if so, who'd bought them would be slightly more challenging.

I'd considered this last night before I fell asleep—with Liam breathing deeply beside me. Why did he really want me to do this? I decided he had kind of glossed over that, but

I doubted any of it had any significance. Those cookies in Truit's pocket being somehow involved with his death? No way. But I assumed the authorities were checking into everything, no matter how minor, to be able to cross it all off their evidence list.

And it did give me one last time to act as an amateur sleuth in this situation that still meant a lot—too much—to me.

Sasha and I went upstairs to the middle deck. Palmer was in the bridge enclosure, so I moved around till he saw me, then waved hi to him. He smiled and waved back. Everything looked just fine, far as I could tell. Another fun tour day to come.

Sasha and I then climbed to the top deck. Rafe was there, organizing the chairs in the middle. No Lettie yet, but that was fine.

I generally said hi to the deckhands when I first saw them, so Sasha and I headed toward Rafe. When he saw us, he scowled and moved a couple of chairs slightly out of their row, as if he intended to use them to keep me away from him. I couldn't help chortling a little as I nevertheless got a little closer. "What?" I said. "You don't want to give me a good morning hug?"

"Only in your dreams," he muttered—but then he aimed a quick grin at me. "Or mine. But don't even think about trying to ask me more questions. The answer will always be no."

"Even if I ask if you're an innocent victim of what's been going on?"

He actually laughed. "Well, maybe then I can come up with a better answer."

A wave of tourists showed up on this deck then, so I wiggled my fingers in a *See ya* wave and headed up to the prow area with my pup.

Rather than just stand there on our own, I approached a middle-aged Asian couple who stood nearby, looking out the window and taking pictures already. "Welcome," I said. "Are you ready for a fun tour?"

"Absolutely," the man said.

"Are you our tour guide?" asked the woman. When I said I was, she got all enthusiastic. They had come to Juneau on a cruise, and she just loved the idea of seeing all Alaska had to offer.

Lettie arrived, and I introduced her to the now-growing crowd around me as my assistant. The boat started vibrating, and then we left the pier.

Sasha and I remained there, leaving Lettie in charge of the initial tour descriptions for a while after Palmer gave his talk. But as we got farther along Stephens Passage, I headed downstairs with my dog. Would I find a moment to ask Betsy anything other than to give me some coffee? Depended on how busy she was serving other people.

Yes, she was busy when we arrived, but I used the opportunity to edge up to the counter in the area where the sweet, wrapped snacks were stored on their metal stand and look them over, even turning the stand a bit as my mouth watered. Oh, I'd enjoyed my usual cereal and milk this morning, but the small cinnamon rolls and cupcakes and cookies—yes, some of them were chocolate chip—made me yearn to eat one. Or two.

"Here you are." A cup of coffee was suddenly right in front of me on the counter. I hadn't seen Betsy draw closer, but she had obviously seen me. "Want a sweet roll?"

Did I ever! But I wasn't going to act on it. Not now, at least. Not with Betsy so busy serving people. I needed some talking time.

"Maybe later," I said. "Thanks." I toasted her with my coffee cup and headed away.

But I did keep an eye on how busy she was for the next hour or so, while Lettie stayed in charge on our tour deck. Sasha and I visited her frequently and I let her introduce us, plus I answered tourists' questions. Lettie told me that Palmer had been there, too, to give an initial short tour talk.

My preference was to get my inquiry of Betsy out of the way before we reached Tracy Arm and I took over the tour, so I made it a point to stop on all three decks and introduce myself even more and answer additional questions till things calmed down a bit in anticipation of getting to Tracy Arm soon.

Was Hansen on board? Oh yeah. I'd seen him on the top deck before I left it, but he'd settled on the middle deck in a chair at the end of a row so he could stand whenever he wanted and look out the window toward the mountainous, sometimes tree-covered and sometimes icy shoreline. Lovely view. But what was he really thinking?

Fortunately, Sasha and I finally reached the bottom deck at a time when no one was hanging around the counter despite the tables being busy. Betsy appeared to be brewing another urn of coffee, so hopefully I'd be able to get her attention once she got it started.

I nudged my dog, and we headed there.

"Hi," I said to get Betsy's attention. "Looks like my timing is good. I'm always happy with your coffee, but I certainly like the idea of a fresh pot."

She pressed a button on the metal container and turned toward me. "It'll be a minute," she said. She was wearing an appropriately dark-brown ClemTours shirt—unusual for our crew but sure to match the coffee she was brewing.

"That's okay. I've got a few before I need to get to the top deck again." I bent and leaned against the counter, and Sasha sidled up against me. Such a sweet dog. I put my hand on her head as I continued, "I don't see our local kind of chocolate-chip cookie. I liked the ones I got here the other day, the ones just wrapped in cellophane, but I like the ChocAlaska ones even better. You had them before, but I don't see them here now.. Do you have any more?"

She seemed to hesitate. "I didn't know those were your favorite," she said, shaking her head a little so that her blond curls moved. "I'll have to try to get some more. I don't think I've got any now. I just take on whatever ClemTours has sent to our boat." Her head was tilted and she was smiling almost contemplatively as she looked at me through her glasses—and it made me wonder what she was thinking.

Did she know something about those cookies?

Or was I just imagining things, hoping to get some answers for Liam?

But if I did, I wanted them to be accurate.

"I assume you had some a few days ago," I said, still leaning toward her. "Not that I spent much time around Truit, but one of the times I saw him insulting Palmer and otherwise talking about starting his own tour company, I thought I saw him pull those cookies from his pocket. Did you have them then and sell them to him?"

"I don't think so." But Betsy appeared a little flustered. "Maybe the other kind, like you got."

"Did you sell some ChocAlaska to anyone else? Maybe someone bought them and gave them to Truit."

Betsy's apparent discomfort morphed into an irritated expression. "Are you still asking your damn questions about Truit, trying to get someone on board that day to admit to killing him, maybe after giving him cookies? That's really weird."

I shrugged one shoulder. "Maybe so. You're right, though. I'm still trying to learn all I can about Truit's day on the *ClemElk* to try to protect Palmer." Okay, I was partially lying. But I wasn't going to tell her the source of my knowledge that Truit had had ChocAlaska cookies with him when he died.

"Well, if I remember when I last had that kind of cookie here or anything else useful, I'll tell you." She abruptly turned her back on me, approached the coffee urn, and poured a cup. She set it before me on the counter, and I noticed a few tourists had started to congregate at the end to my right. "Now I've got some customers to wait on." And she headed in their direction.

# Chapter
# Twenty-One

I guessed I knew what Betsy wanted me to do after that: leave her galley area. Sounded good to me, so I took my coffee in one hand and Sasha's leash in the other and started walking around people and tables toward the stairs.

I noticed someone else headed for the stairs as well, off to my side. A guy, and he looked a bit familiar.

Had he also been on the *ClemElk* yesterday? Or was I imagining things—maybe because of my ongoing discomfort now in trying to help Liam? And even if he had been, so what? He hadn't been hanging around like Hansen, at least.

I was curious, though. Maybe it would help to know more about him. I moved in his direction along the nearly empty way to the stairs, my beautiful husky trailing me.

"Hi," I said brightly. "Are you enjoying the tour?"

He was a tall, thin, dark-skinned guy who wore a Juneau sweatshirt, somewhat baggy jeans, and thick boots. "Definitely," he said. "I'm really looking forward to getting to Tracy Arm and seeing the land and ice formations and animals there."

"And I'm looking forward to pointing them out to you and others. I'm the main tour guide on board."

"I know," he said, as he gestured for Sasha and me to precede him up the steps. "I live in the area and have taken tours before, including this one yesterday. I enjoyed it so much I decided to do it again to really lock all I've seen into my mind—and the pictures on my phone."

Okay. I got it. Yes, I had seen him yesterday, and it was no big deal. Except that I was pleased he'd enjoyed himself.

Sasha and I continued up the steps, and at the top, as the guy got there too, I turned and said, "We'll be at Tracy Arm soon. Feel free to ask me any questions there or otherwise, or my assistant Lettie too. She's the one with the microphone now." I gestured toward the prow area where she stood—yes, with the microphone. She was pointing out some of the landscape, including the amazing craggy hillsides.

"Got it." He bent slightly toward me. "I'm Mitch, by the way. I know you're Stacie."

"Exactly. Well, enjoy." And Sasha and I started maneuvering our way toward Lettie.

We were soon in Tracy Arm. I couldn't help grinning at all who were there to welcome us: harbor seals, including moms and pups, a few otters floating on their backs near the shoreline, pigeon guillemots over the water, a couple of bears along the shore—and, delightfully, a soaring bald eagle.

Heaven, at least as far as I was concerned.

And yes, there were a couple other tour boats too.

I pointed out all I could and encouraged our tourists to do the same and let me know of anything I didn't mention or even interesting points along the shoreline.

I wasn't too surprised when my new buddy Mitch approached and pointed at a large nest near the top of a crag we were just sailing by. "Is that an eagle's?" he asked.

"Yes. Thanks for mentioning it."

"Anytime."

Was the guy flirting with me or just being an interested tourist?

Did it matter? Not really.

I realized then that my stomach had started rumbling, or at least feeling uncomfortable. Drat. This wasn't a good time. But I knew I needed to head to the restroom.

Fortunately, that had never happened on tours—before.

I looked around and saw Lettie nearby at the window, talking to a couple of our younger passengers. "Come, Sasha," I told my dog, after putting the microphone in its holder. It was Lettie's turn to be tour guide once more.

When she noticed me approach, I gestured for her to join me off to the side. "Tummy emergency," I said quietly. "Minor but I'm headed downstairs."

"Got it," she said, and she did get the microphone as Sasha and I made our way quickly to the steps. Because this was one of the prime moments of the tour, there weren't any other people around us, neither crew nor passengers, so we made it downstairs fairly quickly. The restroom was unsurprisingly empty, so I was able to get inside and take care of business, which fortunately turned out to be no big deal.

Sasha sniffed the air inside my stall with her raised nose, which kind of embarrassed me.

When I finally exited the stall and washed my hands, I saw Betsy enter the restroom.

"Hi," I said. No details of why I was there were needed. And I wanted to get back to my upper deck in a hurry.

"Hi," she said. "So glad you're here. I saw you come inside and had to wait a minute before heading this way because of something I was working on, but I wanted to show you something off the prow. I hope it's still visible. There was a seal on a floe a little distance away that probably couldn't be seen from the upper deck because of the angle, but it looked to me as if it was in distress."

"Really? Let's go see." My mind started racing. I hoped the seal was okay, but if she was right, who should I contact? Probably the local Alaska office of the NOAA—National Oceanic and Atmospheric Administration; they could tell me who else to call if they couldn't help. I'd have to use the boat's communication system, of course.

Sasha and I quickly followed Betsy out of the bathroom and toward the prow as she hurried on the wooden deck in her moccasins. Unlocking the door, she led us around the outside of the galley along the narrow walkway right in front of it that hung out over the water. The air was cooler here at the open prow. Where was that seal? I kept looking but didn't see it. I turned to Betsy. "Where—"

Betsy suddenly grabbed me and threw me against the ship's wooden frame. Her hands went after my neck, and I felt her attempting to choke the breath out of me and push me headfirst over the side as the boat rocked while it moved forward. And up here no one would see me fall or maybe even hear me scream. If I could.

Really? I now had a good idea of what had happened to Truit, but if this continued, I wouldn't be able to do anything about it, since I'd be dead too.

Not if I could help it! I'd worry about why she was doing this later.

Too bad she wasn't a guy, since I used my knee to jab into her below her waistline. At the same time I grabbed her arms, even as I attempted to scream—but not much came out thanks to the way she held my throat.

I began gagging even as I attempted desperately to keep my footing on the deck—and not go overboard.

The boat kept rocking. Here, where I was standing below my usual deck and forward, it felt a lot more pronounced than I was used to.

I realized then that Sasha was barking. Good. Maybe someone would hear her and hurry this way to attempt to shut her up.

And save me.

But could that happen in time?

"Damn dog!" Betsy yelled all of a sudden, and let go of my neck. I was able to move enough then to see that Sasha was biting her, hanging on hard to her arm. Smart dog to know where to grab.

I'd always known her name meant defender.

I coughed even as I tried to tell Sasha what a good girl she was. But what was I going to do now?

I definitely wouldn't leave my pup here in danger, attacking this vicious killer.

Yes, I felt certain the same thing had happened to Truit, but he hadn't had a Sasha with him to save him. Betsy might find a way to get control and hurt—

"Let go of me," Betsy shrieked. She'd pulled a knife out of her pocket—a small kitchen knife—and unsheathed it.

She was going to stab my wonderful best friend. I absolutely wouldn't allow that. But unlike her, I didn't have a weapon.

And so I jumped at Betsy, kicking again and trying to grab her arm and turn the knife toward her. Sasha still hung on. Could I get that damned knife—

It was now aimed at my throat. I had to get out of the way, but what would happen to Sasha?

And could I get out of the way fast enough to stay alive?

I ducked and aimed my shoulder at Betsy. Better that she stab my back than my neck—or my dog. I braced for the blade to cut me—

"Drop it," cried a familiar male voice. My new friend Mitch stood there with a gun aimed at Betsy. Really?

Yes!

Mitch grabbed her and pulled her arms behind her without lowering his gun, forcing her to drop the knife.

"Her name?" he growled at me.

"Betsy Jones," I said.

"Betsy Jones, in case you haven't guessed, consider yourself under arrest for the assault and battery of Stacie Calder."

"And the murder of Sheldon Truit," I added.

"That'll come soon if all goes as I think," Mitch said. He pulled handcuffs from his pocket. Gun? Handcuffs? Was he an undercover state trooper? That would explain his saying she was under arrest. Was he here because Liam had sent him?

And fortunately, the door to this area must have stayed unlocked after Betsy opened it—or Mitch had used appropriate force.

Whoever he was, whatever the reason he was here, he'd saved Sasha and me.

"Okay, Ms. Jones," he said. "I noticed a small room this side of the galley. We'll go there for now." I wondered if he wanted me to follow or just to go away. I didn't even have to ask. "Please come with us, Stacie. Once we're in there, I'm going to call for backup on my radio, and I'd also like to have you go upstairs and inform this boat's captain what's going on."

"Fine," I said, my voice raspy. No wonder. She'd been attempting to strangle me. "Do I need to tell him to turn around and return to Juneau right away?"

"No, I'll handle it. But I'd like to talk to him, so please ask him to join us."

"Of course."

"You're going to regret this," Betsy hissed. Her back was still toward us, and Sasha snuggled against my legs as if she was continuing to protect me.

"Oh, I doubt it," I responded lightly.

"Let's go." Mitch held Betsy's cuffed hands and used them to direct her ahead along the narrow passage. We were soon inside the small kitchen area that contained storage cabinets and a junior-sized stove, refrigerator, and sink. It had only one door, and Sasha and I stood outside it as Mitch fastened the handcuffs binding Betsy to one of the sturdy-looking cabinets after testing to make sure it was well attached to the wall. Then he pulled a badge out of his pocket and showed it to me. "In case you're wondering," he said. Yep, he was official. "Okay. I'll make my call now, and you should go up to the bridge and ask the captain to come here."

I had all sorts of questions, but right now this situation needed to be handled. I obeyed Trooper Mitch, of course, breathing deeply and feeling my heart rate lower to normal.

When I got to the table area on the bottom deck, Hansen was sitting there, and he looked at me. Had he heard Sasha barking? Interesting that no one else had come to find out why. Maybe the wind off the prow had smothered the sound. But did Hansen know what had just happened?

Well, this wasn't the time to find out. Sasha and I hurried to the steps and jogged up them.

Both Palmer and Steph were in the enclosed bridge room. I knocked on the door, and Steph opened it. Palmer was at the helm.

"I have something to report." I closed the door again behind us, then I told our captain and his assistant what had happened—and knelt to hug Sasha during it.

"What!" Palmer exclaimed. "But why?"

"That's my next question," I said. "But the trooper who became Sasha's backup in saving me wanted me to let you know what happened and ask you to join him. I'm heading back down to the kitchen next. He's done a good job of keeping the situation quiet for now, at least, so I don't think we owe our passengers any explanation."

"Good. I need to get things in order here a little more so Steph can take charge, and then I'll catch up with you."

"See you then." Sasha and I left and returned to the bottom deck. I chose not to look in the direction I'd last seen Hansen. I didn't want any distractions or delays before returning to the galley room.

Yes, the door to the prow area remained unlocked. I gave one knock on the kitchen door before entering. "It's Stacie," I called. Mitch would know I had Sasha along. I pushed the handle, then we walked inside.

Betsy was sitting on a folding chair I hadn't seen before, and Mitch leaned against the wall across from her.

"Palmer will be here in a minute," I said to Mitch. Then I turned toward Betsy. "So what's this all about?" I asked her. "Bad enough that you threw Truit overboard, or I assume you did." Her expression grew even more defiant, but she didn't respond. "But why would you try to do the same to me?"

"Because you are one nosy bitch and you were asking too many questions," she snapped. "Even about those damned cookies that I figured might be found with Truit, so I threw the rest away, hoping no one would be sure I'd had any there at that time. I don't care about your reason, like protecting our dear Captain Palmer." She almost sang the last part of that sarcastically, as if she meant Palmer was anything but dear.

Why did she dislike our nice boss?

I glanced at Mitch, asking silently whether I could continue. He must have gotten what I meant, since he shrugged and looked back at Betsy as if saying to me, *Have at her*.

"So if you're not overly fond of Palmer, why would you have hurt Truit? I mean, he was going to start a business to compete with your employer ClemTours." I'd pondered this before when I'd heard Betsy might have had a similar idea, so I continued, "Didn't you want the competition when you started your own tour company?"

"Damn you!" she blasted. "And damn him! I'm not admitting anything. But Hansen wasn't the only one Truit had talked about going into business with. He wanted all the information I could give him about ClemTours. And I did tell him, at least some of it."

"But not enough, in his opinion?" I asked speculatively, thanks to the way she spat Truit's name. "Was he going to dump you as a possible partner? Is that why you got so mad at him?"

Fury burst from Betsy's eyes. She started to rise from her chair, but Mitch grabbed her arm and settled her down.

She tried to twist her arm away from Mitch's grasp. "None of your business."

Which gave me the answer. "I'd say otherwise, since you tried to kill me too." I'd already started pondering the answer to something else related to the situation, so I continued, "Did you happen to hide one of Truit's hats in the tarp box on the top deck? Were you trying to make it look like Truit hid there instead of being pushed overboard? I assume that if you had a relationship, it wouldn't have been hard to get one of his hats."

No response but a glare that still gave me the answer. I figured she wouldn't tell me how she'd gotten to the top deck without being noticed, but with all the people on board and thick jackets and hats and even facial masks for warmth sometimes, she could have appeared to be someone else.

A knock sounded on the door. Mitch cocked his head in that direction, and I went to open it. "Who's there?" I asked first.

"Palmer."

I pulled it open and let him in. His stare toward Betsy was furious. Before he could say anything to her, I said, "I'd like you to meet Trooper Mitch. Like I told you upstairs, he helped Sasha save my life. And now—"

"Now he has Betsy in custody, for good reason, considering what you told me at the bridge."

And now Betsy would know he was aware of what she'd done too.

"I assume Stacie told you that Ms. Jones assaulted her and was attempting to do a lot more," Mitch said. "Yes, Ms. Jones is in custody now, but I wanted to tell you, Captain, that I'm going to have some backup meet us now rather than wait the couple of hours or whatever that it'll take us to land in Juneau. I would rather get her into appropriate custody now. But there won't be any subtle way for my colleagues to get her off the boat out here."

"It's okay with me," Palmer said. "I'm sure most, if not all, of our passengers are aware of what happened to Truit the other day. And if it appears to them that we might finally have a solution, all the better."

"Just let me go!" Betsy obviously didn't like that idea. Why? Did she think she'd somehow be able to escape if we had to wait till we got to Juneau before she was jailed?

"Oh, I don't think so," Mitch responded. "Excuse me a minute."

He went through the kitchen door, but I could hear him talking on his radio outside it. Meanwhile, Palmer and I and Sasha remained there with a squirming Betsy. I didn't feel in danger now. I wasn't at the edge of the boat, and Betsy was secured. Plus Mitch remained nearby with his gun.

Even so—I hoped whatever Mitch arranged for, it was quick.

And it was. He was back inside with Sasha and me a short while later when I heard the noise of a helicopter. Palmer had already returned to the bridge and aimed the boat toward the shore as Mitch had asked him. The area around here fortunately seemed flat enough—as I looked out the kitchen's window—for a copter to land on pontoons on the water.

It was. The copter had signage on it identifying it as belonging to the Alaska State Troopers. I could see people getting out of it and pulling out a small canoe and heading toward the shore.

Apparently the deckhands had been told to lower the gangway to water level rather than use the rope ladder as they apparently did most of the time when they weren't docked at the shore. I left the kitchen, headed toward that part of the bottom deck with Sasha, and was delighted to see three uniformed troopers make their way up the gangway.

In moments they reached the deck. One of them headed straight toward Sasha and me.

"Are you okay, Stacie?" asked Liam.

# Chapter
# Twenty-Two

Yes, I was okay. Maybe surprisingly so after all I had gone through.

I was so okay that, after Liam and his colleagues had accompanied a still-cuffed Betsy down the gangway and we had resumed our regular tour, I took over the narration again from Lettie, though my voice was raspy. Betsy had grabbed my throat, after all.

Of course I'd made plans to meet Liam tonight to discuss it all, and I could give him my official statement about what had happened then. And he had admitted to having arranged to have Mitch go undercover on our boat during tours and watch for anything unusual, especially regarding the captain and staff members.

We hadn't had time to discuss anything more. But we would.

And I was determined to serve him a delicious dinner cooked by me. I only hoped I could figure out something quick and wonderful, and that I had the energy to make it.

I wanted to show him my appreciation for his having sent Mitch to be there. Even though Betsy probably wouldn't have had anything against me if I hadn't been snooping around regarding Truit's death, as Liam had encouraged me to.

Although, knowing me, I'd probably have done it anyway in my amateur attempt to clear Palmer.

Okay, up on the top deck. It was almost time to leave Tracy Arm, but I maintained my role as top tour guide, having fun pointing out and discussing the wonderful wildlife here.

And I did manage to stoop and hug my wonderful, brave protector Sasha a lot.

I slid over questions people had about what had happened below as much as I could, just saying there had been a difficult incident that had to be dealt with. I didn't talk about my involvement, though. And I understood that deckhand Rafe had taken over galley duties for the rest of the trip.

Lettie was clearly concerned, so I told her the truth, briefly and quietly, and then said we couldn't talk about it.

Once we swung into Stephens Passage, I let Lettie take over the tour, and Sasha and I went down to the bottom deck. No, I didn't want to spark any memories. But a cup of coffee—even after I'd figured out that Betsy had put something into my prior one—somehow sounded good.

And then there was Hansen. He pulled earbuds out of his ears, then joined Sasha and me at the counter and practically begged me to come over and talk to him, which I did.

I admitted there'd been a problem with Betsy and asked him to tell me, this time, all he knew about her interest in joining Truit and him in starting a tour company.

The large guy had a cup of coffee with a lot of cream and a package of cupcakes—not cookies—on the table in front of him. "I'm glad you're okay." He looked at me with his sad brown eyes. "Don't know what happened there, but I gather Betsy wasn't nice to you."

"No," I said dryly, "she wasn't."

"Well, I guess you should know now that I was aware she wanted to join us in our new tour company. I wasn't too thrilled about it but figured Truit encouraged her for other reasons. I knew they spent a lot of time together offshore, at Truit's home. And I also knew when he told her she ought to go start her own tour company, since he wouldn't have room for her with us after all. She was mad. I could tell. But even when Truit was found, I just couldn't think that nice young lady did it, so I didn't tell all I knew, even when we discussed suspects before." He paused, looking more directly at me again. "Till now. And of course I might have had my suspicions, but I didn't know she'd done it. Not for sure. And I'd have said something more specific if it ever appeared I was going to get arrested rather than just hinting at her interest and Rafe's—which wasn't nearly as strong. So please—tell me what just happened."

"It's not up to me to tell you anything," I said.

I kept my voice soft and refused to get angry, even though I wanted to yell at him. He'd had his suspicions. I suspected it was more than that, but he'd chosen to protect Betsy.

And earlier he might have heard my dog barking— although maybe his earbuds had muffled it. But if he had heard, he apparently hadn't tried to help or find someone who could.

All had turned out well anyway.

"But," I continued, "well, I suspect you'll hear more about it on the news eventually."

We chatted more about wildlife and local tours then. I tried to sound friendly, though I hoped Liam would have his troopers really interrogate this guy, since they apparently hadn't before.

I wondered if Hansen would come on as many tours with us from now on. And whether he actually would try to start another tour company on his own.

I soon stood and grabbed another cup of coffee—from Rafe, who also set out the bowl with water in it for Sasha, and I took that as a sign he was silently apologizing. "Everything okay now?" he asked.

"Sure is," I replied.

Next, I visited Palmer and Steph on the bridge. "So glad you're all right," Steph said. She'd been standing nearest the door, and Palmer had apparently filled her in.

"Thanks. Me too. And I'm also glad that the truth will get out there now, and Palmer shouldn't be harassed anymore about Truit."

"I'm glad too," said Palmer from the helm. "Come over here, you. And Sasha too." We did as he said, and he gave each of us a brief hug. Stepping back, he stared from me to Sasha, then back again, and said, "I owe you both. You put yourselves in danger to help me."

"Hey, I like my job here," I said. And it was true.

I figured I should be able to keep it as long as I wanted now, especially once Palmer told his parents what had happened.

Maybe I'd even get a raise.

I left soon and returned to the top deck, though I let Lettie keep control of the remainder of the tour.

Soon we were docked, and I did my usual thing of joining Palmer and Steph at the gangway and wishing our departing passengers a wonderful rest of their vacation.

Including Hansen, who promised, as he left, "I'll be back."

I called Liam after Sasha and I got off the boat and headed toward the parking lot. To my surprise, he answered right away. I'd figured he would still be dealing with Betsy's arrest and had planned to leave him a message.

He'd already said he would come to my place tonight to take my statement. I offered to cook dinner, partly as thanks for what he'd done to help today, though I didn't mention that. He agreed but said he'd owe me at least one more dinner in appreciation for all I'd done regarding this case. And then he asked, "What'll dinner be tonight?"

"A surprise, but one I can cook fairly quickly. Though I'll need to stop at the grocery store first."

Which I did, leaving Sasha in the car with the windows open a crack. After all, even in May, it wasn't that hot here.

Soon we were home, and I'd barely started to cook when Liam arrived. He'd brought some wine this time.

"I hope this goes well with whatever you're making," he said. It was a white wine, a sauvignon blanc. "I assumed it might be fish, since that's mostly been what we've eaten when we've been out together."

"It'll be great," I said. "You're right about the seafood. We're having shrimp scampi."

First, though, we sat down in my living room. Liam had brought equipment to film and record what I said, and he asked a bunch of cogent questions about what I had gone through on board when Betsy attacked me.

Talking about it exhausted me—but I was still okay to cook our shrimp scampi.

Which I finished making fairly soon. I'd already walked and fed Sasha earlier, so Liam and I sat down at my kitchen table with our wineglasses and scampi.

"Okay," I said right away. "You might also be interested in what Hansen told me today." And I related it to him. Most of it we'd known or suspected, but it still could come in handy. When I was done, I said, "Okay, now tell me everything you can about what's going on with Betsy."

"Sure, since you recognize I can't tell all."

But he did say she was in custody and would be charged tomorrow with at least what she'd done to me. "And here's how it looks—though don't talk about it, since I'm about to tell you too much. But you deserve it, considering how much you helped and how you almost paid for it. We have some evidence and some admissions from her, despite her being represented by counsel now, but are still digging for more. We'll be talking again to Hansen. We'll be charging her with crimes relating to what she did to you. And we have a lot of related speculations."

He described how, according to Betsy, Truit had been planning to go into business with not only Hansen but her too as a partner.

"Hansen did indicate Truit and Betsy had some kind of relationship," I said.

"Right," Liam agreed. "We gather now that he might have even started an affair with her, and she'd apparently cared a lot for Truit. He'd convinced her to learn all she could from ClemTours and steal everything that might help him get his tour company started."

That went along with what Hansen had told me.

But around the time Truit died, he'd apparently told Betsy he wouldn't be taking tours on the *ClemElk* much longer. In essence, he'd made it clear to her that it was time for him to get started. And he was leaving not only the boat but her too. He'd hurt her badly.

"What we understand now," Liam continued, "is that Betsy told Truit she was about to retaliate by letting the Clementoses know what he was up to and how he'd gotten his information. Why do we believe it? Well, Truit's cell phone was found on his body. It no longer worked, but there were some messages from Betsy on his number—suspicious ones, though they didn't amount to proof. Even so, they boosted Betsy up on our suspect list."

So, according to Liam, the troopers' theory now, after what Betsy had tried to do to me and had admitted, was that Betsy had not only been helping Truit and Hansen but had planned on becoming their partner—evidence of which would undoubtedly cause her to be fired from her ClemTours job and possibly not get hired elsewhere if it became known to other potential employers what she had done to hurt her bosses. And Truit apparently had decided he wasn't about to take her on—as a partner or otherwise. So, their theory went, she had hit him and choked him and pushed him overboard to keep her job but attempted to frame Palmer to get any suspicions off her, since he had a good motive.

Liam kept eating while he spoke, but he'd finished most of his scampi and was now concentrating on the wine. He refilled his glass—and stopped talking.

"How much of that do you know to be true?" I asked.

"Okay, yeah, a lot of it remains speculation now, but we're working on it. What do you think? Could it be real?"

"I definitely think so," I said.

Soon we finished eating, and Liam helped me with the dishes. We took Sasha for her last walk of the day. I wanted to keep exercising her because I wanted her to stay a healthy weight—but I kept giving my sweet, protective dog extra treats now.

That night was another one filled with fun with Liam.

And in the morning we talked about what we'd do after I returned from my tour this Tuesday. We agreed he could treat me to a nice dinner.

When we both left my house, Liam walked Sasha and me to my car. I wasn't sure when I'd see him next, so I invited him to take another tour on the *ClemElk* one of these days— at a time he wouldn't be working.

"Absolutely," he said. "I enjoy seeing our wildlife around here too but couldn't concentrate on it while I was on duty." He gave me a good-bye kiss after I'd strapped Sasha into the back and prepared to get into the driver's seat.

How much would we see each other in the future? I was beginning to hope it would be a lot—at dinners and on tours and at night . . .

But not murder investigations.

Right?

# Acknowledgments

Like Stacie Calder, I adore Alaska and its wildlife, and I'm delighted to have the opportunity to tell this story that includes both. Adding in a dog too? Oh yeah! Thanks to my publisher, Crooked Lane, for publishing this Alaska Untamed Mystery.

A very special thank-you to Paige Wheeler, who has been working with me for a whole lot of years.

Thanks also to those wonderful folks at Crooked Lane who have helped with this book, including editorial and production associate Melissa Rechter, publishing and production assistant Rebecca Nelson, marketing associate Madeline Rathle, and senior editor Terri Bischoff.

And thanks to my readers who've followed me to this new series, name and publisher. And to my new readers, welcome!